PRAISE FOR NEW YORK TIMES
BESTSELLER CJ LYONS:

"Everything a great thriller should be—action packed, authentic, and intense."

~ *#1 New York Times bestselling author Lee Child*

"A compelling new voice in thriller writing . . . I love how the characters come alive on every page."

~ *New York Times bestselling author Jeffery Deaver*

"Top Pick! A fascinating and intense thriller."

~ *RT Book Reviews*

"An intense, emotional thriller . . . [that] climbs to the edge of intensity."

~ *National Examiner*

"A perfect blend of romance and suspense. My kind of read."

~ *#1 New York Times Bestselling author Sandra Brown*

"Highly engaging characters, heart-stopping scenes . . . one great rollercoaster ride that will not be stopping anytime soon."

~ *Bookreporter.com*

"Adrenalin pumping."

~ *The Mystery Gazette*

"Riveting."

~ *Publishers Weekly Beyond Her Book*

Lyons "is a master within the genre."

~ *Pittsburgh Magazine*

"Will leave you breathless and begging for more."

~ *Romance Novel TV*

FACE TO FACE

A Hart and Drake Novel

CJ Lyons

This book is a work of fiction. Any references to historical events, real people, or real locales are used fictitiously. Other names, characters, places, and incidents are the product of the author's imagination, and any resemblance to actual events or locales or persons, living or dead, is entirely coincidental and not intended by the author.

Want more of CJ's Thrillers with Heart?
Check out her complete list of books:

Lucy Guardino FBI Thrillers:
SNAKE SKIN
BLOOD STAINED
KILL ZONE

Caitlyn Tierney FBI Thrillers:
BLIND FAITH (coming soon)
BLACK SHEEP (coming soon)

Hart and Drake Romantic Suspense Series:
NERVES OF STEEL
SLEIGHT OF HAND
FACE TO FACE

Shadow Ops, Romantic Thrillers:
CHASING SHADOWS
LOST IN SHADOWS
EDGE OF SHADOWS (coming soon)

AJ Palladino Suspense Series
(co-written with Erin Brockovich):
ROCK BOTTOM
HOT WATER

BORROWED TIME, a Romantic Thriller

LUCIDITY, a Ghost of a Love Story

Angels of Mercy, Medical Suspense Series:
LIFELINES
WARNING SIGNS
URGENT CARE
CRITICAL CONDITION

FACE TO FACE

PROLOGUE

ATHENA, GODDESS OF WAR. Athena, goddess of wisdom.

Athena, goddess of a godforsaken burnt-out condemned tenement in the middle of Pittsburgh, rubbed her swollen belly and tried her best to breathe without making a sound.

She'd been wise enough to outsmart Lucien these past two weeks, and strong enough to escape his Rippers yesterday when two had caught up with her and tried to pound the truth from her.

Maybe her mother had chosen her the right name from that ragged book of myths and fairytales she'd treasured all her life.

The first Athena was a sly and clever goddess, able to hide in plain sight. Just like her. How many other teenagers, waddling with pregnant bellies and marked by the scar Lucien had left on her face, could escape death, not once—but twice? Plus, find a safe haven for her and her unborn Baby Jane smack dab in the middle of Lucien's turf, in the no man's land of a smoldering gang war about to erupt in the July heat?

If only she could breathe. Every tiny gasp brought tears of pain to her eyes. Her back hurt, too. She'd been peeing blood ever since Lucien's boys beat her. Baby Jane was all right, though. She knew from the way the baby kept doing somersaults, compounding her momma's misery, but also giving her the strength to survive. Even if Athena was reduced to living like a rat, creeping through the burnt-out building, and crawling beneath charred graffiti-covered debris to her hole in the wall.

The shadows she spied through her peek-hole told Athena it was light out. She sucked on a finger, and tried to produce enough spit to ease her parched throat. Daylight or not, she had to go out, get water, and food. If not for her, for Baby Jane.

She eased her way to her knees and crawled through the maze of obstacles standing between her and free air. A wrenching pain seared through her, stabbing from her belly all the way to her back. Different from the other pains. This was Baby Jane, calling out, refusing to be denied.

No, Athena told her baby, *not now. It's too dangerous. Not now.*

Another cramp made her cry out, her voice strangled as she shoved a fist in her mouth. A gush of water followed.

Athena curled up in a ball of agony, biting down on her hand so hard she tasted coppery blood, and knew her mother had been a fool after all.

She was no goddess, no pillar of invincibility.

She was a sixteen-year-old girl, pregnant with a baby coming too soon, carrying a secret that could mean the deaths of dozens.

And she was only human after all.

Chapter 1

Friday, July 10

DR. CASSANDRA HART LAY in bed, the weight of the dead smothering her.

Once an ER physician at Three Rivers Medical Center, Pittsburgh's busiest trauma center, Cassie was no stranger to death. She had long ago grown accustomed to her patients' faces haunting her dreams, reliving their last moments, asking herself: *could she have saved them?*

That was before she became a killer.

She kicked free of the stranglehold of sweat–soaked sheets and buried her head beneath her pillow. The dead followed her, relentless.

Her eyes squeezed shut. She felt the heft of the tire iron in her hand as she swung it, felt the crushing impact on the man's skull, the spurt of warm blood splatter her own face. Heard his gasp of breath turn into a gurgle as he collapsed at her feet.

Watched him die all over again.

He'd killed her best friend, shot Drake, and was slicing Cassie, preparing to kill her, when she'd swung that tire iron. Justifiable homicide, maybe, but there was no question about it: she killed him with her own hands.

They'd been hands of a healer. Once upon a time.

In her dream, Cassie dropped the tire iron, hands dripping with blood and turned to see her ex-husband. Richard King wasn't dead, but his life as a surgeon was over, stolen by an overdose of drugs that left him brain damaged. The overdose was meant for Cassie, meant to kill her. Body twisted in convulsions, face blue from lack of oxygen, he looked directly into Cassie's eyes. *Why?* He asked through ashen lips foaming with saliva. *Why didn't you choose me? Love me?*

Then little Mary Eamon appeared on the stage of Cassie's sleeping mind. Mary's nightgown, tattered and torn, hung from her thin body. Her large brown eyes looked out from a heart-shaped face splattered with freckles. Mary did not cry, did not beg to return to her life. Death seemed to have brought her well-earned peace. Instead, the three-year-old gazed at Cassie with an expression that said: *Whatever I did, I'm sorry, so sorry I made him do this to me.*

Tears streamed down Cassie's face and she was powerless to stop them. She thrashed on the bed, reaching her hand out to Drake, closing on empty air.

She was alone.

⎯⌁⌁⌁⎯

DETECTIVE MICKEY DRAKE STOOD on the patio behind Hart's house, coffee mug in hand as he watched the July sun unveil its merciless gaze. Only dawn, and already over eighty degrees. Pittsburgh choked beneath a blanket of heat and humidity. Drake had to get out of this town. Today.

It was July tenth, his last day of reprieve.

They'd leave tonight, he reminded himself. He had the weekend off, and didn't have to be back until Monday—by that time everything would be all right.

He hoped.

A soft thump followed by a creak came from the open bedroom window above him. He glanced up in concern. Hart with another of her night terrors.

He sighed and moved back inside, setting his untouched coffee on the counter and ignoring the overweight tortoiseshell cat sitting hopefully beside an empty food bowl. The oak steps squeaked as he jogged up them.

Everything in Hart's house was old. She had the same appliances and same furniture she'd grown up with. Even slept in the same bed her grandfather built sixty-odd years ago. The headboard was intricately carved from red maple, strewn with Gaelic runes and designs.

Drake smiled as he thought of the music they'd coaxed from that creaky bedstead last night. The bed at his apartment was chrome. A modern version of what some anonymous designer thought represented romance. It had suited Drake well enough when sex was the primary objective of his relationships.

After his first night in Hart's smaller, hand-hewn heirloom bed, he realized his posh king-sized bed had nothing to do with romance or intimacy. In Hart's bed there was no room to run and hide. You dealt with life together or neither of you got much sleep.

Finally, he understood why many of his happily married friends said they never went to bed mad. Now he couldn't imagine trying to sleep without Hart's body curled tight against his.

He pushed through the bedroom door. She lay face down, her small form drenched in sweat, the T-shirt she wore clinging to her body. Her long, dark hair tumbled around her shoulders in a tangle of curls, and her fingers twisted in his pillowcase.

A detective with the Pittsburgh Police Bureau's Major Crime Squad, Drake faced the worse Pittsburgh had to offer without blinking an eye. But the sight of one small woman trapped in the throes of a nightmare and he came completely undone.

Damn. Never should have left her. She'd been sleeping soundly, and he hadn't wanted to wake her with his own worries.

Drake slid into his proper place beside Hart. He pulled her sleeping form into his body, dodging her hands as she shied away as if warding off evil spirits. Hart had saved his life, had saved so many lives. Why couldn't she be visited by *those* memories in her dreams?

Like a toddler in the midst of a tantrum, she fought him, struggling against the restraint of loving arms. He ignored her efforts and held her so that her head rested against his chest where she could feel his heartbeat.

Drake stroked her hair and crooned to her until she relaxed, free from her nightmare, her breathing steady once more. "It's all right," he whispered. "I won't let anything hurt you."

Then, knowing she was still buried in the depths of sleep, he added the words he often told her while she was awake, but she still didn't fully accept. Before she met Drake, Hart lived her life by one creed: *trust no one.* Mere words wouldn't change that. Not after the damage done to her by her ex, Richard King, who had seduced her into a fairytale romance, and then a marriage that became a trap of psychological and physical abuse.

Hart had escaped, had saved herself. But it came at a cost. The scars surrounding her heart were too thick for her to trust in love. At least not yet.

Still, he murmured the words over and over, a subliminal message of hope. "I love you."

Easing into the rhythm of her breathing, he continued to caress her. He watched her sleep, wishing he could as well. It'd been four days since he'd had a full night's rest. Instead, he'd lie awake, watching over Hart, his mind spinning with gruesome scenarios.

During the day he'd sleepwalk through his work, lashing out at friends and strangers alike, irritating everyone he came in contact with. His friends questioned him, but he didn't want to bring anyone else into this. It was bad enough his presence might be placing Hart in danger. But how could he protect her from a distance?

He clenched his fists, twisting the sheet into a wretched knot that matched the one churning in his belly. Whoever stalked him was smart—and knew Drake all too well.

The letters came first. Anonymous. No trace evidence on the envelopes, the paper a mass market brand available at any Wal-Mart.

It was a simple message, clear and concise in its threat: *Never forget.*

The actor had obviously been studying him for some time. The letters turned up in places Drake felt secure. The first slid under the door to his building, the second wedged under the wiper of his car parked in the police employee lot, the third he'd found nestled among the bottles at the bar owned by one of his best friends and frequented by other cops, the fourth included in a stack of paperwork for the Liberty Center's building permits, and so on. Two or three letters a day, rearing their heads from unsuspected places until Drake looked twice at any scrap of paper within sight.

Yesterday the photos started. Crime scene photos, some enlarged, some glued into bizarre collages of blood and horror. Autopsy photos revealing sacrosanct secrets of the body of a woman Drake had once been intimate with.

A woman who killed herself with Drake's own gun. While Drake slept a few feet away in her bed. After they made love.

Pamela Reynolds, age twenty-six. By all accounts unstable, off balance, in desperate need of psychiatric help, angry, despairing, and hopeless after learning she was HIV positive—a secret she kept until her autopsy.

Drake had ended their relationship weeks before her death, her boomerang moods and childlike neediness too much for him to handle. But then, July eleventh of last year, after too much to drink, Pamela seduced him back into her bed once more, one final time. He squeezed his eyes shut against the memory of that last night. He'd awoken to find her standing at the foot of the bed, smiling as she raised his gun to her head. Then came the explosion of sound and blood that reverberated through his soul.

Never forget. As if he ever could.

He squeezed Hart tighter than he'd intended, clutching her against his body as if she were lost to him as well. He felt her stir and awaken. She took his hand in hers and raised it to rest over her heart. He opened his eyes to see her dark ones staring up at him in concern.

"You going to tell me what's going on?" she asked.

Hoping she wouldn't see the lie, he looked away. "Can't. It's work."

She took his face in both of her hands and gazed into his eyes, frowning. "You know you can tell me anything," she said. "Anything."

He nodded. Her fingers danced over his forehead, soothing away the furrows. Her lips followed, gently caressing and soothing. Then she moved down, kissing each eyelid, his nose, the scar on his chin. He ran his hands under her T-shirt, sliding over the sculpted muscles leading from her shoulder blades to curve deliciously down to her hips.

Finally, after a tantalizing pause, her mouth found his. As his mouth opened beneath hers, he felt his need for her rise with an urgency he couldn't control. He was a drowning man, and Hart was his only hope.

CASSIE STRADDLED DRAKE, HOPING to distract him from his dark worries. Whatever the case was that consumed him, it had insinuated itself between them. Over the past few days, sex had become the only outlet for his emotions. He refused to talk to her about what troubled him. Whenever they were together, his eyes were either dark with worry or darting about the room, searching for hidden enemies.

She knelt over him, tugged her shirt over her head, and flung it away. If it was sex he needed, she'd use it—if only to break down the invisible wall that had suddenly grown between them. They'd been together for almost five months now, and survived rough times. She'd seen him get shot; he'd been there when she killed a man.

After all that, Cassie thought they'd found a balance, a comfortable give and take between their disparate personalities and life styles.

Before this week, he turned to her for help on his cases. This was the first time he refused to discuss one with her.

Which made her both fearful, and grimly determined to help him in any way possible.

She fisted her hands in his hair, tilting his head back as she leaned over him. Their kiss was passionate enough to drive demons away. She felt his arousal and pulled back, just enough to allow his mouth to move to her breast. His hands ran down her hips, along the back of her thighs, stroking, kneading, as she squirmed against him.

When they were both ready, she moved her hips down over his.

She felt him respond, and then he tensed.

"Wait." Through clenched teeth, his voice a ragged whisper. He moved her weight off him and reached toward the bedside table, fumbling for the condoms there.

"It's okay," she told him, laying her hand over his. "You've been tested."

His eyes clouded for a moment, passion replaced by something else for a brief second. "The results of the last one won't be back until next week."

Cassie sighed. He'd taken the cocktail after his HIV exposure from Pamela Reynolds, tested negative three times since—but still he insisted on condoms, even though the odds were very much in their favor. It annoyed her, this martyr complex, this penance he'd assigned himself.

And he accused her of being stubborn. She said nothing. Instead, she tugged his shorts off and allowed her fingers to stroke him, sending ripples through his muscles as he fought to control his arousal. He turned to her, and she smiled a wicked smile. If he wanted to torture and punish himself about a mistake he made a year ago, then fine, she could go along with that.

A harsh rasp escaped his throat. She plucked the unwrapped condom from his limp fingers, taking her sweet time as she smoothed it over him. His head fell back, knocking against the headboard, eyes squeezed shut.

"Cassie," he moaned.

She smiled. Drake only used her first name when he was seriously annoyed. If he was that irritated, she could guarantee he wasn't thinking about his case. She slid her body over his, torturing him for a few moments longer before guiding him inside of her. They immediately found their rhythm, their bodies moving together as the bed creaked in harmony. His hands on her hips, hers clutching his shoulders. She searched his gaze, found no fears, no worries there, and she was pleased. *Mission accomplished.*

Long minutes later, they collapsed onto the sweat soaked sheets. Cassie turned her head to one side, found the strength to open her eyes. Drake's hands idly feathered their way over her back. His face was smooth, unlined with worry for the first time in days.

Raising a hand to comb through the sparse, dark hair on his chest, she sighed in contentment. She could lie forever just like this. Let the rest of the world go to hell. She had all that she needed, right here.

How many people could say that? A tingle of awe at her luck ran through her. For all his annoying habits—she still hadn't trained him to put the toilet seat down—Drake was all she ever wanted to make her life complete. And to think, before she met him, she'd given up on men completely. No surprise, given her disastrous marriage to Richard King. A fairytale romance turned into a bloody nightmare.

A nightmare she'd walked away from, she reminded herself. She was no victim. A fool occasionally, but never a victim. She took responsibility for the people she brought into her life. For better or worse. A lesson hammered into her by the grandmother who raised her, her father's mother, Rosa.

Cassie traced her finger along Drake's strong jaw line, that enchanting scar on his chin, those luscious lips, and smiled. It was a gift, a very precious gift to find this. It wasn't that Drake *made* her happy, rather she was happy merely because he was there with her.

He opened his mouth and sucked on her finger.

"Breakfast?" she asked. She pulled her finger away from his playful nip.

"Too hot."

No surprise, he seldom ate before noon. Not her—her stomach

growled at the mere thought of food.

"It'll be cooler up at the Lake," he continued. After his shift, they were driving up to his Aunt Nellie's house, meeting his mother and aunt for the weekend. "I could call in sick. We could leave this morning." He gazed down at her. "Why don't we do that? We could be there in a few hours."

His voice was eager, and she hated to disappoint him. "Can't. I have to meet with the District Attorney about my testimony in the Mary Eamon case."

"I've got a gun," Drake muttered. His hands tensed into fists at her back. "How about if I just take the bastard out and shoot him like the dog he is?"

She arched up and looked at him full in the face. This wasn't Drake. He was the one who worked within the law, and used the system to get the bad guys. Usually it was Cassie who ran afoul of authority with her casual disregard of rules and regulations.

She laid a finger over his lips. "Shhh," she whispered. "You don't mean that. I'll take care of Ronald Brickner. I'll bury him in court. The jury will convict him so fast it'll make his head spin."

He kissed her hand, but the shadows had returned to his eyes. What the hell was this case that had him so worried? She hated being powerless to help him. "I'll call, see if we can meet earlier," she promised him. "Maybe we can leave by lunch."

His expression lightened a little. "You going in to work on the clinic this morning?"

Of course. Where else did she have to go, after losing her position in the ER at Three Rivers Medical Center? "Almost done hanging drywall on the first floor." She forced her voice to remain light. "Told Tammy I'd meet her there by eight."

Drake nodded at that. Once the construction on the Liberty Center was finished, he'd be free to return to his apartment on the third floor of his building, and get back to work on the paintings he'd left neglected in his studio. But first he had to deal with the sick sonofabitch stalking him.

He wanted tomorrow to be over with, wanted Hart safe at the Lake, and wanted to get his hands on whoever was stalking him. He saw the frown crease her forehead and forced himself to smile.

After tomorrow, he'd tell her everything, he vowed. Just had to see her safely through the eleventh. Just had to get the hell out of this city.

Before he lost his mind.

Chapter 2

DRAKE WAS THE FIRST out the door. He paused on the porch, scanning the street for anything suspicious, while Hart got her stuff together and set her house alarm. His car, a candy apple red '68 Mustang convertible, sat parked at the curb. Everything seemed fine.

None of the envelopes had come here. Hart's house was his last safe refuge. In more ways than one, he thought, remembering how accepting of his silence she'd been, never once bringing him to task for his recent irritability.

Just had to make it through today.

He had a plan. Hart was a master improviser; while Drake liked to know where he was going. Even when he began a painting he knew the exact effect he wanted to achieve. Which was why it had taken him so long to finish the triptych his agent was currently yammering at him to deliver.

The paintings were a series titled *Steadfast*. In the first panel, a dark-haired angel knelt, her wings folded around her, head bent low, seemingly defeated, shrouded in shadow. In the second, her face brightened, wings beginning to unfold, shoulders lifting, eyes blazing in defiance. And in the final, she rose to her full power, wings unfurled, brilliant banners of light and color bathing her face and body, her face calm but determined as she continued her battle.

Drake created special mixtures of vegetable dyes and oils to get the right consistency and transparency. He played with the light and shadow, wrestled with negative spaces and contours for weeks before he was happy with the end result that matched his memory.

The figure was Hart, of course. Almost all of his work was anymore. He'd done the original sketches the first week after he met her. At a time when he'd seen her brought low by the murder of her best friend, by threats on her own life and the shadows of suspicion cast onto her, and, finally, had witnessed her triumphant emergence from the darkness.

He settled his forty-caliber Glock into its accustomed place at his right hip. Hart hated guns, and insisted he remove his service weapon and the Baby Glock he wore in an ankle holster as soon as he came into her house. He kept a Beretta as a backup in a lockbox in the Mustang's trunk when it wasn't sitting close at hand below his driver's seat. Hart didn't know about that one—no sense asking for an argument.

Satisfied that at least the morning was starting out well, Drake crossed the porch. He stopped short. Saw the envelope centered on the cushions of the porch swing. Jagged red letters spelling out his name scratched across the front.

His breath caught. He glanced through the living room window to ensure Hart wasn't watching as he approached the swing. Generic manila envelope, but the first one with handwriting on it. Not enough to identify the actor, he was certain. To be safe, he pulled out a clean handkerchief and wrapped it around his hand as he opened the thin package.

Drake knew he should wait until he got to the station house to open it. But none of the others yielded any useful evidence and he desperately needed to see what was inside, to weigh any threat his stalker might be announcing. Particularly if that threat involved Hart.

He slid the photos out, just enough to take a quick glance at them. Photos of Pamela's death scene. And a new twist: photos of Drake lying in a pool of his own blood.

The message had changed as well, now a single word: *Tomorrow*.

Drake's breath hissed out as if he'd been sucker punched. The photos of him were computer generated, but eerily accurate. The actor must have read the police report of his shooting five months ago. Or talked to someone who'd been on scene. It could be a paramedic, state trooper . . . the list was too long to be helpful.

"I thought you'd left already." Hart's voice made him jump. "What's that?"

He fumbled the photos back into the envelope before turning around. He held it by its edges, turned so that she couldn't see the writing on it.

"Just something I need for my case," he told her, keeping his voice steady, his face impassive.

She looked at him hard, but didn't challenge his lie.

"How about if I drive you to the clinic?" he suggested. "I need to grab some things from my place anyway."

"I need my car to go downtown to the District Attorney's office, remember?"

"Right, I forgot. I'll follow you, then." He gestured for her to precede him down the porch steps, hoping she didn't notice his hand on his Glock. He almost ran into her when she stopped to wave to her neighbor across the street, Mrs. Ferraro, who was watering her Impatiens.

Go, go, he thought. They were sitting targets out here. His gaze boomeranged up and down Gettysburg Street. Everything was quiet except his pulse jackhammering through his brain. Sweat pooled at the base of his spine, while the small hairs on the back of his neck prickled in warning.

He saw her safely to her car, a blue Subaru Impreza, parked two spaces down from his. *Bomb?* He whirled to grab the keys from her, but too late. She started the car before he could intercept her. He couldn't stop the flinch that interrupted his inhalation. Turning, he got behind the wheel of the Mustang, all focus and attention on Hart's car in front of him.

By the time they drove two blocks, he was already exhausted from his vigil. Christ, how long could he keep this up?

CASSIE STARED AT DRAKE in her rearview mirror. Hunched over the wheel of the Mustang like a tank commander going into battle.

What the hell was going on? she wondered, and not for the first time. For once in her life she was following the rules. She hadn't pried, had tried to give him time and space to deal with whatever worries this new case brought. But this was getting out of control.

He wasn't sleeping. He was constantly on edge, jumping at the slightest thing. And for some reason, all the more solicitous of her. Taking her to the clinic, coming by to get her for lunch, picking her up, and spending more time at her house. No matter what he claimed, it wasn't the dust from the clinic renovations that had driven him from his building and to her house the past week. Nothing could keep him from his art.

The only other time he stopped painting was after he'd been shot, when he suffered from post-traumatic stress, having panic attacks, and a fear that something might happen to her.

She almost stalled the car at the light on Beechwood. Drake once stopped painting because he was anxious about her.

Could his current case have something to do with her? She decided to test her theory. The next light was yellow. She hit the accelerator and crossed the intersection just as it turned red. Looking in her rear view mirror, she watched as Drake followed her, not even bothering to check for traffic.

Damn, she'd been a fool. This *did* have something to do with her. As usual, Drake was too busy playing the knight in shining armor to bother her with any trivial details.

Once heated, her temper moved quickly from a simmer to a boil. She thought he trusted her, why not with this?

Cassie screeched to a stop in the parking lot of The Liberty Times building, Drake's building at the end of Ravenna Way, originally home to a 1920s newspaper. She slammed her car door.

Not waiting for him, she flung the back door open and sprinted up the steps to the first floor, which would house the medical clinic, counseling offices, and legal services. The second floor was almost done, ready to receive the food bank and daycare. The Liberty Center Community Clinic had been Drake's dream, his and her old boss, Ed Castro. Together they had scrounged the funding necessary to make the dream a reality.

Cassie ignored the dust-coated oak floors, stepping through framed but empty walls to assess the work before her. She had insulated and dry walled the main dividing walls, giving the social services' offices and the legal clinic in the front of the building their own space. The rear two-thirds of the first floor was the medical clinic, which was only rough framed so far. She put her hands on her hips, turning in a circle, deciding which project to tackle first.

Besides tackling Drake. If he didn't trust her enough to talk to her, confronting him would only make things worse. That much she'd learned in the five months they'd been together.

Feeling the urge to pound something, Cassie strapped her leather tool belt around her hips and spotted a likely candidate. She'd hammer together the two by fours she cut yesterday to make a radiator cover.

Hard to worry with a tool in your hand, Gram Rosa, would say. Cassie swung the hammer a few times and smiled. As usual, Rosa was right.

Who could Drake be protecting her from? Cassie thought, settling into the rhythm of her work.

Or what?

Chapter 3

DRAKE RAN AFTER HART, following her up the outside steps into the rear of the building. Then he spotted the determined set of her jaw and angry blush coloring her cheeks. He should have told her sooner. He stepped forward, ready to fill her in, to convince her to leave for the Lake immediately, but then she started to swing the damn hammer loud enough to wake the dead.

He watched her for a few moments before beating a retreat upstairs to his apartment on the third floor. He'd tell her later. After she calmed down. Otherwise, there was a very good chance she'd rush out, determined to do something, and end up causing more harm than good.

Hart was like that. She acted before she thought, relying on her instincts and gut level determination to pull her through any situation. So far it had worked. Drake thought about some of her close calls and grimaced as he crossed the open space of his living room and dining area.

Better to stick with his plan. Safer for all involved.

In the bedroom, he shoved the few things he'd need for the Lake trip into a gym bag. He wouldn't be staying there long. Once

Hart was safe at Nellie's house, he would return to the city and find his stalker. Or rather, let his stalker find him.

It was a game of cat and mouse. One Drake intended to win. Now that he knew this actor was serious, he'd bring Jimmy Dolan, his partner, on board. Maybe Sarah Miller, Commander of the Major Crimes Squad, as well. As soon as he had Hart safely out of the way.

Drake tucked extra ammunition into the bag and zipped it shut with a final glance at the chrome headboard. Hart's hand-carved one was so much better. Her face, flushed with their lovemaking as the old bed creaked and sang beneath them, flashed through his mind.

He just needed to make it through the day. Then their lives could get back to normal.

He ran down the steps, pausing on the first floor landing, the scent of fresh-cut lumber filling the air. Hart hammered in synch with the Aerosmith that echoed through the high-ceilinged space. He smiled. Her taste in music was even more eclectic than his own. On any given day her MP3 player shuffled between heavy metal, classic rock, Irish folk music, R and B, jazz, and zydeco.

At least she wasn't still mad. One good thing about Hart. She had a quick temper, but never held a grudge.

Drake stood in the doorway. He admired the way her lithe muscles, rock hard from her Kempo training and the construction work she'd done on the Liberty Center, rippled beneath the fabric of her denim overalls and tank top. She swung the hammer with efficient movements. *Tap, tap, bang*, and a nail was in. She mouthed the words to "Love in an Elevator" while she swiveled her hips in time with Steven Tyler's warble.

The slam of a car door sent Drake's hand flying to his gun, shattering the moment.

He pivoted and saw a familiar figure climb the outside stairs. Tony Spanos. Drake dropped his bag and moved to intercept the burly ex-policeman. At six-four, Spanos had four inches and several pounds on Drake. That didn't worry him; he and Spanos had tangled before and he'd always come out on top.

"What the hell are you doing here?" Drake asked him, pitching his voice so Hart wouldn't hear them. He kept advancing, forcing Spanos to retreat out the door, onto the concrete stoop, and two steps down the handicapped ramp.

"Cassie invited me. Didn't she tell you?" Spanos asked with a smirk.

Drake clenched his fists and resisted the urge to wipe that superior grin from Spanos' face. He wasn't worth it. After resigning from the force two months ago, Spanos was now a civilian and thus off limits.

But damn, it would feel so good. Drake had little sympathy for the younger man. Once upon a time he thought Spanos might make a good cop, even if they didn't get along. That was before Spanos lost his nerve during a hostage situation, forcing Drake to take a dangerous headshot to take down a gunman.

Since Hart had been the hostage in question, Drake would never forgive Spanos for jeopardizing her safety. Hart didn't know she was the reason Spanos lost his badge. To his credit, the ex-cop tried to make up for almost getting her killed by helping out at the Center, but that didn't mean Drake had to like him hanging around.

"How's life been treating you, DJ?" Spanos used Drake's nickname as if they were old drinking buddies. "I figure if Cassie's calling me to come over, maybe you guys are having a bit of trouble. Guess years and booze will do that to a man." Spanos hooked his thumbs in the belt loops of his jeans. He was twenty-eight, six years younger than Drake, with brown hair, dark eyes and a smile he seemed certain drove the ladies mad.

Drake ignored his jibes, noting the logo embroidered on

Spanos' denim work shirt. Guardian Security. Hart had mentioned the alarm system installation this week.

"Hi, Tony." Hart's voice came from behind him, interrupting the crude reply Drake was formulating. Drake's bag was slung over her shoulder.

"Thanks, honey," he said, taking the bag from her. Before she could protest his use of the hated saccharine diminutive, he kissed her passionately. Only after he left her breathless and flushed by the unexpected display of public affection, did he release her.

"I'll call you about lunch." He strode to the Mustang, tossing the duffle into the back seat of the convertible.

As he drove out of the parking lot, Spanos gave him a middle-fingered salute.

⌁⌁⌁

CASSIE WALKED DOWN THE steps. Drake peeled out of the parking lot like an adolescent trying to impersonate James Dean. She put her hands on her hips and turned to Tony who wore a look of extreme innocence on his face.

"Want to tell me what that was all about?"

Tony shrugged. "Drake's a nut job. I don't get what you see in him."

Cassie knew the ex-cop had a crush on her. Five months ago, they started off on the wrong foot, but she had since earned Tony's admiration and he'd apologized, blaming his rude behavior on his animosity with Drake. Now he often helped out with the Liberty Center. He'd even convinced his new boss to give them a break on the security system the Center needed.

She liked the tall, hulking Greek. Beneath the Neanderthal exterior he'd revealed a soft heart—at least as far as the Center and Cassie went. Though he never forgave Drake for replacing him in

Pamela Reynolds' heart or the role he felt Drake had played in her suicide.

"You ready to get started?" she asked, changing the subject away from Drake to one she and Tony could comfortably talk about.

"Sure." He grabbed a notepad from his pocket and began taking notes. "I'm thinking a code key back here and out front. This entrance will be limited access, right?" He gestured to the door behind them.

"Right. Everyone except a few staff members will come in the front entrance."

"Do you want a camera out here and in the front?" He gestured to the gang graffiti that was renewed daily. "Might not be a bad idea."

She considered his suggestion as she regarded today's artwork sprayed on the Center's brick wall. Alongside the usual gang tags was a portrait of a young couple holding hands, vibrant flowers flying about them as if they walked on air. Tagger, the artist, was in a playful mood she noted, tilting her head to take in the neon swirls.

"Too expensive," she decided. "Besides, we'll never have the manpower to actually keep an eye on them. Let's put our resources into better locks and sensors at the most critical areas."

"All right."

Cassie scanned the area beneath the dumpster for telltale shadows of an eleven-year-old's skinny legs. Tagger was nowhere to be seen today. Usually he'd wait for Drake to leave, then appear as if from nowhere. Of course, most days she wasn't accompanied by a man in uniform.

Taming Tagger was harder than coaxing a wild animal from its den. But, after weeks of tempting the eleven-year-old with offerings of food and art supplies pillaged from Drake, she finally made headway to the point where he would occasionally stop long enough to join her in a meal or to offer warnings of the latest gang activity. Gangs were a constant threat with the Center perched in the no-man's land separating the Ruby Avenue Rippers and the Garfield Gangstas.

They moved back inside and she showed Tony the second floor daycare area.

"I can't believe how much you've finished since the last time I was here," he told her. "You've done a really good thing, Cassie."

"Thanks." She found herself blushing as he ran a hand over the mitered corners of the molding she'd so painstakingly cut to match the original trim. She'd spent hours getting it just right.

He turned and smiled at her, taking her hand in his larger one and running a light finger over her new calluses. "You might have found a second career here—just like I have."

She pulled her hand away, not sure how to handle his praise. "It's been fun," she admitted. Although not as much fun as a fresh trauma or scene run. Not to mention the hours she spent working alone at the Center—a far cry from the camaraderie she experienced with her team in the ER. "But I'll be happy when it's finished and I get back to being a doctor."

"Have you heard anything about King's lawsuit?" The last time Tony came over to the Center, she'd been served another notice in Richard's malpractice case. Nothing like having your ex-husband sue you for almost letting him die.

Tony had helped her over her anger by challenging her to a Spackle battle and they'd ended up with more of the mud on themselves than on the drywall.

"They keep changing the date."

"Damn lawyers. They're just trying to keep you off balance."

"I let Juliet handle it now." Juliet Nguyen was the Liberty Center's attorney and would be running their legal clinic.

He squeezed her hand. "King's an idiot. You did everything you could. He would have died if you weren't there."

That didn't matter to Richard. He wanted Cassie back—and if he couldn't have her, he'd be just as happy to destroy her life instead. Like he'd almost done while they were married. Possessive, controlling, narcissistic . . . that was Richard. At least when he was a surgeon, before the drug overdose. The overdose meant for her. A fact Richard's family would never let her forget. As if she ever could. If she'd drunk from that cup instead of Richard . . .

"Hey, I'm sorry." Tony brushed against her arm, bringing her back to the present. "I should have never said anything." He turned around the brightly lit room with its sunny yellow walls and wide windows. "So this is going to be the kids' area. Guess we don't want any locks in here. Kids are the best burglars around, except they usually end up on the wrong side of the locked door." His hand brushed her arm again as he stood close to her.

Too close, she realized, and flinched involuntarily. She appreciated Tony's friendship and help with the Center, but there could never be anything more between the two of them. She moved away from him, toward the one wall not filled with windows. "Drake's going to help the kids paint a mural over here."

Tony frowned at the mention of Drake's name. "Has he—" Tony's voice dropped. "Been getting any weird mail?"

"What do you mean?"

"You know about Drake and Pamela Reynolds, right?" He scuffed one toe against the hardwood floor, a faint sheen of sweat visible at the back of his neck as he bowed his head.

She nodded.

"I was seeing Pamela, too. She broke off with me to start up with Drake." Tony looked away as if the memory was painful. "It'll be a year tomorrow," he went on, then shook his head. "If only she'd called me that night instead of Drake. Maybe I could have done something, stopped her, gotten her help."

"There was nothing you could have done," she said, placing her hand on his arm.

"We'll never know, will we?" Bitterness tinged his voice. "Anyway, these past few days, I've been getting letters about Pamela. Anonymous ones. Like someone blamed me for her death." He took a deep breath. "I wondered if Drake might be getting them as well."

"If he is, he hasn't told me." She didn't mention Drake's bad mood. Had he lied to her about it being because of work? She didn't want to even think it. The one thing they had going for them was that, no matter how painful, they always told each other the truth.

But she had an awful feeling Tony had found the reason for Drake's strange behavior.

"Pamela had a sister. I think she's behind the letters, but I haven't been able to track her down. I thought maybe Drake— anyway, maybe you could talk to him about it? It wouldn't work, coming from me. We'd only end up fighting about Pamela. Like we always do." He looked down at Cassie, his eyes filled with concern. "But if it's her, she needs help. Before she does something rash . . ."

Like kill herself, Cassie finished silently. Like her sister did.

"I'll talk to him," she promised.

They strolled into the central space that held a large communal kitchen between the children's area and the food bank, serving to segregate the adult and pediatric clientele. He nodded thoughtfully at the layout; the entrance to the area was also central so the volunteers working in the kitchen could keep an eye on everyone coming in and out.

"How 'bout panic buttons?" he suggested. "Here, in the dining area and the daycare?" He gestured to the high ceilings. "And we'll tie the smoke detectors into the system as well."

"Good idea," Cassie said, more comfortable now that they were talking business once more. They walked out to the second floor landing.

Tony glanced up at the steps leading to Drake's apartment on the third floor. "You want an alarm or motion detector at that door?" he asked, not using Drake's name. "Anyone could get up there unnoticed." Before Cassie answered, he jogged up the steps, and examined the locks. "I can redo these with the rest, no charge."

"Thanks. Let me talk to Drake about it."

He shrugged. "All right." They climbed back down to the first floor. "The social worker's and Juliet's offices will need motion detectors and extra locks," he noted. "Anyone else going to have confidential information that will need protected?"

"We've got a grant from the Gates Foundation for an electronic medical record system that's supposed to be secure," she told him. "But we'll still have some drugs and equipment that will need protected."

"Not to mention the computers." He moved around, checking the height of the windows from the ground, and the layout of storage areas. "Panic buttons in all the patient and client areas?" She nodded, and he made more notes.

The clamor of racing footsteps interrupted them. "Cassie, Cassie!" A small, dark whirlwind sped past Tony and into Cassie's arms. Antwan Washington, just turned four, jumped up and down. "Where's my joke?"

Cassie grinned and set the boy back down on his feet. "How do you get a Kleenex to dance?" she asked, squatting down to his eye level.

"I dunno," he said after careful consideration.

"Blow some boogie into it!" she answered, giving him a

raspberry kiss and swinging him off his feet in a parody of the boogie-woogie. She was rewarded by joyous peals of laughter.

"Hey, Little Man," Tony greeted the youngster.

"Tony!" Antwan was ecstatic. He leapt from Cassie's arms into Tony's. "Spin me!"

"Your wish is my command." Tony began to whirl Antwan, lifting him to ever dizzying heights.

His mother, Tammy, appeared in the doorway, her arms filled with juice boxes, books, and a bag of toys to occupy her son while she and Cassie worked.

"Sorry we're late," she said, her hand smoothing her black hair from her dark skinned face. The young mother's usually worry-lined face lit with a smile as she watched Tony with her son.

Tammy had come a long way from the overworked, overburdened mother who had watched her son fight his way out of a coma four months ago. She was one of the few paid employees of the Center, and would eventually be their receptionist, scheduling appointments, managing walk-ins, and keeping track of the kids in the daycare and the volunteers. The job didn't pay much, but with the free daycare provided for Antwan, it would be enough to get them through.

"That's enough, Antwan," she said in a firm voice. "Mr. Tony has work of his own to do."

"It's all right, Tammy," Tony said as he set the squirming toddler back on his feet. "Antwan can help me. You can count to ten, right, sport?"

"Onetwothreefourfivesixseveneightninetenleven—" Antwan began breathlessly.

"Let's go." Tony took him by the hand. "We've got to count doors and windows."

"Bring him back if he bothers you," Tammy called after them.

She turned to Cassie. "He's so good with kids," she said, watching Tony lift Antwan onto his broad shoulders. "Don't think he'd like to take on a single mom, do you?"

Matchmaking was definitely not Cassie's forte. "Just ask him out," she said. "What could it hurt?"

Tammy frowned and shook her head. "You've got it so easy with Drake."

Remembering this morning and Drake's moodiness over the past few days, she rolled her eyes. "I'll trade you for Antwan any day."

"I might take you up on that."

Tammy moved to pick up a sander. Cassie raised her hammer once more, and then froze when a familiar shadow filled the doorway.

Tammy spun around, the sander in front of her like a weapon. "Go away, we're busy."

Alan King stood on the edge of the construction zone, his hands brushing invisible dust from his Armani as if entering the Center threatened to contaminate his polished appearance. With his blonde hair and light colored eyes, he appeared every inch of the noble prince his family raised him to be.

The King family took their wealth, prestige, and family name seriously. Everything else in life came second. Cassie glared at Alan, her hand clenching the hammer, fighting the urge to pound something, anything.

Her ex-brother-in-law merely smiled, eyebrow raised, as he gazed upon the tool in her hand. "If you're not going to use that, you might consider putting it down," he said in his cultured tones. "After all, I am an officer of the court, here on business, and some could construe that as a threat."

"Not me," Tammy said, stepping forward to stand at Cassie's

side. "I'll be a witness. You're harassing her."

Alan flicked a look at Tammy as if he she was a gnat too small to bother smashing. But Cassie knew you didn't attract the attention of the King family without paying a price and she didn't want Tammy sucked into the morass her impending malpractice suit had become. Slowly, she re-holstered the hammer and removed the tool belt.

"It's all right," she told Tammy. "I'll just be a moment."

"Nice place you have here," Alan said, looking around as if appraising the building for back taxes. "I hear you've put a lot into it." His gaze returned to her, sliding from her mouth to her breasts and back again as if she were a piece of property as well.

"What do you want, Alan?"

"Thought I'd stop by to deliver this in person." He drew a sheath of papers from his coat pocket and handed them to her. As managing partner of Pittsburgh's largest and most powerful law firm, Alan King didn't usually serve summons.

The reasons behind this visit were much more personal. As Richard's older brother, he held Cassie responsible for the downward turn Richard's life had taken after the overdose. It left Richard with brain damage and destroyed his career as a surgeon. Alan made it perfectly clear that not only would he not settle the suit against Cassie, he wouldn't accept anything less than her complete and total ruin.

Cassie ignored her former brother-in-law and scanned the papers. "The deposition is tomorrow? I can't—"

"Oh, but I think you can," he practically purred with satisfaction. His hand grazed over her arm in a possessive way, and she jerked away from his touch.

Typical of the King men. Total power over everyone around them. It was the only language they understood, the only position they would accept.

She choked back her impulse to send a snap kick into his groin. Maybe if there weren't any witnesses . . .

"Sorry, you'll have to reschedule." She broke away from his grasp and moved past him to the exit. She needed fresh air; room to breathe that wasn't polluted with the stench of wealth and corruption. "I have plans."

He followed her outside onto the stoop, but remained in the cooler shadows of the building. Blood sucking vampire.

Richard had his share of problems. Being the youngest born to a powerful, rich family had a lot to do with his need to exert total control over everyone he met, especially Cassie. A need she hadn't recognized until after they were married and he became abusive.

But Alan was the worst of the bunch. A man with one code: power was everything, and no one stood in his way. She knew he'd manipulated Richard into forcing her resignation from Three Rivers and bringing the lawsuit against her.

"Cancel your plans," he said.

She held her ground, basking in the hot sun. Maybe it was time Alan King learned the world didn't revolve around him and his family. "No."

He pursed his lips in mock consideration at her refusal and reached into his coat for another stack of papers. "Then, I'll be forced to file these." He held them out to her, translating as she shuffled through them. "We'll need complete accounting of the Liberty Community Center's funding from all principles involved. The Center's assets and accounts will be frozen until we're satisfied and the audit is completed."

Cassie felt the blood drain from her face. "You couldn't—you wouldn't. If the Center doesn't open by September first we lose our matching grants."

Not to mention forfeiting Drake and Ed Castro's personal lines of credit they used for startup costs. It would set them back months, maybe even permanently. Ultimately destroying the one place that offered hope to the residents of these ravaged neighborhoods where kids couldn't even get to school because no bus drivers would venture near.

"Why?" She forced the words from between numb lips.

"Sources claim you're using the Center to shield your money from possible forfeiture if you lose the case." He shook his head, *tsking* like an old schoolmarm. "Really, Cassandra, you should know better."

"Everything I gave to the clinic was before you filed the lawsuit. You know that." Cassie knew she should just let Juliet handle Alan. He was bluffing, she was certain. But she couldn't risk the Center, Drake's dream. She pounded her fist against her thigh, unable to strike out at the true object of her fury. "Do you hate me so much you would destroy a place that will only help the people of Pittsburgh?"

He shrugged, the smile on his face revealing his delight at her discomfort. "I'm obligated to act in the best interest of my client. The man who lost his entire future because of you. But feel free to take it personally."

Cassie bit her lip and turned away, looking past the overflowing construction dumpster toward the ravine behind the building. A pleasant breeze swirled through the oaks and maples that towered from the sides of the ravine. From this vantage you could barely hear the sound of the busway, and could almost imagine being far away from urban life.

Safe from the machinations of lawyers.

"What do you want?" she whispered. At his look of triumph she cursed herself for asking. She knew damned well what Alan King wanted.

Everything she had. Her reputation, her medical license, her house, her money, and her pride.

He thought he could take it all, make her suffer a painful public humiliation as payment for the pain she'd caused his brother and their family. It was all about the Kings and their reputation.

Her stomach clenched as she tried to control her anger and keep herself from lashing out, making things worse than they already were.

"I'll be there tomorrow." It was the only way to protect the Center and everything she and the others had invested here. She turned her head, looking through the open window beside her as Tony and Antwan raced past, the four-year-old giggling with glee. So many people had worked so hard to make this dream come true. She couldn't let them down.

"I thought you would. See you tomorrow, Cassandra." He brushed past her, his body pressing against hers for a too-long moment, before he continued down the steps to his Porsche.

Cassie watched in frustration as he squealed out of the parking lot. Tammy joined her.

"Anything I can do?" she asked.

"No, I'll work something out," Cassie said with grim determination.

"Doc Cass, Doc Cass!" A shout accompanied by pounding footsteps came from the alleyway between the vacant warehouses across the street.

Tagger emerged from the shadows, panting, clutching his side as he ran across the street and into the parking lot. The eleven-year-old wore ragged jeans two sizes too big, sneakers decorated in a rainbow of color, a torn Steelers T-shirt, and his ever-present black ball cap. "Come quick," he said, grabbing onto her hand. "She's having a baby. Come on, now."

"Who's having a baby? Where?" she asked, extracting her hand from his. She moved to her car a few feet away and grabbed her daypack from the trunk.

He jerked his head. "Over in the Spookhouse. You know, the burnt one, where the Rippers hang out and get high."

"What were you doing in Ripper territory?" Tammy asked. Tagger's brother had been the leader of the Garfield Gangstas, archrivals to the Ruby Avenue Rippers.

He gave a rebellious one shouldered shrug. "Just doing my art, s'all."

"Show me," Cassie said, spinning away from the Center. "Tammy, call the paramedics."

"You're not going over there," Tammy protested.

"Don't worry," Tagger said, tugging Cassie's hand. "I'm with her."

"Wait for Tony, at least."

"He can meet us there." Cassie and Tagger sprinted across the cul-de-sac and between the buildings, a short cut over to Ruby Avenue, two blocks away.

"Hurry," Tagger cried out, yanking on her hand as she stumbled over torn up pavement. "She's dying in there!"

Chapter 4

"TELL ME WHAT HAPPENED." Drake took the seat beside the victim at the small table in the interview room of the Major Crimes Squad.

She pushed her long, straight hair from her eyes and looked up at him. Then she started to cry.

Aw hell. He hated it when they cried.

"It's okay. Just take your time." He looked around for the box of tissues. Missing in action. Damn it, where was Jimmy when he needed him?

She found her own Kleenex and was blowing her nose when Drake's partner, Jimmy Dolan, entered the room balancing three coffees between his large hands. Jimmy set a cup before the victim, then gave Drake one. Drake rolled his eyes as Jimmy took two packets of sugar and carefully stirred them into the victim's coffee.

"Two sugars, right, Ms. Burns?" Jimmy said soothingly. The victim nodded her thanks. Her name was Monica Burns. She was twenty-four and scared to death.

"I'm sorry," she sniffed. "It just hit me, that man—he was in my house while I slept, anything could have happened—"

"Yes ma'am," Drake tried to sound sympathetic. It was hard though, especially since Burns kept whipping her hair back and looking at him, like she expected more from him. Some miracle CSI magic like on TV. But he just couldn't muster the energy to do more than be annoyed. Not today.

The only reason Robbery dropped the case onto Drake and Jimmy was Burns had complained about their handling of her case and requested Jimmy. So the powers-that-be tapped Major Crimes to play diplomats. It still made it a dump. The lady said only a few pieces of inexpensive jewelry were taken. But the value of what was stolen seldom mattered if you were the victim.

He could deal with all of this a hell of lot better if it wasn't the hottest day of the year and if the air conditioning was working properly and if there was a snowball's chance in hell they were ever gonna solve this case. The boys at Robbery knew that when they gave it to them—which really made him just so happy to be sitting here with this crying lady in a room the size of a closet with sweat pouring from him.

But Mr. Niceguy, Jimmy, ate it up. Enjoyed Drake's torment. If Drake's hands were large enough to fit around Jimmy's former-Marine bull neck, he'd throttle him right here and now, witness and paperwork notwithstanding.

Jimmy sat down across from Drake and smiled as he sipped his coffee. "You feeling better, Ms. Burns?"

"Yes, thank you." She answered Jimmy, but her eyes stayed on Drake. Large doe eyes in a pale face, hair a shade of blonde not quite found in nature.

"Why don't you tell us what happened," Jimmy continued.

"I don't know where to start—" Her eyes darted around the room, looking for a means of escape.

They all got that look sooner or later, Drake had noticed during his five years as a detective. No one liked telling their story to the cops—not the victims, not the witnesses, and certainly not the criminals. Today he heartily sympathized with Monica Burns. He too wanted for this to be over with so that he could get out of this room, out of the station house, and out of this city.

"Start at the beginning," Drake prompted her. "When did you first notice the items were missing?"

Burns shook her long hair out of her face again. Drake wondered how hot and heavy all that hair must feel on a day like this. The heat didn't seem to bother Burns, in fact she was dressed in a black T-shirt and black jeans. If you passed her in the street you would take her for a starving artist with her pale complexion and hollow cheeks.

"When did I notice them missing? This morning," she answered.

Come on lady. Don't make me work for this. "And did you notice anything unusual last night?"

She hesitated, then shook her head no. Drake cut his eyes at Jimmy and passed the ball to his partner.

"What kind of security do you have?" Jimmy asked.

"It's a house converted to apartments. There's a lock on the main doors and one on my door. But, with the heat—"

"You've been keeping the entrance doors open," Jimmy supplied. It was a common practice in the older buildings that lacked central air. She nodded. "And your own door, was that locked last night?"

Drake was continually amazed by how many urbanites forgot something so simple as turning their dead bolt. These were the same people who often decried the police for their inability to protect the public.

"I'm sorry, I just can't remember. I might have forgotten it. I know I didn't put the chain on because I never do." She said the last as if they should reward her for her excellent memory.

Drake had enough. This wasn't getting them anywhere.

"Thanks a lot, Ms. Burns. Listen, why don't you work on making us a list of what was stolen. Try to be as detailed as possible." He motioned to Jimmy, and they went out into the hallway, leaving their victim to puzzle over the paperwork.

"Jeez, what a dump," Drake sighed when they were back at their desks.

"DJ, will you just chill out?" Jimmy said. Most cops called Drake DJ—or Drake Junior—since he'd joined the force while his father was still alive and on the job. "What's going on with you today? I know you're anxious to get out of here, but—"

"It's this heat, I can't stand it."

"Yeah, I don't remember it being this hot last July—" Jimmy paused and looked at Drake. "It was this time last year that Pamela killed herself, wasn't it?"

"I'm fine," Drake snapped at his partner.

Another of the detectives, Janet Kwon, handed a stack of case files to Jimmy. "He PMSing or what?" She gestured at Drake.

"Just in dire need of a vacation," Jimmy answered as Drake snatched the files from his partner.

"But I'll settle for a weekend off if everybody gets off of my back. Shit, are these all of the BE's and burglaries from the zone?" Drake leafed through the case files.

"That's just the last thirty days," Kwon supplied helpfully.

Drake groaned. "What's so special about this weekend, anyway? You have something planned?"

"He's taking Hart to the Lake. With the family." Jimmy propped himself on the edge of Drake's desk.

Kwon whistled. "Sounds like lover boy's getting serious about this one."

"Yeah," Jimmy replied, reaching over to lift a framed photo of Hart from the desk. "First time I've ever seen him bring a picture of a girlfriend in here." They both turned to stare at Drake as if he were a zoo specimen.

"You two want to move this coffee klatch somewhere besides my desk?" Drake asked, snatching the photo from Jimmy. It was taken after Hart passed her brown belt test last month. She was dressed in a white *gi*, dark hair matted with sweat but her smile was wide and her eyes flashed her triumph at the camera. "In case you haven't noticed, I'm trying to work here."

"Well, excuse the hell out of me," Kwon said. "I was going to offer to go through those files, but—"

"Thanks Janet." Drake shoved the files back at her before she could say anything more.

"Why don't we get Ms. Burns to sign her statement? Then we can go check out her building."

That suited Drake. "Let's put this baby to rest for the weekend and pick it up again on Monday. It's not like there'll be anything happening over the weekend, not on a dump case like this one."

Chapter 5

THE SPOOKHOUSE, AS TAGGER called it, was a three-story half-burned derelict yellow-brick apartment building that had been on the city's demolition list for several years. The Stackhouse Apartments' fire had polarized the city, almost starting a race riot. Seven people lost their lives, five of them young children. Residents blamed the City for not enforcing housing code violations, the fire department for not responding fast enough, and the police for blocking civilian efforts to rescue the trapped children.

Few mentioned the Garfield Gangstas, the Black Gangster Disciple Gang that had cordoned off the area with abandoned vehicles to block emergency response units and who had began the fire in retaliation for the drive-by shooting of one of their members. Fewer still mentioned the Ruby Avenue Rippers whose turf included the Stackhouse and whose members raced from the fire, abandoning their families to the inferno.

Cassie pulled up short before they exited the cover of the alley, pulling at Tagger's shirt collar to halt him. Across the street was the Stackhouse. Its windows boarded over, covered by gang graffiti, its front door totally gone, giving it the appearance of a gape-toothed jack-o-lantern. Beyond the front entrance lay an impenetrable darkness.

What pregnant woman in her right mind would pick that building to crawl inside to have her child? Cassie shuddered and turned her attention to the group of young men milling in the alleyway beside the building, tossing coins against the wall, hip-hop music reverberating from the brick walls.

Ripper territory. She glanced down at Tagger. He was wearing a black ball cap with the GG's insignia. She yanked it off, and shoved it into her pack.

"Hey! That's my pride, you don't mess with that." He gave her a squinty look as if he were a whole lot meaner than she knew he was.

"Right now your only job is to get that girl safely out of there. Don't give me any grief or I'll find your auntie and tell her you've been playing wannabee with the Gangstas."

He huffed, and squared off his shoulders. "Don't you diss my boys. My brother died a G."

"Yeah, at the ripe old age of eighteen. Let's try to beat his record, okay?"

She didn't wait for the pre-teen's answer. She grabbed his arm and pulled him along the empty storefronts until they were out of sight of the alley. No obvious watchers, but she knew they were there, somewhere. A white woman with a black kid would stand out. Sooner or later, the Rippers would know she and Tagger had come calling.

If they caught him and he started mouthing off about the Gangstas . . .

"Go back to the Center," she told him. "Tell Tammy to call the ambulance again."

"No. You'll never find her in there. Not without me, you won't."

He hauled her across the street and up the steps to the Stackhouse's front entrance. "Don't worry none about the Rippers," he said once they were inside what used to be the foyer, waiting as she grabbed a Maglite from her pack. "They're all a bunch of punks."

Out of the mouth of babes. She only hoped Tagger never learned how deadly punks could be. Then she remembered his older brother and knew he already had.

Gloom engulfed them in a claustrophobic embrace. Tagger gripped her wrist as she flicked the flashlight on. The narrow beam illuminated an alien landscape, reflecting off garish fluorescent graffiti, the gleam of crack pipes, and abandoned bottles of cheap booze and forty-cans. That was all she could see before the charred remains of furniture and drywall swallowed the beam of light whole.

She shuffled her feet over used condoms and other debris. The stench of urine, vomit, sex, and rotten food mingled with the wet, stifling smell of burnt plastic and decaying wood. Each breath brought with it a new and unwanted odor. Cassie waved her hand before her face as if she could brush away the stench clinging to her like cobwebs.

"This way," Tagger said, moving past a half-charred sofa dumped in the foyer like it was a dentist's office waiting room. He ducked his head under a fallen piece of drywall.

Her foot crunched down on a child's plastic doll. It wasn't singed by fire, and looked relatively new. As if this burned out crack den was a playground. The realization pricked at the back of her eyes. Tagger's unique graffiti splattered over the walls, psychedelic sunflowers and neon star-filled skies reminiscent of Van Gogh, a bright ray of hope in an otherwise godforsaken cavern of despair.

He led her through a maze of charred timbers, walking through the walls of the apartments, stepping over melted baby toys,

appliances, and unidentifiable objects, grazing against fried wiring
and broken pipes that gleamed in the dark like goblin's teeth and
barked her shins when she wasn't careful.

"The hallway's blocked, ceiling collapsed," he answered her
unasked question. "Whole other side of the building is lots worse
than this—couldn't make it more than a few steps over there."

Cassie had somehow gotten used to the stench and bizarre
sights, and was even able to ignore the sensation that the walls and
ceiling were about to fall in on her, squeeze all the air from her
body, and abandon her in the blackness. Then she saw where Tagger
led next.

"C'mon," he urged when she stopped. "She's down here."

Oh no, no, no. She shook her head, words failing her as her
breath caught in her throat. He couldn't be serious. No way.

He had crouched at the opening of a plumbing access panel,
low in the wall, and had climbed halfway inside. "It's the only way.
It's not far now."

She waved the light, trying to make the two-foot square
manmade tunnel appear larger. It didn't. In fact, as the light was
swallowed by the darkness, the area looked smaller. And a lot more
deadly. Jagged spikes of copper piping jutted from every surface—
just waiting to impale her. Tagger had no compunctions. He slid on
his stomach through the opening as easily as Alice down the rabbit's
hole.

"Hurry," his high-pitched voice echoed from the darkness.

Cassie sighed, clamped the flashlight between her teeth, and
pushed the backpack before her, stalling for one more breath of
air before she entered. How the hell had a pregnant woman gotten
through this? There had to be a back way to where her patient lay.
There had damn well better be, because no way in hell were any
paramedics going to find them through here.

Her thoughts and Tagger's urging kept her mind occupied, helped her ignore the bile churning her gut and burning her throat as her claustrophobia ambushed her. *Just a little farther*, became her mantra. Accompanied by a refrain of: Drake was going to kill her if he ever heard about this.

She realized her cell phone was in the charger in her car, protected from the drywall dust. If this was some kind of elaborate trap, if Tagger was using her to score points with the Gangstas . . .

No. He seemed honestly scared, and wanted to help the woman, despite the fact she chose to have her baby in Ripper territory. He risked his life coming back here with so many Rippers around. No, it wasn't Tagger she had to worry about. It was everyone else. Not to mention the building falling down on her.

Or figuring out how the hell she was going to get Tagger and a pregnant lady out of here.

Beware what you wish for, Rosa would say. Cassie had been searching for a path out of the purgatory her resignation from Three Rivers had exiled her to, and had been yearning for a way back into medicine.

She got what she wanted, in spades.

The backpack slipped from her grasp as the floor vanished beneath her.

Chapter 6

DRAKE SAT IN THE unmarked Intrepid's passenger seat as Jimmy parked a few doors down from a brick Tudor on the wrong side of the demarcation between trendy Shadyside and not-so-desirable East Liberty. He didn't move, relishing the cool breeze emerging from the car's AC vents. Jimmy turned the ignition off. Drake inhaled one last time to savor the crisp oxygen. The air outside shimmered as if alive, beckoning them with deadly intent.

Jimmy circled around to the sidewalk. Drake waited until the last possible moment before exiting the car. No good. The blast of heat still swamped him, made him feel as if he'd fallen into quicksand. This kind of air you could cut like a knife, drown in.

Even Jimmy, the impervious former Marine, was flushed and sweating by the time they climbed to the top of the stoop. Drake hid his smile. Misery loved company. The front door stood wide open, inviting any hint of a breeze and any two-bit push-in artist to enter.

"What floor?" Drake asked.

"Fourth, top."

"Figures." He looked up the narrow steps sporting frayed carpeting. The entire house smelled of cabbages and cigarettes.

"Flip you for it?"

"Nah. You work the scene, I'll start banging on doors."

It was their usual division of labor, each following their strengths. Drake could read a crime scene better than any of the detectives on the squad, while Jimmy could make anyone talk whether they wanted to or not. Still, Drake felt a prickling behind his neck as he began up the first flight of stairs.

It was a dead end burglary, nothing to get so excited about. Just nerves. Not sleeping for four days would put anyone on edge. It didn't help that Burns lived in the same neighborhood as Pamela. In fact, Pamela's building was just a few blocks from here.

He pushed aside all thoughts of Pamela and tried to concentrate on the case. Instead, all he could think about with each step was a cold breeze coming in off the Lake, water lapping against him as he ducked his head under, emerging to find Hart beside him, her fingers tracing the beads of water down his chest and moving lower still . . .

The top of the steps came all too soon. Drake shook his sexy daydream away, promising himself to revisit it at his next available moment, and knocked on Monica Burns' door.

She opened it and stood there for a long moment, arm against the doorjamb as if she was posing for a perfume ad. She'd changed into a black midriff tank top and filmy, gauze skirt, both of which clung to her, revealing every jutting angle of her emaciated ribs and sunken abdomen. In contrast, her full breasts strained the tank top's spaghetti straps.

Did other guys really find that attractive? Give him Hart with her well-formed muscles, compact breasts that fit oh-so-well into his hands, her narrow hips and tight abdomen—trimmed by work, not from starvation.

He focused his eyes on Burns' face, kept his gaze expressionless as she slowly lowered her arm and stepped back inside, motioning for him to follow. Instead, he squatted, examined the locks on her door. No dead bolt. Only a simple snap lock anyone with a credit card could spring, and the chain she'd already admitted to not using.

"Might want to think about investing in a dead bolt." He straightened. She'd moved to stand where the light from the window backlit her, effortlessly cutting through the thin fabric of her skirt. What the hell? He remembered the way she'd brushed against him at the station house. Was she coming on to him?

"Yes, sir," she replied. Then she stood there, silently, expectantly.

Drake felt his forehead knot into a frown and cursed himself. Burns was pissing him off with her demur glances and silent invitations. She just wasn't his type.

A stirring in his pelvis begged to differ. He couldn't pull his eyes away as she inhaled deeply, her breasts swelling, straining the fabric of her top. Burns *was* exactly his type, a cookie-cutter image of so many women he'd been with. *Before* Hart.

The tall, Barbie-doll blonde before him was Hart's opposite in so many ways, he couldn't even begin to list them. Just as Hart was Pamela's opposite—

Shit. Back to Pamela. Focus, damn it, he was on the job here.

"Where were the items taken from?" He swallowed to clear the gravel that clogged his voice.

"The bathroom." The bathroom was through the apartment's sole bedroom. She led the way, stopping short so he bumped against her. From her expression, he had the feeling that was her intention.

"I'm sorry, I guess I shouldn't have touched anything," she said, standing in the open doorway. "But it's the only bathroom."

Drake entered the tiny space. Teal green and black tile on the walls, black and white tiles on the floor, claw foot tub, commode, and pedestal sink. The single small window above the toilet was open, but no air moved in the cramped room. Burns joined him, her body adding to the heat. The scent of almonds and apricots swirled around him, thick like an exotic liqueur. Sweat glued his shirt to his chest and back as he turned around to survey the area.

Actor would have had to come through the bedroom to reach the bath. No way anyone could have gotten in through the window. "Are you a heavy sleeper?"

"Yes, why?" Then her eyes went wide as if she'd just now realized the implications. "You mean he was in my bedroom." She shuddered dramatically. "Anything could have happened."

Drake wasn't surprised when she grabbed his arm. Like some kind of knight in shining armor. Jeezit, did she have the wrong cop. He looked at the empty porcelain cup that sat on the back of the toilet. "That's where the rings were?"

"Yes. And my bracelets were beside them in the saucer." She jangled her wrists and raised one golden chain clad ankle to demonstrate. "Usually these are all I sleep in, so he didn't get these. But I had some others—sterling silver and turquoise, one carved coral—a whole bunch."

"You touch anything—" he started. Of course she had. He amended his question. "The cup or saucer?"

A pretty frown creased her brow as she concentrated. "No. Just the flusher, the sink, the door handle—" She spun around in the cramped quarters, brushing against him once more, releasing another wave of the fruity fragrance. "And the bath tub. That's all."

That was enough. Something about this didn't feel right. Escaping the confines of the bath, he exited into her bedroom. The bed was rumpled with brightly colored mismatched sheets, and silk pillows of every size and shape. Instead of curtains, mosquito netting was draped over a rod at the window. Candles festooned every available surface. Drake moved to the open window, searching for a morsel of fresh air. Burns followed as if worried he'd miss a vital clue.

No fire escape. The actor would've come from inside, through the front door. Walking right past the stereo, TV, and DVD player just to snag some cheap rings and bracelets? And risk waking the resident? It didn't make much sense as a burglary.

His breath caught as his gaze snagged on the building opposite. They faced the rear of an apartment building. A building he knew well. Against his will, the hairs on his neck prickling, he counted windows until he reached the fifth floor. And found himself staring into what had once been Pamela Reynolds' bedroom.

The last place he, or anyone, had seen her alive.

Chapter 7

CASSIE TOPPLED INTO SPACE. The flashlight dropped, clanging as it spiraled down. Her hand slammed against a concrete step. The darkness gave the illusion she'd fallen a great distance, but in reality it'd only been a few feet. Just enough to disorient her. She pulled the lower half of her body from the hole in the wall and crawled the rest of the way into a stairwell. Tagger grabbed her flashlight and guided her with its beam.

Her lungs felt as if they'd been squeezed tight. Sweat and grime covered her. "How far did we come?"

Tagger retrieved her backpack. "Dunno. We was in the walls behind a kitchen and bath. The hallway has holes in the floor so I thought this way would be safer. That all right?"

He looked at her with a worried expression that said he'd forgotten she was an old person. Cassie ignored him as she did a mental calculation. Kitchen and bath—maybe twenty feet they'd crawled through? Seemed as if she'd tunneled beneath the entire Allegheny Plateau.

She felt her way down the steps to join him. She'd done it, made it through. That was what counted. "How did you find this?"

"Rippers chased me in here one day." He shrugged, the light bobbing with his movement. "It's not so bad here once you get used to it. I can think, do my art. Lots quieter than home."

"With your aunt?" Another silent nod. "Why, what happened?" They moved into a relatively intact basement area surrounded by cement block walls covered in Tagger's artwork. His reply came to her from the darkness as if that was the only way he could share secrets like this one.

"Ever since Rodney died, she's been going out lots more. One of her friends—she's gots lots, always bringing them by—he came into my room . . ." His voice trailed off.

Cassie could guess what happened next. "He tried to touch you?"

She barely caught the nod of his head and shrug of his shoulders. But the sniff as he wiped tears away echoed loud through the darkness. "Tried to make me . . . anyway, I bit him. Hard." Pride edged his voice. "He cried like a baby and hit me. Then he hit my aunt and left, and she came after me, hollering that I was spoiling everything. Then she was trying to beat up on me, so's I left, too."

"How long ago was that?" she asked as she bent low to avoid a sawed-off pipe. Scavengers took anything they could.

"Two-three days. S'all right, I can take care of myself." He turned one more corner in the maze. "C'mon. She's in here."

There was a click as he turned on a portable lantern hanging from a twisted piece of rebar in the ceiling. Cassie blinked in the unexpected brightness. They were in the basement laundry area, a windowless room where Tagger's art covered every surface. Part of the ceiling was collapsed at the far end, legs of a kitchen table straddling the opening. The faint sound of whimpering punctuated by gasps came from behind a fallen piece of charred drywall to one side of the collapse.

Tagger moved toward the sound. Cassie rushed to join him, her gaze raking over the precariously stacked debris. Through the hole, a faint glimmer of sunlight from the apartment above dared to part the shadows. The entire wall looked like it might tumble down on top of them with one wrong breath.

Then she saw her patient. This was no woman. This was a girl. Thin. Much too thin for someone so far along in their pregnancy, cheeks and eyes sunken in a finely boned face, ebony complexion marred by a wicked scar burned into her forehead.

Cassie had seen similar scars in people grazed by a bullet. It didn't look very old, maybe a week or two. Pink granulation tissue still glistened in the center of the wound.

This girl looked maybe fifteen, sixteen, tops. What had she done to be shot at, then abandoned here to have her baby alone? What kind of hell had this girl already survived?

"Told you I'd get help, Athena." Tagger squeezed the girl's hand as he knelt at her side. "This is Doc Cass. She's the best."

"You know her?" Cassie assessed her patient's pulse, noting the signs of dehydration as well as the clear fluid puddled on the floor beneath the girl's hips.

"Athena was Rodney's girlfriend," he said. His brother who'd been killed two weeks ago.

The girl's eyes fluttered open and she gasped in fear, tried to pull away. Cassie grabbed a water bottle from her pack and held it to the girl's lips.

"Drink, slow," she urged. The girl complied, so weak Tagger had to lift her head.

Cassie wished she had IV fluids, but all she had in her pack were basic first aid supplies. "How far apart are your contractions?"

"Baby Jane and I had a talk, she's gonna wait," the girl said. "They've slowed down."

Cassie didn't have the heart to tell the girl that might be a bad sign. "How far along are you?"

"Eight and a half months, give or take."

Thirty-four weeks. That give or take might mean all the difference to the baby. Cassie felt the girl's belly. "Anything hurt?"

Athena winced when she palpated her left kidney and Cassie noticed bruising along her side. Fresh bruises, only a few days old at most. The baby didn't move under her touch. It felt like it was vertex, though, that was good. A breech delivery in these conditions would be a nightmare. She grabbed her stethoscope. Even though it wasn't an obstetric one, this far along, she might be able to make out the baby's heart tones. Athena and Tagger watched her anxiously as she strained to hear. Finally she caught the faint heartbeat. Slow, maybe eighty beats a minute. Too slow.

"Tagger, we have to get her out of here. There has to be another door, right?"

His eyes darted past her before he nodded. "In the stairway. Opens onto the alley."

Now she understood why he'd taken her through the claustrophobic labyrinth. If Tagger showed his face in an alley full of Rippers, they'd kill him.

But she couldn't leave Athena to go herself. This baby had to be delivered soon—or it might die.

"Athena, I'm going to examine you down there. Try to exhale, blow your breath out, it might feel a bit uncomfortable." Nothing compared to a baby passing through the same area, but she didn't tell the girl that. Cassie slipped on a pair of vinyl gloves and did a manual exam. Athena sucked her breath in and clenched her muscles for a moment. Cassie tried to help her relax. "Jane, is that what your baby's name is going to be?"

"Plain, simple Jane," Athena said. Tagger gave her another

drink as Cassie finished. "Nothing fancy like mine—nothing she has to live up to. She's gonna be her own woman."

Cassie gave the girl a grim smile. "I think you've done a fine job of living up to your name, Athena."

"Is my Baby Jane all right?"

"She will be if we can deliver her soon. Her head's all the way down, she's ready to go, but I don't think she can wait much longer."

"Why not?"

"She's been too stressed and now her heart is beginning to slow. When you feel the next contraction, I want you to try pushing."

"I can't, they hurt too much and I'm too tired." The girl sounded desperate, at the end of her strength. Cassie could only imagine. How long had she been hiding here, without proper food or water? Living in the dark like an animal. No place to bring a new life into the world.

Athena's body writhed in pain as another contraction shot through her. Cassie pulled one of the girl's legs back, nodding to Tagger to do the same with the other.

"Good girl, Athena. Just breathe. Like this." She demonstrated a panting type of stacked breaths. Athena's eyes squeezed shut as her entire body strained to push her baby out. "Good, good. Just like that," Cassie coached her. A glimpse of dark hair appeared as the baby crowned.

Athena collapsed, gasping for air. Cassie relaxed the girl's leg. "It won't be long now." She opened her knapsack, and gathered her supplies. She'd cut the cord with her Leatherman, bundle the baby in her foil emergency blanket, tie the cord with a piece of nylon cording. As long as Athena didn't hemorrhage and the baby didn't get stuck, things should work out.

Except for the dozen Rippers between them and escape. No

wonder the paramedics hadn't arrived yet. Probably drove past the place and decided it was a prank call. Surely Tony Spanos wouldn't give up that easily. But could he find them?

The idea of having the burly Greek at her side as they faced the Rippers gave Cassie a little hope. Only person she'd rather see would be Drake.

She listened to the baby's heartbeat again. Down to seventy. Another contraction tore through Athena, who bit down on her own hand in an effort to remain quiet.

Cassie admired the girl's fortitude. Last thing they needed was a bunch of Rippers barging in during the delivery. She positioned Tagger so he could hold Athena's legs and she would be free to catch the baby.

"The head's right there," she told Athena. "Keep pushing, you can do it." Had better do it. She wasn't sure how low the baby's heart rate would drop with contractions. The added stress might be too much for Baby Jane. "C'mon, little girl. You made it this far, just a few more inches. Your momma's waiting for you."

Cassie gently ran her fingers along the rim of the birth canal, helping Athena's muscles to stretch. She hadn't caught a baby in a while. This one sure had a lot of hair for being so early. She felt Athena's strength flag even though the contraction was still strong.

"Breathe, Athena. Now!" she commanded as the girl's eyes fluttered and her body went limp for a moment. "You can do it! Push!"

Athena scrunched her face and bore down. The baby's head popped free, into Cassie's waiting hand. She had no suction available, so she did her best to clear the baby's airway with a piece of gauze. "Good girl, hold on just a moment. The head is out."

Cassie rotated the baby's head, checked for a cord around her neck. None. Good, one less thing to worry about. "All right, one more push. Now!"

Athena complied, her breath escaping in a strangled moan. Cassie delivered the baby's shoulder, the rest of the body following effortlessly. She laid the baby on the space blanket and dried it off.

C'mon, breathe. Please, just breathe, Cassie prayed.

"Tagger, tie the cord in two places and cut between it," Cassie told him, her attention focused on the baby who had yet to take her first breath.

"What's wrong?" Athena gasped, tears filling her voice. "Why's she so quiet?"

Cassie was too busy trying to check Baby Jane's heart rate to answer. Eighty. C'mon, Jane. She mercilessly flicked the baby's feet and rubbed her back while bending over, blowing in her face.

"She's beautiful," Tagger whispered in a reverent tone.

Only if you liked a dusky shade of purple. Cassie was about to start mouth to mouth on the limp baby when Jane's eyes popped open and she gurgled in a deep breath, followed by a lusty cry that brought tears to Cassie's eyes. "Good girl."

Once Jane's color was a healthy pink, Cassie bundled the baby in the blanket and placed her in Athena's arms. The loud squeals of a good set of healthy lungs echoed through the room.

Thank you, God, Cassie thought.

Now what about those gang-bangers hanging outside the door?

Suddenly light spilled in from the direction of the stairway accompanied by the sound of heavy, running footsteps.

Cassie sucked in her breath, desperately scanned the area for a weapon. Her fingers closed on a length of rebar and she held it at the ready, standing between the three children and the intruder.

Chapter 8

"SOMEONE CALL FOR A taxi?" Tony Spanos' voice boomed through the narrow room.

"In here," Cassie called. The knot twisting her stomach finally relaxed. Athena cooed to her baby; both mother and child seemed out of danger. They could deliver the placenta at Three Rivers, and get Athena antibiotics and pitocin. Not to mention evaluate her other injuries.

"What did you do with the Rippers?" Cassie asked as Tony crouched beside her. She stripped the bloody gloves from her hands and shoved everything back into her pack.

"After they scared the medics away, I knocked a few of them senseless and the rest went scrambling. The cops are on the way, but the Rippers will be back soon, so we'd best hurry."

She heartily agreed. She had no desire to spend another second down here in this dark hellhole. "You carry Athena. I'll take the baby."

Athena clutched Jane to her chest as if frightened she'd never see her daughter again. Cassie gently disengaged the girl's hands and cradled the baby herself. "It's all right, Athena. It's only until we get to the hospital."

Tony effortlessly scooped Athena's thin frame into his arms. "Good thing I heard that baby crying or I never would have found yunz."

Tagger stood to one side, staring at the door with apprehension. "Maybe I'd best go out the way I came in."

"No." Athena reached for his hand.

"She's right, Tagger. You'll be safest with us." Cassie handed the flashlight to the boy, hoping that having a weapon, however small, might give him some courage. He nodded and followed Tony out. Cassie hesitated then gripped the rebar. She was more than happy to be leaving the dark confines of the Stackhouse behind.

"Are you ever going to have a story to tell when you get older," she whispered to Baby Jane as she scrambled up the steps.

DRAKE FLED FROM BURNS' bedroom. Call him a coward, but he was tired of Pamela ambushing him from every direction. He was ready to get the hell out of Dodge. Now.

He stopped short in the living room, and tried to regain his composure. There had to be a dozen buildings in this neighborhood you could see Pamela's apartment from. He'd probably been inside most of them without ever noticing. It was the stalker, worming his way into Drake's brain with his sick mind games.

"I'm going to send some guys to check for fingerprints," he told Burns. Fat lot of good it would do, but worth a shot.

She nodded mutely, then burst into tears. Aw hell, not again. Before he could offer her his handkerchief, she grabbed her purse and rummaged through it.

"Hold this," she said, handing him a black patent leather wallet that matched the purse. Then she withdrew a delicate piece of embroidered linen and wiped her tears, while he stood there holding her wallet in one hand, the purse in the other, wishing he'd called in sick this morning.

If he had, he'd already be at the Lake. He and Hart sailing, and catching cool breezes not found here in this pressure cooker of a city. He could see Hart laughing, the wind dancing over her hair as he showed her how to handle the small Sunfish. Just a few more hours. He could hang on that long.

Burns sniffed one more time and looked up at him with large, hazel eyes dripping with need. "Am I all right here?" She reached a hand out, resting it on his arm. "You'll protect me, make sure nothing happens?"

Not him, lady. Not until after this weekend anyway.

"We'll do the best we can," he tried to reassure her. "But you might want to stay with a friend for a few days. Until you get the locks changed, at least."

She straightened, trying and failing to appear brave. "Could I—could I call you if anything happens, Detective Drake?"

He gave her his card, the one with the station house number, not his private numbers. "You can call this twenty-four hours a day."

She looked down at the card, a small frown crossing her features as if she realized a brush-off when she saw one. He sure as hell hoped she did.

Jimmy's heavy steps sounded from the staircase. "I've got to get going. Don't touch anything more until the crime scene technicians are done. And remember to ask for their ID before you let them inside."

She nodded her head like a little girl chastened by past mistakes and anxious to please. "Yes, I will. Thank you." He was already halfway out the door, eager to be leaving her presence. "I'll see you later, Detective Drake."

Not if he saw her first. Jeezit, did the Burglary guys owe them big time on this one. He stole a glance back at Burns who was hanging over the railing at the top of the steps, watching him leave. Maybe she was pretty in that Hollywood too-thin way.

If only he didn't already have Hart. He stopped short. Had he really fallen so far he couldn't even look at another woman? In just five short months?

No, no way. He always promised himself he'd never be tied down, never be one of those men who let a woman control their entire existence. True, he loved Hart, he really did. But she didn't own him or anything.

He stood his ground, and in defiance of the feelings spiraling through him at the thought of Hart, he raised his head and met Burns' gaze with a smile. The smile she returned was full wattage as she leaned further, giving him a glimpse of her ample cleavage.

Drake fled down the steps, already regretting his impulse, meeting Jimmy on the third floor landing. Christ, he was a heel. What the hell was he thinking, smiling at a victim like that—just to prove he could, that he still had it in him to make a woman look at him with lust in her eyes?

And the worst thing was, his body had responded to Burns' interest even as his mind kept thinking of Hart.

"What's wrong with you?" Jimmy asked when Drake stood there like a mope.

"I'm an idiot."

"Could've told you that. What's the deal?"

"Not your typical B and E. I think we might have a peeper who got lucky—hopefully won't be escalating anytime soon, but we should have CSU take a look, see if they can find any prints worth running."

"No one else in the building saw, heard, or lost anything. Looks like our actor climbed right up to the top of the building."

They continued down the steps and out to the car. "So he knows Burns—or at least where she lives."

"Name's on the mailbox," Jimmy supplied, "with little hearts drawn around it."

Next time Drake saw Monica Burns, he was going to lecture her on life in the big, bad city.

"We'll get the boys working on it. Not much else we can do today." Drake slouched in the seat as Jimmy steered the Intrepid back toward East Liberty and the House. "Might as well call it quits."

To his surprise, Jimmy stopped in front of the Blarney Stone, the bar Drake's first partner, Andy Greally, owned. Jimmy turned and looked at him. "You going tell me what the hell is going on?"

Drake was silent. Last thing he wanted was to get anyone else involved. Pamela's suicide raked up, his co-workers doubting him again. Especially not Jimmy. He stared at the vent, wishing the air conditioner could go higher.

Jimmy turned the ignition off but made no move to leave the car. "I can take the heat."

The car quickly grew stifling. An oven roasting in the relentless sun. Drake debated his options—all of which conspired to make him look a fool. Or more of a fool than he already appeared. Besides, if you couldn't trust your partner . . .

"All right. But inside, where it's cooler."

"My thoughts exactly."

Chapter 9

THE BLARNEY STONE WAS a traditional policeman's pub: high-backed booths promising privacy, back room with an old fashioned jukebox and antique pool table, red-cheeked bartender behind the lovingly polished bar, waiting to hear confession.

Only the man behind the bar was no priest. And certainly no saint. Andy Greally was a retired patrol officer who had been Drake's father's partner and then Drake's training officer. Drake nodded a greeting as he settled himself into the back booth—the most private. Not that there was anyone else in the bar with the breakfast crowd gone and the lunch one not yet begun.

Jimmy heaved into the bench opposite, immediately loosening his tie, but leaving his suit coat on. Andy arrived balancing three cups of coffee and a manila envelope.

"What's that?" Drake asked, pushing against the back corner of the booth at the sight of the envelope. He knew the answer. Hard enough explaining what a fuck up he was to Jimmy—but now he had to let Andy in on it as well?

Andy dealt out the coffee mugs, flipped the envelope onto the table, and slid in beside Drake, trapping him. "You tell me. Kenny found it when he was closing up last night. Gave it to me to give to you. Reeks of cheap perfume. You got another psychofreak like Pamela hounding you? Does Hart know?"

Andy never approved of Pamela. Thought she was unstable. A badge bunny who needed rescuing on a constant basis. But he was a staunch supporter of Hart. The doctor was one of the few women up to the challenge of keeping Drake in line.

Drake swiped at the envelope. Jimmy beat him to it, flipping it over to reveal Drake's name scrawled in angry red lipstick. He opened his knife, slit the bottom and slid the contents onto the table. This time the photos were smeared with what looked like blood, a few drops thicker, others with the edges spread thin like real blood did when it separated.

"You didn't call?" Jimmy asked Andy as he shuffled through the photos, taking care not to smudge any possible prints. Not that there would be. This actor was smarter than that.

Drake didn't bother more than an initial glance to make sure there was nothing new besides the blood. Same old, same old. Pictures of him looking dead, lying in his own blood, autopsy and crime scene photos of Pamela, her face blown off, the gun—his gun—near her hand, the rumpled bed they shared that night.

"Didn't know I needed to," Andy replied, obviously miffed at playing catch up.

"This one," Jimmy nodded to Drake, "thought he could handle it on his own. Was just getting ready to fill in his partner." He stressed the last word as if it might be a temporary position.

"When did they start?" Andy asked. He and Jimmy stared at Drake like Drake was a witness. A victim. Anything but a fellow cop.

Drake glared into his untouched coffee, too tired to even lift it to his lips to drink, and told them everything.

"And you have no idea who might be behind it?" Andy asked.

"No. Well, some ideas, nothing concrete—"

"Did Pamela have any family?"

"A sister. I never met her. Lived in California. I never knew about her except she was listed in the obituary." It wasn't like Drake had attended the funeral of the woman he helped kill.

He'd wanted to. He almost did until Jimmy talked him out of it, told him it might help Drake's guilt but it wouldn't help Pamela's family. Now he wished he had gone, if only to have a visual memory of the people in Pamela's life.

"What about Spanos?" Andy put in. "He was with Pamela before you."

"Yeah. I thought about him." Drake heaved his shoulders in a shrug. "Can't find anything to tie him to this." He swept his hand at the photos. "So far there's been no evidence. But maybe with the blood—"

"Don't be an idiot," Andy scoffed. "It will be chicken or cow's blood. Besides, no way can you get results back fast enough to help."

"The actor knows that," Jimmy said thoughtfully. "Otherwise he'd have used the blood earlier to increase the intimidation factor."

Drake was grateful Jimmy didn't say "fear factor." Although it sure as hell wasn't intimidation keeping him awake and worrying all night. "This morning there was an envelope waiting on Hart's front porch."

"Shit. Does she know?" Andy asked.

"No."

Both men hunched their shoulders, ready to protect Hart.

"I have a plan."

"You're not using Hart as bait." Andy glowered at his former trainee.

"Of course not." Drake found the energy to straighten and glare back. Andy broke it off first.

"What's your plan?" Jimmy asked, playing peacemaker.

"I'm taking Hart out of here. Tonight. Up to my aunt's house at the Lake. She'll be safe there while I come back to set a trap for . . ." He stalled. "For whomever."

"Good plan. Except for one thing. You and Hart stay up at the Lake and I'll take care of this actor," Jimmy said, gathering the photos and sliding them back into the envelope.

"No. This is about me. I'll—"

"You can't investigate a case you're personally involved in. And this is about as personal as it gets."

"Besides," Andy put in, "it will do you good, some time alone with Hart."

"We won't be alone. My aunt and mother will be there."

Andy and Jimmy exchanged glances. "So, where's the ring? How're you going to pop the question?" Andy asked while Jimmy beamed his approval.

"Ring? No, I'm not—"

"Sure you are. We can have the bachelor party right here."

Drake pushed his coffee away, lay his head down on the table, and groaned. Someone out there wanted to hurt him, and maybe Hart, and these two were planning wedding favors? Could this day get any worse?

CASSIE HUGGED BABY JANE to her chest, her other hand gripping the length of rebar as they climbed up the steps to the alley door. A primal drumbeat surged through her veins. After her disastrous marriage to Richard, she never dreamed of having children. The thought terrified her. The enormity. The responsibility.

Yet, in this moment, the baby so light and warm bundled in her arms, she would die for Baby Jane. She knew it. Protecting Baby Jane filled her with the same fierce determination as rushing to save a life did back in the ER.

She reached the last step and crossed the threshold. Bright sunlight blinded her and she didn't have a hand free to shield her vision. As she blinked, the rumble of gangsta rap echoed through the narrow concrete canyon. Tony had backed his van into the alley to make for a quicker getaway. Just as he opened the side door and laid Athena inside, a black BMW with rims spinning sparks rolled into sight, blocking their escape.

Tagger shouted a warning. Cassie stepped forward, hand with the rebar rising as if she could miraculously fly across the ten feet and protect him.

The *rat-tat-pop* of semi-automatic and automatic fire cut through the air. Tagger dove to the ground. Cassie dropped her useless weapon and jumped back inside the doorway, both arms now holding Baby Jane.

Naïve to think the Rippers would come at them with fists and warm bodies. Of course not. They'd retreat and return armed with Mac-10s spitting bullets.

Tony returned fire with his pistol. Cassie dared to edge a glance beyond her cover. Bullets flew from above as well as from the car. That's when she realized. The car was black. Garfield Gangstas, GGs. The Rippers were on rooftops returning fire.

Leaving them hopelessly caught in the no man's land between the warring gangs.

Cassie hugged the baby tight. No matter what, Baby Jane would survive.

But it wasn't Baby Jane's face that floated in her vision. It was Mary Eamon's. The little girl Cassie couldn't save.

Huddled in the dark, back against a charred cinder block wall, Cassie remembered the little three-year-old. Her blonde curls floated out around her head, her face so pale it blended in with the white sheets, still beautiful despite the blood tinged tube running down her nose and the other, larger tube taped to her mouth. Her naked body on the trauma stretcher, exposing Mary's terrible secrets to the world.

As they'd cut away Mary's pink nightie, stained with blood and vomit and bile, the damage had been obvious. So obvious that one of the paramedics, a Lieutenant who'd seen the worse Pittsburgh had to offer, made a noise caught between a retch and a growl, balled his fists and turned for the door before Cassie intercepted him. His ears were scarlet with rage, body tense against the palm she placed on his chest, and she wasn't sure he wouldn't storm right through her.

It took a beat. The only sounds in the room was the whoosh of the respiratory therapist pumping air into Mary's chest and the steady rhythm of the cardiac monitor. Cassie stared at the man almost twice her size, felt his anger coil into a tight fist. "Help me help her."

Slowly his eyes refocused and he nodded. Cassie turned back, her team knowing what to do, all hands feverishly working to save the little girl who'd already been through hell.

In the end, when they'd lost Mary, the Lieutenant vomited into the scrub sink.

The gunfire in the alley increased, snapping Cassie back to the present. The barrage of noise made Cassie curl her body over Baby Jane's even tighter. Then, sudden silence. The smell of gunpowder mingled with the other odors of the Stackhouse. The heat and humidity added weight to the stink, clogging Cassie's lungs.

"We want the girl!" a man shouted.

Cassie risked a glance beyond the threshold. Tagger had
crawled under the van, now riddled with bullet holes, while Tony
had positioned himself with the engine block between himself and
the GG's car.

"C'mon out, Athena! You know what we want!"

Athena. They were after Athena. What could a pregnant teen
have that the Gangstas were willing to kill for?

Gunfire erupted from above as Tagger made his move and
jumped into the van. Whatever Athena had, the Rippers were also
willing to kill for. Or they were pissed at the outsiders trespassing
on their turf. Or maybe it was simply too damn hot and target
practice made them feel better.

Whatever the hell it was, Cassie wasn't about to wait around
to see. Tagger pushed open the rear van door and beckoned her.
Tony fired at the Rippers above, providing cover. Cassie hauled in
a breath and ran for it, crouching low to the ground, body between
Baby Jane and the bullets.

Sirens screamed in the distance, but neither the Rippers nor
the Gangstas seemed to care. Tagger slammed the door as soon as
Cassie cleared it. Tony jumped into the driver's seat and gunned the
engine. In reverse. "Hang on!"

Athena lay motionless on the floor, blood seeping from between
her legs. Cassie clutched the baby tight with one hand and tried to
hold on to Athena with the other. Tagger's one arm dangled useless,
tears of pain streaking his face, but he didn't make a noise as he
grabbed the inside door handle.

"Were you hit?" Cassie asked, reaching for his arm. There was
no blood, but it was obviously broken.

He shook his head. "Fell."

Tony finished reversing, then rammed the gearshift into drive
and took off, tires peeling, aiming directly at the Gangsta's BMW

blocking their way.

The windshield cracked as bullets hit it, but the BMW's driver must have cared more for his car than stopping them because at the last possible moment he tore off down the street, one tire bumping over the curve as the van clipped his rear bumper.

The van took the corner too fast. Cassie's stomach lurched into freefall, the floor and ceiling tilted as the van's wheels left the ground, then bumped back down to earth.

"Next stop, Three Rivers," Tony shouted.

His only answer was the gurgle of Baby Jane's cry.

Chapter 10

WHEN THEY RETURNED TO the House, Jimmy took all of Drake's notes and sequestered himself in the interview room, his favorite hideout when he needed to get work done—leaving Drake to field the routine stuff, including a phone call from Monica Burns asking him what brand of locks to buy.

After half an hour fending off her inane questions and hints at meeting outside of work, he finally referred her to Tony Spanos' security company, hoping maybe she'd transfer her attention to the ex-cop. He was still pissed at Spanos for the scene with Hart this morning at the Liberty Center, and figured he owed Spanos a little payback.

Just as Drake was seriously considering leaving early, Jimmy returned. "I think I got a line on your stalker."

Drake looked up, and made sure no one was within listening distance. Everyone was out, seeking solace by grabbing any case that took them inside air conditioned comfort.

"That was quick," he said, wondering how Jimmy could have a lead when all Drake had was dead ends.

"This actor knows you. Too well. He knew you'd keep it quiet, and knew how you'd investigate it—looking into the evidence logs, checking with the coroner's office. So I did exactly the opposite of what you would have done."

"What did you find?"

Instead of answering Drake's question, Jimmy asked, "How's Spanos fit?"

"Spanos?" Drake felt his shoulders hunch with an urge to pound the ex-cop's face. Spanos. Yeah, something like this would be just his style. Vicious, sneaky, downright dirty pool. "I can see that."

"Don't get hot and bothered. I don't have any solid evidence."

"What do you have?" Drake wondered if he'd made a mistake sending Monica Burns to Spanos. But the ex-cop had it in for Drake, not some innocent ditzy victim.

"Asked the whiz-kids in tech support for help. The photos from Pamela's crime scene and PM are part of an electronic database the coroner put together for teaching purposes. Anyone can go online and access it."

"You're not serious?"

Jimmy shrugged one shoulder. "It's all public information. The faces are blanked out, but the whiz-kids say anyone with photo software can fix that. Anyway, they traced the recent downloads and one of the email addresses was an ASpanoscop."

Drake jumped to his feet, already headed to the door. Jimmy stopped him with a hand on his shoulder. "Hold up, it's not proof. Anyone could have set up that account in Spanos' name."

"I don't need proof. It's him." Spanos thought Drake stole Pamela from him, blamed Drake for her death, and he was infatuated with Hart. Now he was driving a wedge between Hart and Drake, using Pamela's death to unbalance Drake while Spanos moved in and played the hero for Hart. "It's the only thing that makes sense. Pamela didn't have any family other than a sister in

California. It has to be Spanos."

"Give me the weekend," Jimmy asked. "Let me see what more I can find. On Monday, if I have enough probable cause, we'll go after a warrant for his Internet accounts and his computer."

Drake shook his head. That would mean making it an open case. Last thing he needed was the guys at the House getting into his business, thinking he couldn't handle things on his own.

No way. Especially since a good number of them still blamed him for Pamela's death. He could understand why. He'd been with her that night—should have seen the mood she was in, how unstable she'd become. He was ten feet away when she pulled the trigger, and all he could do was watch?

Who was he kidding? He was at fault and everyone knew it. This past year, he'd tried to atone for her death and what good had it done?

Pamela was still dead.

"At least you won't have to worry about Hart," Jimmy continued, interrupting Drake's self-indulgent pity party. "Spanos would never hurt her. He's smitten."

"I need to call her, tell her about him."

"Not until we have solid proof. Unless you want to look like a fool and send her running into his arms. Give me the weekend. I'm catching anyway, so I'll have time to dig deeper."

"I can't just leave all this to you."

Jimmy scoffed. "Sure you can. Look at yourself. You're driving us all crazy. Go. Take Hart. Go to your aunt's. Have fun, get some rest, relax. Spanos isn't going anywhere."

"But tomorrow, the deadline—"

"Forget about tomorrow. So Spanos is throwing a party. No one says you have to show up for it. Better that way, might slow him down a bit."

"So would breaking his legs."

"Don't do it, DJ. You go after Spanos and it gets bloody, what do you think Hart will think? Not to mention the powers that be."

Drake blew his breath out. Jimmy was right. Hart didn't even let him wear his gun inside her house. She wouldn't tolerate senseless violence—however deserved it might be. And their boss, Miller, she'd fry his ass for sure.

"The joke's on Spanos. While he scurries around trying to ruin my life, I'll be with Hart on the Lake enjoying myself." The wispy memory of his earlier fantasy tantalized him. Drake couldn't help but smile.

"Don't worry," Jimmy said. "She's going to say yes."

Drake had no intention of asking Hart to marry him. "I told you—" Drake started, then stopped. Jimmy smirked. "Whatever. I'm out of here. See you Monday."

It was going to be all right. He and Hart were leaving the city and its memories today.

CASSIE REMAINED WITH ATHENA and Baby Jane as they were rushed up to the OB floor, while Tony stayed with Tagger in the ER.

The OB-GYN nurses quickly started two IVs. Minutes later, the OB resident delivered the placenta and declared Athena "damn lucky." She ordered an abdominal CT scan to rule out any injury from the beating Athena received. Baby Jane was also doing well, although the pediatricians put her in a heated isolette while they checked her for infection and monitored her breathing. Cassie ducked out to check on the baby.

"I want to see her," Athena said, gripping Cassie's hand when she returned with the good news.

"They said as soon as she's stable."

Another nurse came in and adjusted the IV pump. When Cassie moved to get out of her way, Athena wouldn't let her go.

"You're not leaving. Please." The girl's voice slurred as her eyes drifted shut. But her fingers remained clenched around Cassie's. Even unconscious, Athena wouldn't drop her guard.

"Of course not," Cassie promised, smoothing her hand through Athena's matted hair. Athena's eyelids fluttered without opening and she began to snore.

"You don't have to stay," the nurse said as she tossed Athena's stiff, blood-soaked clothing into a biohazard trash bag. "We'll take care of her. We'll call the police and Children and Youth."

"Children and Youth? She just gave birth, even if she's a minor, technically she's emancipated."

"Not for mom." The nurse brushed her hands together as if, despite the gloves she wore, she still risked contamination from Athena. "To take the baby."

Athena whimpered, fighting off invisible demons. The nurse stepped back. Cassie grabbed a gauze pad from the bedside and wiped a small trail of spittle from Athena's mouth.

"Would you mind bringing me some three inch gauze and Xeroform?" she asked before the nurse could abandon her.

"What for?"

"To dress her burn." No need to mention the wound looked like a gunshot graze. It would only be one more thing the police would have questions about. Best to hide the gunshot wound before they arrived. Right now Athena needed rest more than interrogation. "And some shampoo and a comb, please?"

The nurse looked at Cassie like she was nuts, but then shrugged. "Whatever you say, Dr. Hart."

Cassie was certain the nurse rolled her eyes as soon as her back was turned. No matter. She never did get along with by-the-book nurses anyway. A few minutes later, the nurse returned with the supplies as well as a basin of warm water and a stack of washcloths.

Athena woke a short time later, almost lunging from the bed as a nightmare overtook her. Cassie held her down. "Shhh, it's all right. Athena, it's all right."

The girl stopped struggling and her eyes snapped open. "Baby Jane?"

"She's fine. Over in the nursery."

"I want to see her."

"I'll take you over as soon as your doctor says you're ready."

"I'm ready now." She tried to sit up and immediately crumpled back onto the pillows. "What are these? Take them out." She shook her arms with the IV lines as if they were ropes binding her to the bed.

"Medicine and fluids. You were dehydrated. Your kidney was bruised—"

"I was pissing blood."

"Who hit you?" Cassie tried to keep her tone mild, nonjudgmental. But the girl flinched and looked away.

"Nobody. I fell."

Right. And shot herself in the forehead in the process. Although the gunshot wound looked a few weeks older than the assorted other cuts and bruises covering Athena's body.

"Is there anyone we should call?" Cassie tried another tack. "Family?"

Athena shook her head, biting her lower lip.

"Want to tell me your last name?"

"Smith." The syllable emerged so grudgingly Cassie felt sure it was a lie. "You call the cops?"

"Not me. The nurses did—they had to."

Athena tried to get up again, managed to achieve a sitting

position. "I gotta go."

"How old are you?"

The question earned Cassie a defiant glare. "Eighteen. I'm an adult. I know my rights. I'm going to take my baby and leave."

"And go where?" Cassie asked gently.

Athena's mouth opened then closed again. Her cheeks hollowed as she sucked in her breath hard and fast. She sunk back, collapsing in on herself, closing her eyes once more.

"It's all right," Cassie said, squeezing her hand. "Tell me who you're running from. Maybe I can help."

"Maybe ain't good enough. Baby Jane is safe, is all that counts." The girl's head was turned away from Cassie, her eyes squeezed tight. But she still allowed Cassie to hold her hand.

Her hand trembled with terror. Cassie blew out her own breath, trying to figure out a way to reach the young girl. No way she was eighteen. Sixteen, tops.

And she looked a very old sixteen. Just like Gram Rosa. By the time she was sixteen, Rosa had already seen her family slaughtered by Nazis, had escaped them once, and started her own resistance band of fighters. By sixteen, Rosa had already killed.

Cassie looked down on the battered and bruised girl in the bed. What had Athena been forced to do to save her baby's life?

"My grandmother, Rosa, was only your age when she was trapped in a hospital," she said, remembering one of her grandfather's stories.

When she was a kid she thought Padraic's stories about Rosa were made up, but then in high school a teacher showed her where to find Library of Congress recordings from survivors of the war, verifying the fantastic tales Padraic had spun. American, British, and French soldiers were all saved by one gypsy girl. The only voice not heard from was Rosa herself—she never shared her stories. She said it was bad luck.

"You got it easy," Cassie continued. "Rosa was trapped by Nazis in a hospital in France. She was trying to rescue a bunch of English prisoners."

That got Athena's attention. And skepticism. "How's a kid going to fight off a bunch of soldiers all by herself?"

"She wasn't alone. My grandfather was with her. They figured the best way to rescue the prisoners wasn't to fight."

Athena sat up straighter. "What do you mean, not fight? Sure you gotta fight—can't let them win."

Cassie wasn't sure they were still talking about Nazis, but continued with her story. "Ah, but my gram, she was smart. She waltzed right into that hospital and left with eight prisoners before the Nazis even knew she was there."

"How'd she do that?"

Gotcha, Cassie thought. "She stole an ambulance. She dressed as a nurse, my grandfather a Nazi officer. They forged transfer papers for the prisoners—eight RAF pilots—and whisked them away to Marseilles where they hid them in a brothel."

Athena smiled at that. "Your gram sounds like a smart woman."

"Yes. She was."

"What would she tell me to do?" Athena's smile fled, replaced by fear. "How do I keep Baby Jane safe?"

"Tell me what the gangs wanted. Let me help."

For a moment, Cassie thought she'd broken through to the terrified teen. But then Athena pinched her lips tight and shook her head.

Cassie relented. "Life is hope," she whispered. "That's what Rosa always said."

Athena sighed in disappointment, Rosa's words too simple to be taken as serious advice, and closed her eyes.

ONCE THEY ROLLED A still-sleeping Athena down for her CT
scan, Cassie checked on Baby Jane, and then went down to the ER
to see about Tagger. He was in the Ortho room, lying on a gurney,
fingers dangling from wire traps as the resident wrapped fiberglass
around his forearm. She glanced at the x-rays: transverse fractures
of both the radius and ulna but no displacement or angulation. For
a kid, it was the kind of fracture that should heal just fine in a few
weeks.

Of course the big question was: where would Tagger be in a
few weeks? It didn't sound safe for him to go back to his aunt's
house. She'd make sure the ER staff got social services involved.
But if CYS put him in the wrong foster care home—one with rival
gang bangers—he'd be in even more danger.

She spotted Ed Castro, the head of the ER and Drake's partner
in the Liberty Center, standing at the nurses' station, noting
something on a chart.

"Ed," she called. He turned and smiled. "Are you and Natalie
still licensed as emergency foster parents?"

His smile widened. "Two steps ahead of you for once," he said.
"Tony Spanos told me all about your escapade. I called Natalie.
She'd love to have a baby in the house."

"How about the eleven-year-old who helped save the baby's
life?" She nodded to the open door where Tagger lay. She still
didn't know his real name, but that didn't matter. He'd shown more
courage on that street than most adults twice his age. And more
common sense.

Since his own kids were all girls, Ed had a soft spot for boys
trying to find their way. After Cassie finished telling him Tagger's
story, he grabbed the phone. "I'll let Natalie know there will be one

more for dinner."

Cassie went to give Tagger the good news and was surprised to find Tony with him in the cast room.

"Is the baby okay?" Tony asked.

"And Athena?" Tagger added.

"They're both fine. Nice cast," she told Tagger. The ortho resident finished it with a layer of Steelers logo-emblazoned fiberglass.

Tagger wiggled his fingers. "Gonna be hard to do my art with this thing on."

"Maybe that's not a bad thing," Tony said. "After today, I don't think either the Rippers or Gangstas are gonna be happy to see you on their turf."

"How'd you like to get some home cooking tonight and stay in a house with a big backyard?"

Tagger stared at Cassie like she'd said something stupid. "No way. I'm not staying with anyone. I'm gonna stay here, and look after Athena and Baby Jane. I promised Rodney I would."

"Rodney? Your brother?" Cassie sat down beside Tagger, taking care not to jostle his arm. "Tagger, is Rodney Baby Jane's father?"

He didn't look at her. "Baby Jane's why they killed him."

Tony stood at alert. "Who? The Rippers or the Gangstas?"

Tagger's street-born suspicion kicked in. "Doesn't matter. I promised Rodney if anything happened to him, I'd take care of them."

Rodney died two weeks ago—about the same time Athena got shot. "Athena saw it?"

"Yeah. Said she has proof of something. Said it's the only thing keeping her and Baby Jane alive." He looked up at her, eyes filled with anguish. "I gotta stay with them, keep them safe. I gotta."

Cassie wanted to hug the boy, but held back, knowing he'd hate it. "I'm sorry, sweetie. But a real good friend of mine, Dr. Castro, is going to take you and Baby Jane home with him. I'll tell the police and guards here to watch over Athena."

Tagger didn't look too convinced. His concern grew when Ed appeared in the doorway and beckoned to Cassie. "That girl you brought in? Athena Smith? She vanished from CT."

Chapter 11

THE LAST THEY TRACKED Athena was a blurred shot on the security footage of her wearing nurse's scrubs and a lab coat, climbing onto a bus headed for East Liberty. Cassie didn't tell the others she'd inadvertently planted the idea of a disguise in Athena's mind with her story about Gram Rosa.

Tagger was livid. He wanted to go hunt for her, but Ed finally calmed him down with Tony's help.

It was late afternoon by the time Cassie left. Tammy had driven Cassie's car to Three Rivers, so Cassie drove her and Antwan home before heading back to the Liberty Center. She just pulled into the parking lot, still smeared with blood, sweat, and grime, when her cell rang. She grabbed it from the charger, hoping it was Drake.

No such luck. It was Lisa Dimeo, the Assistant DA handling Mary Eamon's case.

"Cancel any plans you have for tonight," the prosecutor started.

"Why?" The last thing Cassie needed was something else going wrong today. She let herself inside the Center, almost tripping on the tool belt she'd dropped when she rushed out this morning.

"Haven't you heard? Brickner has a new lawyer. He got all of our DNA evidence tossed. Been out on bail since yesterday."

"What happened?" Cassie asked, astounded the confessed child molester and murderer was out walking the streets.

"The body was left unattended in the OR for almost half an hour before the coroner arrived. That means no chain of custody."

Cassie felt an overwhelming urge to hit something. She couldn't bring herself to put a hole in the drywall she and Tammy so painstakingly hung, so she hit mute and shouted a string of obscenities into the empty room.

"It gets worse," Dimeo went on. "The defense filed a motion to exclude your testimony. If it's granted, we'll have to drop the case for lack of evidence."

"What's wrong with me testifying?"

"They're saying since you've testified as an expert witness before, you knew anything you learned in the course of a medical history could be used as evidence. They're saying that's the same as a coerced confession, that you manipulated Brickner and he had no benefit of counsel."

"So they're using my own expertise against me? That's insane. I can't help it if Brickner confessed to me."

"Mary's mother and grandmother will testify you orchestrated the interview hoping he would confess, even though you knew it wouldn't do Mary any good. That you in fact acted as an investigator rather than a physician."

"How am I supposed to take care of a patient if I don't get a complete history?" Cassie argued.

"This has nothing to do with taking care of people. I have to give Judge Flory my response tomorrow morning. He'll review the motion over the weekend and there'll be a hearing on Monday. Without you, I don't have a case, and Brickner walks."

"So you need me Monday?" Cassie held out hope she could

salvage at least part of the weekend. Drive up this afternoon, and come back tomorrow in time to meet with Alan King for her deposition on Richard's malpractice case. She knew how important this weekend was to Drake, and wanted to be there for him.

"You don't understand. We're going over your stuff tonight. I need to put it in my rebuttal and we have to prep your testimony for Monday."

"Tonight?" Cassie stared out the rear windows of the clinic, straining to catch any hint of a breeze. The air was so thick, the dust seemed permanently suspended, defying the laws of gravity.

"You have a problem with that?" the harried prosecutor snapped. "Just say so, and I'll stop wasting my time and drop the case. You want to let scum like Brickner walk the streets free, it's fine with me. I don't need this bullshit—"

Drake said Dimeo was a tight-ass, expecting perfection from those she worked with and no less from herself. Intense was the word he'd used.

Intense didn't quite cover it, Cassie thought as the prosecutor continued ranting. "Lisa, I'm there. What time?"

"Be here by seven. You might want to bring your PJ's," she said as if inviting Cassie to a slumber party.

Cassie sighed. There went any chance for a quiet weekend at the Lake. There was nothing she could do about it. Drake would just have to go by himself. Maybe he'd come back in a better mood.

"All right."

⁓⌁⌁⌁⌁⁓

DRAKE PULLED INTO HIS parking lot feeling better than he had in days. They were going to make it out of this city. Hart would love Nellie's lake house, and he couldn't wait to teach her how to sail. He'd bet she was a natural. Hard to imagine anything Hart wouldn't be good at.

Spanos' van was gone. Good. But who belonged to the BMW parked near the back entrance? He noted the handicapped tag on the plate and frowned. Just what he didn't need, a visit from Hart's ex, Richard King. He squared his shoulders and climbed the steps to the handicapped accessible entrance.

He didn't give a shit why King was here. Probably something about his damn lawsuit. King was determined to make Hart's life just as miserable now as it had been when they were married.

It wasn't going to happen. Not today. He and Hart were out of here; they were going to the Lake. They were leaving now.

He found King sitting in his wheelchair at the elevator in the rear of the building. Despite the heat, King wore a stylish suit, but Drake noticed his shoes weren't so stylish, although probably expensive. Black leather high tops wide enough to accommodate the splints King wore on his ankles.

No sign of Hart or anyone else. Drake frowned, glanced around. Tools lay haphazardly on the floor, a bucket of mud with an open lid.

Weird. Hart was a bit of a slob when it came to her personal space, but a fanatic about her work at the clinic. She'd never leave tools around where Tammy's kid could get into them.

"Who the hell let you in?" he asked King, wondering if Hart's ex was the reason she hadn't gotten any work done today. If King had done something to upset her . . .

King spun his chair around and shot Drake a glare. "I came to check on Cassandra. Why weren't you with her? How could you let her go there?"

Drake stared down at the wheelchair-bound man. King lost a good part of his memory after his overdose but he'd never been irrational before. "What are you talking about?"

"You don't even know, do you?" King tilted his chair up then gave it a small bounce of exasperation. It was sleek, black, and looked built for racing. "What the hell good are you, Drake? You're a cop, goddamn it! If you can't keep her safe—"

"What happened?" Drake's patience snapped. "Is she okay? Where's Hart?"

"She was attacked by a bunch of gangbangers."

"Here? They attacked her here, in the clinic?" Nightmare images hammered at Drake's mind. She'd be all right. She had to be. Probably at Three Rivers. He turned to leave, but King stopped him.

"She's upstairs," King said. "At least I'm guessing—your land line's been busy and she's not answering her cell." He gestured to his wheelchair. "I just got here and was trying to figure out your elevator controls when you arrived."

Drake didn't bother to ask how King had access to his private phone number. He was more concerned that King knew what happened and he didn't.

"Tell me everything," he said, his words emerging in a taut staccato. "Now."

King gave him an elaborate shrug, obviously delighting in his superior knowledge. Drake had once entertained the idea that King could be his stalker, but there was no way a man in a wheelchair could have gotten the letters to the places they were delivered. Now he saw the spark of malice in the other man's eyes and his suspicion returned. Even a man in a wheelchair could hire a delivery boy.

"I wonder why Cassandra didn't call you herself," King said.

"What happened?" Drake practically spit the words out, his jaw clamped shut against his anger and fear. He was torn between waiting for King to explain the details and wanting to rush upstairs to Hart. But he knew Hart—she'd minimize everything. Better to learn whatever he could on his own.

"She went to the Stackhouse to deliver a baby. On her way out they were jumped by a bunch of gang members—"

"Ruby Avenue Rippers," Drake supplied automatically.

"Whoever. She wasn't hurt, but a kid with her got his arm fractured in two places. The baby's doing fine, in case you're interested."

Hart wasn't hurt. The magic words. "Thanks, you can go now."

"I have no intention of going anywhere," Richard sputtered, hands grabbing the wheels of his chair like he was ready to run Drake over.

"This is my building and you're leaving. Now." Drake held the door open. He could give King a push. If he got lucky, maybe the asshole would miss the handicapped ramp and go flying over the steps, all the way down the ravine and out of their lives forever.

Nah, he'd never be that lucky.

King glared at Drake for a long moment. "You know she'd be better off with me. Happier. Safer."

"What the hell are you talking about? Are you threatening me?"

King's expression hardened, his smug smile etched into his face. "Maybe I am. Think about this, Drake." He wheeled past Drake over the threshold. "I can give Cassandra everything you can't. If you care about her at all, you'll let her come back to me. Where she belongs."

"Go to hell, King." Drake banged the door shut, made sure it was locked, and bolted up to his apartment. He ran inside to find Hart, her clothes streaked with blood and grime, talking on the phone.

"Thanks for the update, Ed." She hung up and turned to him in surprise.

Drake stood inside the open door and stared at her. Her hair was plastered to her head with sweat, her shirt was ripped, and there were scratches on her forearms.

"Are you all right?"

"I'm fine," she said. "Nothing a shower won't cure." To his surprise, her face lit up with a wide smile. "You should've seen me. I was worried maybe I'd gotten rusty, lost my edge, but it was great—" She continued in a rush, her face flushed with excitement. "I felt like a real doctor again!"

He took her hands in his, scrutinizing her injuries more closely. All superficial. But that didn't ease the anger churning through his gut. At her for not calling him. At himself for not being there. King was right, it was Drake's job to protect her, but he seemed repeatedly doomed to failure.

Of course Drake couldn't keep Hart safe, a small voice whispered inside his head. After all, he was only ten feet away when Pamela pulled the gun and he couldn't save her.

"Want to explain why I had to hear about your—" he paused, searching for words, "adventure from Richard King?"

She jerked her head up at his tone and he tried to take a breath, calm down. Instead he remembered King's words mocking him and his fury grew.

"Richard?" she asked. "Why were you talking to Richard? How did he know?"

"How the hell should I know? Seems like he has some kind of psychic hotline when it comes to you. Seems like everyone does except me. Why didn't you call me?" His voice was loud enough to bounce off the high ceiling, reverberating back at him as she pulled away.

"There wasn't a chance. I didn't have my cell." Of course not. She never carried the damn thing. Especially not when she needed it. One of these days he swore he was going to surgically implant a

Bluetooth into her.

"You were at the hospital, weren't you?" He advanced on her and she backed up. Another step and they were inside his studio, the afternoon sun cascading through the windows, shimmering off the canvases positioned around the room, most of them revealing Hart's image. "They still have phones at Three Rivers, don't they?"

She planted her feet, hands fisted on her hips.

All the fear and anger and anxiety building in him all week reached a crescendo as he glared down at her.

She returned his stare measure for measure.

"I didn't call from Three Rivers because I'm not a doctor there anymore," she began, her voice low and calm. Too calm by far, he realized. He saw where she was heading and immediately regretted having pushed her there. "So I didn't ask to use a phone at the nurses' station. I could have used the phone in the visitor's lounge." Her voice faltered. He reached for her, tried to stop her, but she pulled away as if determined to get the words out. "But that would have meant . . ." Her words trailed off and she broke eye contact.

His anger still simmered but it wasn't powerful enough to blind him to her pain. Aw hell. This wasn't what he wanted. They were supposed to be on their way out of here. He moved forward, and gathered her in his arms.

"You didn't want to admit you were a visitor, an outsider," he finished for her, his fingers stroking her hair, untangling the snarled mass of curls. He knew how much her job at Three Rivers meant to her—losing it was like losing a piece of herself. She loved the clinic and would be the best thing that ever happened to her new patients, but her heart still ached for the adrenalin rush of the ER.

"It's all right," he whispered, his face cradled against her head. "It won't be long. We'll have the clinic running and you'll be saving lives right and left."

Her arms tightened around him. What the hell was wrong with him? He was losing it, letting King get his goat like that. She'd only been trying to help someone in need. It wasn't her fault there was a gang war brewing in this neighborhood.

"Your patient, is she all right?"

She nodded, pulling back enough to tilt her face up to his. "Mother and beautiful baby girl did fine, thank you very much." A shadow crossed her face and he guessed there was more.

"King said some kid got hurt?"

"Tagger. Fell and broke his arm. He's all right. In a way it's for the best. He's going into foster care—at Ed Castro's."

Drake smiled at that. Ed's wife would soon straighten Tagger out. He was glad the kid wasn't seriously hurt. He liked his artwork. He'd like it better if it wasn't on the side of his building, but the kid had style, a natural flare. Banksy meets Van Gogh.

Hart stepped back, her gaze skimming over him with appraisal. He felt a flush of shame as he remembered his momentary lapse of reason, flirting with Monica Burns earlier.

"You ready to talk yet?" she asked, hands on her hips.

Drake grimaced. He hadn't fooled Hart. Not at all.

"I'm sorry," he began. The thought of the photos he'd received this morning clamped his jaws shut before he could continue.

"Good start. Want to tell me what about?"

"I'll tell you after we get to the Lake," he hedged. Once he got her to safety, his head would be clear, he could think straight. Most importantly, she would be far away from his stalker.

"I can't go."

His chin jerked up at that. "You have to. We need to get out of here—"

"I can't. Not this weekend, at least. Maybe—"

He was reduced to begging. He didn't care. "No. Tonight.

Now."

"It has to do with Pamela, doesn't it?" Her hands circled around his waist, snuggling him against her body, sharing her warmth, her strength with him.

He held her tight, pillowing his face on her hair again, inhaling her scent, imprinting it on his memory. Lace curtains billowing in the breeze, vanilla and cinnamon, splashing barefoot through puddles after a summer shower. This was the essence of Hart. No amount of dirt or grime could mask it, not from him.

How could she stand to be with a fool like him? A man who'd been careless before with fragile feelings offered to him, even if they had been offered by a deluded, unbalanced woman.

More than ever he regretted his poor judgment. The irresponsible, immature recklessness that had led to the mistakes he'd made with Pamela. It was easy to blame it on the drink, but Drake knew the real fault lay within himself. His shame over the man he'd once been now left him nauseous, as if some bilious disease had contaminated him.

As if he might contaminate her by staying close. Selfish bastard, he berated himself. *This is your fight, not hers. You need to finish what you started.*

"Pamela died a year ago tomorrow," he told her, moving away from her comfort. She followed, placing a single hand on the small of his back, letting him know she wasn't shrinking from his words. That he allowed her hand to remain shamed him further. "Someone has gone to great lengths to be certain I don't forget that fact."

"Strange letters? Threats?" she asked.

He looked at her. Maybe he wasn't as good at hiding his emotions as he thought. "How did you know?"

"Tony Spanos told me he was getting them too. Said he thought they came from Pamela's sister but he couldn't prove it, couldn't track her down."

A surge of anger flared through him. Spanos talked to Hart about this? What the hell was the man thinking, dragging her into this? He almost told her what Jimmy found, that Spanos was his number one suspect. He stopped himself just in time. Hart considered Spanos a friend, casting suspicion on him without proof would only drive a wedge between them. Exactly what Spanos wanted.

She was silent for a moment. "Does Jimmy know?"

"I told him this afternoon." He turned to her once more, taking her hands in his. "Now can you see why we need to leave here? Tonight? After tomorrow I can track this actor down, take all the time in the world—but until then—"

"You're not safe here," she finished for him. "You need to go to the Lake," she continued, nodding as if explaining that two plus two made four, as if it were that simple for a man to turn tail and run, abandoning her.

He shook his head. "No. *We* have to go. I am not going to leave you here."

"I can't go," she said in that firm way of hers that broached no argument.

He inhaled, the air searing his lungs as hot as the anger threatening to spill over onto her. Damn Spanos for putting him in this position. And Hart, who gave so much to perfect strangers— why couldn't she give him this one thing? "Why not? What's so important that you can't leave for a few days—if only to give me some peace of mind? I've seen you put your life at risk to help a friend or a patient. Why can't you do this for me?"

"I want to. Believe me, I wish I could, but I need to—"

"No but, just do it!" Her eyes hardened at his impervious tone. He forced himself to soften his voice. Why did she have to be so stubborn? Might as well ask why the sky was blue. It just was. Nothing he did would ever change it. Or Hart.

But he needed her to see reason. He grabbed her wrists. "Goddamn it, Hart! This is not a game. I mean it. Get your things. We're going, now!"

Her eyes blazed at that and she broke his grip with a quick movement. "Get your hands off me!"

God, how could he be so stupid? Laying hands on her when he was angry. After what she'd been through with King . . .

"I'm sorry. I'm sorry."

She wouldn't look at him. Her eyes focused on his hands, her body shifted automatically into a defensive stance. As if he could ever—would ever hurt her.

He sucked his breath in, and blinked against an angry burning that blurred his vision. "I have to go. If you—" He shied away from the L word, afraid it would push her farther away. "If you care at all for me, if you want to help me, you'll come too."

For a split second he thought she would change her mind, and come with him. She still wouldn't meet his eyes, stared down at the floor, head bowed, hair curtaining her face, an impenetrable shroud.

"I'm sorry. I can't—"

Pain and anger drove him out the door before she could finish. But what kept him from turning back was pure fear.

Blood swirled through his vision as the images his stalker planted in his mind played in a macabre slideshow. Pamela dead. Drake dead. But the one image he couldn't let go of, that made him so dizzy he almost tripped down the steps, was the one his own imagination created: Hart dead.

If he stayed, she was in danger.

He had no choice. He had to go. His stalker would follow him. It was the only way to keep her safe.

Chapter 12

CASSIE WATCHED IN DISBELIEF as the door slammed behind Drake. He was leaving her. Just like that. No chance for her to get a word in edgewise and he was out the door.

Her own face, enhanced by Drake's talent, looked back at her from every corner of the studio. If it had been her reflection in mirrors she would have gleefully shattered them all. But they were Drake's vision, the product of his talent, and Cassie couldn't vent her fury on them.

She ran from the studio to the front window in the living room just in time to see Drake's Mustang fishtail its way out of the parking lot. She crossed into the bedroom to watch the twin taillights run the stop sign at the end of the street, and then lost them in the lights of the city.

She should have found a way to explain, to make him understand why she couldn't leave.

But he hadn't given her a chance, had he? And when he grabbed her, she'd let her own anger and fear take over. She sank onto his bed, hugged her knees to her chest. Her eyes ached as if she should be crying but no tears came. The high ceilings of Drake's bedroom gathered shadows, shrouding her in darkness.

She understood why Drake couldn't stay. Hell, she told him to leave. It was the look of hurt and disappointment in his eyes that haunted her. Truth was, maybe she needed some distance to sort all this out.

For about the millionth time, she entertained doubts about continuing her relationship with Drake. It felt like all too often she failed him—usually when he needed her most. Just as she failed everyone she loved, no matter how hard she tried.

Cassie, I need you to be strong. Her father's last words to her echoed through the dim room. If she closed her eyes, his face, shattered by pain after the car accident filled her mind. Followed by others—Mary Eamon, for one. And Richard, a tragic mistake she was still paying for.

She stripped free of her ruined clothes and took a long, cool shower in Drake's oversized claw foot tub. The ghosts of her failures followed. When she was twelve her father had needed her to get him help in time. Now Drake needed her to go with him, Mary Eamon needed her to stay here and bring her justice . . . they all needed something from Cassie, but she couldn't save everyone. All she could do was try.

She dried off, threw the towel over the shower curtain, and then stopped. Drake liked his towels hung neatly on the rack behind the door. It was the least she could do, seeing as how she couldn't give him what he really wanted.

Swallowing her pain, she quickly dressed in a tank top and pair of khaki shorts, then left to spend the evening dissecting the murder of a three-year-old little girl.

DRAKE DROVE THE MUSTANG with the top down, radio

blasting. He took the back roads to avoid the other Friday evening travelers, people rushing to get anywhere but where they were. He understood their need; he often felt that same restlessness. New faces, new thrills, new places. It was one of the things that attracted him to law enforcement.

He hadn't had those restless feelings as much lately. Not since he'd met Hart. With her he finally felt content to stay where he was. Maybe he'd grown up at last? He always thought he'd be disappointed to see the same face day after day, to be with the same woman this long, but he didn't feel that way at all. At least not until tonight.

They had plenty of arguments before—her stubbornness and independence assured that. As far as he could tell, he did little to provoke them. Well, maybe that wasn't fair. They were both adults, used to living on their own, doing things their own way. They had both made compromises in this relationship. But he'd never seen her so adamant, unwilling to bend, to address his needs. It made him wonder if he meant as much to Hart as she did to him.

Drake thought about that as he drove, replaying the argument in his mind. The only lights came from a farmhouse in the distance, the road curving gently between fields of corn. It hadn't really been an argument, he realized. More like a tirade. He hadn't given her much chance to explain her reasons, had he?

Maybe because he was disappointed she hadn't put his needs first? Hart knew better than anyone how Pamela's suicide had affected him. He didn't need her sympathy—and he certainly didn't want her pity. Maybe this whole situation was a warning, a red flag he had grown too complacent. Expecting Hart to know his needs and wants without him saying anything—wasn't that every man's fantasy? Is that really what he wanted in a woman: a security blanket rather than a partner?

Drake shook his head, stirring his headache into a fierce primal pounding. Life used to be so much easier. Go out, find a girl, have a few drinks, a few laughs, go home and have sex, and part ways in the morning. No ties, no complications. Of course that was what he'd had with Pamela, and look how that ended up.

Two hours later he pulled into his aunt's driveway. He sat in the car for a few minutes, still thinking hard. Who was he running from? Pamela? Hart? His anonymous stalker? Or himself?

The door to the two-story cottage opened. Nellie and his mother emerged, smiling to greet him. Drake pushed all thoughts of other women aside as he got out of the car and went to hug them.

"Remy, it's so good to see you. It's been so long," Muriel Drake gushed, using her pet name for him. "Where's Cassie?"

Nellie joined them on the driveway as Drake grabbed his overnight bag from the trunk.

"Think it might rain?" he asked. "Maybe I should put the top up."

"No rain this weekend," Nellie promised, taking Drake's other arm as they walked into the house. Drake's uncle would be joining them tomorrow. He dropped his bag in the foyer and walked with Nellie and his mother through to the kitchen. The back of the house faced the lake with a deck coming off the dining room and an enclosed porch off the kitchen. On it, Nellie had a picnic table set with four places.

"You two go sit," she told Drake and his mother. "I'll get dinner. Muriel made a pasta salad and we have fresh bread. We thought you wouldn't be very hungry with the heat and all." Nellie busied herself in the kitchen while Drake and Muriel went into the sun porch.

Drake stood at the screen door looking out over the back yard and dock. The lights of other houses and several boats reflected from the water. Further out on the lake was dark, but he could hear the sound of the water lapping against the dock. He kept his back turned from his mother but he knew what she was thinking as she removed the extra place setting.

"We didn't have a fight—" He lied, answering her silent question. "She got busy at the Center."

"Did I ask?" Muriel came up and gave him another hug. "It's so good to have you here."

Drake kissed her on the cheek. "Hey," he called out to Nellie. "Where's my other best girl?" He moved into the kitchen. "When do we eat around here? A man could die of starvation."

"You won't get anything until you get out of my kitchen," Nellie waved him back onto the porch. She brought a tray with a loaf of bread, a bowl of pasta salad, and three bottles of beer out and joined them at the picnic table.

"Cheers." Nellie lifted her bottle of beer in a toast before they began to eat.

They clinked bottles and Drake smiled. His aunt was the only person he knew who could turn drinking a bottle of beer into a refined occasion. That was one of the things he loved most about her, her aptitude for putting people at ease. It was one of the talents that had made her such a good journalist. But that was a long time ago. He looked closely at his mother and aunt and for the first time realized they were growing old. For a moment he felt the cold hand of mortality grip him as well.

Suddenly he wished more than anything he was back in the city, despite the heat, despite the danger. No, it wasn't the city he missed. It was Hart, plain and simple.

He took another sip of beer but it tasted bitter in his mouth. The urge to apologize to Hart was so great he excused himself from the table and tried to call her. No answer, and when the voice mail came on, he couldn't fumble the right words out. All he could manage was, "I miss you. Please call."

He hung up, clutching the cell phone like it was a lifeline to Hart. Willing it to ring. It didn't. His mother's laughter called him back to the other room. He forced a smile for their sake, wishing he could do better.

Chapter 13

"START AT THE BEGINNING," Assistant District Attorney Lisa Dimeo instructed Cassie between bites of her Primanti Brothers' Reuben.

They were in Lisa's tiny office, whose only saving grace was that it had a ceiling fan. It made a wheezing noise that occasionally grew into a sickly cough, the blades strained against the heavy air.

Cassie pushed the reams of paper on the desk to one side, making space for her own turkey and prosciutto. "Why? You've read all the reports."

"Because I think we might lose this one and that thought makes me want to puke, all right? You were there. Maybe there's something I can use, something not in the reports. Don't leave anything out."

Last thing Cassie wanted to think of was that day. That sun-filled, crisp January day that still haunted her dreams. When Mary Eamon arrived at Three Rivers Medical Center's ER.

"Med Five en route with a three-year-old." She remembered the dispatcher's impassionate voice sounding over her trauma radio. "ETA two minutes."

The little girl was tiny for three, and so pale, Cassie had to resist the urge to smear her fingertip against her cheek to see if it was white makeup. One medic forced oxygen into her lungs through a tube inserted into her trachea while the other steered the gurney.

"Heart rate's still good but we couldn't get a BP even by palp. Color's a little better since we tubed her."

This was better? We're in deep shit, Cassie thought, as she helped push the gurney around the corner into the resuscitation bay where her team waited.

"What's the story?" she asked as they moved the patient across to the ER's bed.

"Mother said she'd been vomiting for two days and complaining of belly pain. She called grandmother for advice this morning when she couldn't wake Mary, that's the girl, up. Grandmother came over, took one look at her and called 911. When we arrived she was unresponsive to deep pain, so we scooped and ran, tubed her on the way in."

She leaned over her tiny patient, listening to her lung sounds. The nurses were working around little Mary, cutting her clothes off, trying for an IV.

"Jesus Christ!" The exclamation came from one of the paramedics as Mary's nightgown fell open. Linda, the nurse who had cut it off, took a step backwards.

There was silence in the room for a few heartbeats as they looked at the now naked child. A multitude of bruises covered her body. Her abdomen was grotesquely distended, giving the preschooler the appearance of some kind of obscene pregnancy.

The paramedic, a seasoned Lieutenant, raised his fists, ready to bolt the room. "That sonofabitch."

Cassie stopped him. She needed all the help she could get. So did Mary.

"Get me peds surg stat and have an OR ready," Cassie commanded. "I want trauma labs drawn and two lines. In the meantime get me two units of Oneg on the warmer. Let's get an NG and Foley in her. What's her rhythm on the monitor?"

"Sinus tach, still no blood pressure even with Dynamap."

"She's hard to bag," the respiratory tech spoke up.

Cassie listened once more to her breath sounds. "No pneumo. It's the belly distention. I'm going to relieve the pressure with a paracentesis."

She grabbed some Betadine and prepped the little girl's belly, trying to focus on her task and ignore the reality of the torture this child had endured. Not only from the beatings but also from the severe pain of a perforated bowel.

Linda worked beside her, trying to place a Foley catheter into Mary's bladder before Cassie stuck a needle into the belly to relieve the pressure. The nurse dropped the Foley and had to open a new kit.

"What's the problem?" Cassie asked as she drew on sterile gloves. "We don't have time to waste here."

"Look for yourself." The nurse had gone a pale shade of green and her hands were trembling. Cassie didn't want to know what made a seasoned ER nurse react like that, but it was her job to know.

She bent over and looked. Mary had suffered more than just a beating.

"Christ," she sighed. "Okay, Linda, you're doing fine." Cassie talked her nurse through the procedure in a level voice but she really wanted to scream in frustration. Who could do this to a child? Out of the corner of her eye she saw one of the paramedics retch and turn to the scrub sink, hands over his mouth.

Linda's eyes watered with tears but her hands were steady. "I don't want to hurt her," she whispered.

"It's okay. She's not feeling anything." Linda was able to thread the Foley catheter and Cassie turned back to the belly. She prepped the abdomen and inserted a catheter to relieve the pressure. As soon as it entered the peritoneal cavity there was a rush of air, like a balloon releasing.

"I can bag better now," respiratory said.

"I lost her pulse!"

"Start chest compressions and keep pushing the fluid. Where's that blood?"

"It just got here."

"I want it in as fast it can go. Give her two of epi." Cassie went to the head of the bed and reassessed her patient. No signs of pneumothorax or tamponade; her heart had probably stopped because of the shock and blood loss, which they were working to correct. Thirty long seconds passed.

"Stop compressions for a pulse check," she commanded as she felt the carotid. She took a deep breath. It was faint but there was definitely a pulse. "I've got one. Where's the surgeon? She needs to be up in the OR."

"He's on his way."

Cassie looked at the clock, she'd been working on the girl for less than ten minutes but it seemed an eternity.

She turned back to the little girl, combing her fingers through Mary's blonde curls. It was frustrating to admit, but there was nothing more she could offer the child. Mary needed to be in surgery.

In answer to her prayers, Kurtis Waite, the pediatric surgeon appeared. He must have rushed straight from the OR because he still wore his paper cap and shoe covers.

"What's the story?" he asked, his eyes taking in the girl and her bruises.

"Three-year-old, found unresponsive, history of vomiting. When she got here she was in sinus tach with no blood pressure, her belly so distended it was interfering with ventilation. We've given her three fluid boluses and she's on her second unit of O-neg."

He nodded. "How's ventilation after you decompressed the belly?"

"Better, but then she arrested. We got her back after the third fluid bolus and a dose of epi."

"Is the OR ready?"

"They said they'll need another ten minutes."

"Fuck that, tell them they have two. C'mon, let's roll." Waite pulled on the stretcher, not waiting for help. Cassie nodded to her nurses and they quickly grabbed the monitor and IV pumps, rushing behind him out the door.

Cassie leaned against the counter in the suddenly quiet critical care room, taking deep breaths in an attempt to calm herself. The paramedic still stood there, as if frozen.

"I've never seen anything like that," he finally said.

Cassie looked up at him. He was a fifteen-year veteran of the worst the streets of Pittsburgh could offer. She sighed. "Me neither."

They stood there in silence, mourning Mary's lost innocence, when Cassie's phone rang.

"The family's here. Dr. Waite asked if you could talk to them," the clerk told Cassie.

Cassie could imagine just how colorfully Kurtis Waite made that request. He was an excellent surgeon but with little patience for dealing with situations like this.

"Police and children services notified?"

"They've been called."

"Who all are there?" she asked.

"Gramma, mother, and stepfather."

She went down to the family area. There she saw a middle-aged woman weeping on the sofa, face in her hands. On the other side of the room was a young couple, the woman in her mid-twenties and the man just slightly older.

"I'm Dr. Hart, I was taking care of Mary while she was here in the ER." Cassie sat on the ottoman near the door so she could make eye contact with them. "Can anyone tell me how Mary got hurt?"

The grandmother looked up, shaking her head. "Is she going to be all right? I want to see her."

"She's in very serious condition and is being operated on right now. There's a chance that she might not live," Cassie said softly.

The grandmother let out a low moan. "Oh, my baby, my poor baby."

Cassie looked to the mother and stepfather. Both stared at her silently, neither moving to comfort the older woman.

"You know what happened to Mary, don't you?" she asked in a level voice, not accusing, just stating a fact.

They looked at each other, then nodded.

"I'm sorry," the stepfather whispered. His body seemed to deflate as he slumped down into the chair. "I'm so sorry." He ran his fingers through his beard, covering his mouth as if ashamed of his words.

He was an ordinary appearing man. Slightly overweight. Skin a little sallow, like maybe he spent too much time inside watching football on TV, drinking more beer than was good for him. Like so many ordinary men here in Pittsburgh.

Plain clothes, jeans and a flannel shirt, working man's boots scuffed but with new laces.

Ordinary, hard-working man who'd just admitted to being a monster.

Cassie concentrated on finding air to breathe. The room felt smaller as the truth the stepfather admitted filled the space between them.

"It's important I know when this happened and exactly how Mary got hurt. We need to know what kind of injuries to look for," Cassie continued in that same soft voice. Her stomach churned with nausea and she wanted to run from the room and the evil contained there, but she controlled her feelings and forced herself to make eye contact with the mother.

Mary's mother perched on the arm of the chair, an arm around her husband. "It wasn't Ron's fault," she said, her voice high pitched like a schoolgirl's. It made Cassie wonder if she was younger than she appeared. "Mary never listened. He told her not to make a fuss about going to bed. He counted to ten. He warned her . . ."

"Did this happen last night or the night before?"

Silence for a moment, then Ron spoke up. "Two nights ago. Cindy was trying to get out the door to go to work so I put the kids to bed. Mary kept getting back out of bed, wanting a drink, wanting a story, wanting to watch a video, she just wouldn't listen!"

"Then what happened?"

"I put her back in bed and told her if she didn't stay put, I would spank her. I went back downstairs, and said goodbye to Cin. After that I heard Mary get out of bed again. I grabbed her and carried her back to her bed, and she just started to cry and scream and I lost it—" He shook his head. "I don't know, I just hit her. I wanted her to stop crying, that's all."

"Ronald, be quiet."

Cassie turned to the grandmother in surprise. The older woman stood, holding her hands up above her waist like a conductor calling for attention. "Cindy, tell him to be quiet before he gets us all in trouble." The grandmother stepped between Cassie and the couple. "Doctor, we want to know when we can see Mary, will you please go check?"

Cassie stared at the woman, but she held her ground, arms folded across her chest.

Without a word, Cassie left. Her heart thumped so hard she felt it in her throat, blocking her as she tried to swallow. Those people, what they'd done . . . she shoved her emotions aside. She still had work to do and wouldn't be any good to anyone, including Mary, if she gave into her anger.

She stopped at the nurses' station to call up to the OR and tell Kurtis Waite the injuries occurred two days ago. She was surprised when the surgeon came to the phone himself.

"How's she doing?" she asked, dreading his answer. Only one explanation for him to be available.

"She just died," he said, confirming her fears. "There was a belly full of blood and several feet of dead gut festering in there. There was nothing I could do."

The phone was suddenly her only grasp on reality as she broke out in a cold sweat. "Thanks, Kurtis," she whispered. "I'll tell the family."

She retraced her steps back to the family room, not certain if she could contain the fury growing in her. For the first time in her career, she found herself utterly depleted of compassion for the loved ones of a patient. She didn't want to talk to these people again, didn't want to be in the same room as them, breathe the same air.

There were two police officers and a caseworker from Children and Youth now with the family. Ronald and Cindy held hands, both with stubborn sullen looks on their faces as the grandmother yelled at the police to leave them alone, they did nothing wrong, no one had known Mary was sick. Then she saw Cassie and her expression changed from righteous indignation into hopefulness.

"How's Mary, Doctor? How's our little girl? Is she going to be all right?"

Cassie stood with one hand on the door, ready to escape as soon as possible. It was difficult to watch, these ordinary monsters and their performance.

"Mary just died. There was nothing we could do to save her. Her injuries were too severe," Cassie said, her voice sounding flat and distant.

The police officers exchanged glances; now this was a homicide case. Cassie turned her back and walked away. She ignored the grandmother's shouts of malpractice and threats to sue them all.

Cassie felt dirty. Like she needed to wash herself clean of all this.

She'd headed back past the nurses' station, grateful the board looked under control, when an angry woman strode out of one of the rooms.

"Nurse, will you find me a doctor?" she demanded. "My son has a sore throat and cough and we've been waiting for over an hour! You tell the doctor he's sick and needs to be seen right now!"

It took every ounce of will power for Cassie to turn and face the woman without lashing out. She looked past the woman to where her teenaged son sat playing a handheld video game, looking anything but ill.

"We just had a very serious trauma, ma'am," she replied as politely as she could. "Your son will be taken care of as soon as possible."

The woman huffed and stood in the doorway, a scowl on her face. "I'm never coming back to this hospital again."

Cassie ducked into the utility closet and leaned against a shelf, rubbing her eyes with her hands, trying to erase what they had seen today. After a few minutes of the quiet darkness, she took a deep breath, then blew it out.

She remembered looking down at her watch. Five hours left on her shift.

Now Cassie stared out Lisa's streaky window at the city lights, her sandwich long forgotten. Lisa looked up from her note taking, licked some grease from her fingers.

"So you took no part in the evidence collection? The rape kit was done in the OR?"

There was a long pause before Cassie could pull her mind back to the present. She felt as if Mary was in the room with them; patiently waiting for the grownups to finally get it right, bring her the justice she deserved.

"Kurtis did it after he declared her," she finally answered. "I remember there was another trauma alert—roll over MVA. He came down to help, but he would have left the kit with a nurse to guard it. He knows the routine."

The lawyer's mouth tightened. "Only problem was, the specimens were still drying, so they weren't sealed yet. The nurse got called away to another emergency and it was twenty some minutes until she returned. Then she sealed and tagged everything."

Cassie stared at her. The frustration and anger she felt when Mary died returned with a vengeance. "So Ronald Brickner is claiming someone waited until the nurse just happened to get called away and this anonymous someone just happened to have a sample of his DNA that they just happened to be carrying around and they somehow inserted it into the rape kit? Not to mention the body—the ME did their own evidence collection as well."

"The body was in the same unattended room as the rape kit. It's all out," Lisa said in a tone that made it seem like this was a perfectly reasonable situation.

"This is crazy! Doesn't anyone care what happened to that little girl? The hell he put her through? Do you have any idea how much pain she was in during those two days while her intestines literally rotted inside her belly?" Cassie was shouting, but she didn't care. They were alone on this floor—hell, as far as the legal system cared, they were alone in their crusade to protect Mary.

"It's the law," Lisa said with a shrug. "The law is there to protect everyone. Just sometimes it backfires, is all."

Cassie slammed her palm onto the table hard enough to rattle their Snapple bottles. The crack echoed throughout the room. "Goddamn it!"

She blew her breath out. She hated losing control like that, hated feeling so helpless. She hadn't been able to save Mary's life, but she had sworn to get justice for the little girl.

Cassie slumped back into her chair, and pushed her sandwich away. Her appetite was definitely gone.

"How can you be so calm?" she asked Lisa who was still scribbling notes.

Lisa looked up. "I'm not. Remember on the phone when I called you? That was me coming off my own rant. It's not productive for both of us to freak out simultaneously. Feel better now?"

"A little." Cassie was surprised it was the truth. After Drake's experiences with the ADA, she hadn't expected to like the woman, but she did. They were a lot alike. Driven, obsessed even, when it came to the people they had taken a vow to protect and serve. "Thanks."

Lisa waved her hand dismissively. "Hell, I get worse all the time from the cops. Including *your* cop. Always thinks he's right. Of course the bitch of it is, he usually is." She frowned. "Don't tell him

I said that. Ready to get back to work? We still have a lot to cover."

The ceiling fan gave a final groan and died. Cassie couldn't help but wonder if it was an omen.

Chapter 14

IT WAS ONE-THIRTY IN the morning by the time Cassie let herself back into Drake's place. She couldn't face her own house and its familiar ghosts tonight, not after stirring up the memories of Mary's death. Pacing through Drake's empty apartment, she refused to acknowledge her disappointment when he wasn't there waiting for her.

Yes, she'd told him to go. He needed to go. The best way to keep him safe.

But damn, she wished he was here with her now. She was exhausted. A keyed up kind of fatigue; one that wouldn't allow any release into sleep.

It was late, but she needed to hear his voice. She started to dial his cell from the landline, then stopped, replacing the phone in its cradle. What would she say? Come back and hold me so I don't have nightmares?

Did she really want him back in Pittsburgh where some deranged woman was stalking him? Besides, she could take care of herself.

Right.

She roamed the apartment, wishing Drake was less of a neat freak so she could clean. Maybe a workout? No, she didn't need physical exhaustion to relax her.

What she needed was some peace of mind. Something that lately she'd only found in Drake's arms.

She returned to Drake's bedroom and rummaged in his closet, lifting a broadcloth shirt from its hanger and wrinkling her nose. The burnt smell of starch and a Laundromat.

In Drake's clothes hamper she found the pale blue button down he'd worn to work yesterday. She inhaled deeply. Much better. Musk and tang of his sweat. Not overpowering, but definitely there.

She slipped into the shirt, rolling up the sleeves. The hem swished at mid-thigh, its light touch a teasing stroke, reminding her she'd rather it was Drake, not his shirt, touching her. She crawled into his side of the bed and burrowed her face into his pillow. This was bad, very bad, a warning voice echoed through her mind as she inhaled his scent and imagined his arms around her.

Wasn't this exactly what Richard promised her? He'd vowed to protect her, take care of her. Cinderella, that had been his nickname for her. He treated her like a princess. And she'd bought the fantasy. She had been so tired of being alone after her parents and Rosa died, so desperate to believe.

But even with Richard, she never allowed a man to get so close that she yearned for him when he was gone. She never allowed herself to need anyone like she needed Drake. It was a weakness Cassie didn't want to admit. She'd promised herself after her disastrous marriage she'd never fall in love, never open herself up to that kind of pain. Never again.

This wasn't love. Only lust, she told herself as she drifted to sleep. And lust didn't count.

CASSIE WOKE, YANKED FROM sleep by a surge of fear and adrenalin. She listened for the sound that had invaded her sleep.

Then she heard it. Someone breathing in the dark. Her heart revved into overdrive. Cassie held her breath, trying to pinpoint the location.

A floorboard creaked with weight. A solid shadow passed the windows. Cassie sat up, fumbling for the bedside light, hoping the sudden movement would spook the intruder. Footsteps turned into running feet. The door slammed moments later.

Cassie ignored the light and ran after the intruder.

Was it Pamela's sister, come to find Drake? She grabbed the only weapon that came to hand, a hammer she'd left on the hall table with her tool belt. She raced barefoot down the steps.

A shrill peel of an alarm blared through the stairwell as she turned the corner at the second floor landing. She was in time to see the steel door at the bottom closing.

Cassie ran to the door.

"Stop right there!" a commanding voice came from behind her.

Cassie whirled brandishing her hammer. Tony Spanos stood before her, the cordless drill in his hands aimed at her.

"Cassie? What the hell?" he yelled over the blare of the alarm.

She ignored him and pushed the door open. Nothing moved in the night. Tony crossed to a small keypad beside the door, and seconds later the alarm was silent.

Cassie returned inside, still clutching the hammer. She leaned against the door. Tony sank onto the steps with the drill dangling between his knees. The only sound was their ragged breathing as they regarded each other.

"You scared the shit out of me," he told her. "I thought you and Drake were gone this weekend."

"It's three in the morning," Cassie said when she caught her breath. "What are you doing here?"

"Working a security shift at a club in the Strip District. No way to sleep after six hours of technofunk blasting in your ears, so I thought I'd come over and enjoy some peace and quiet while I worked on your system."

She nodded to the new alarm on the door. "You just put that in?"

"Finished about twenty minutes ago. Guess it was good timing." He smiled as if seeking her approval for protecting her. "Think it was Pamela's sister, leaving another message for Drake?"

"I didn't get a look. Whoever it was moved fast. All I saw was the door swinging shut."

Tony's eyes narrowed. "How'd you get down here so fast anyway?" he asked, his gaze moving up toward the third floor landing. "I was on a ladder installing a smoke detector, and you beat me—"

"I was chasing the intruder. She . . . he—whoever—was in Drake's apartment."

Tony leapt to his feet. He dropped the drill and took her by the arm. "I'm taking you home. It's not safe here."

Cassie wrenched her arm away. "Tony, it's all right. They're gone now. Besides, Drake said they know where I live."

"They must have gotten inside the building before I got here. Are you all right? Did she hurt you?" His gaze dropped, examining her, and Cassie remembered she wore only Drake's shirt and a pair of cotton underpants. She crossed her arms over her chest and tried to ignore the flush that burned her face.

"I'm fine. He—or she—didn't touch me."

Tony poised in indecision. She could see the ex-cop wanted to check Drake's apartment for evidence, but didn't want to leave her unprotected.

As if she couldn't take care of herself. She made up her mind for him and started up the steps.

"Let me search the building, make certain there's no one else here," Tony said, moving to lead the way.

They reached Drake's landing and the door Cassie had left standing open. Tony carefully examined the locks without touching them.

"No obvious signs of force," he told her. He went inside, holding the hammer as he prowled through the apartment. "No signs of any disturbance at all." He moved into Drake's studio before Cassie could stop him.

"What the hell," he said in amazement as his eyes moved over the sketches and canvasses that filled the room. "Drake did these?"

Now Cassie was in trouble. Drake hadn't told anyone outside of her and his family about his second career as an artist. Not even Jimmy Dolan or Andy Greally, his best friends, knew. And now she'd given his secret to Spanos. A man not exactly high on the list of Drake's confidants.

"Tony, you need to promise me you won't tell anyone. Drake doesn't want anyone to know."

He whistled low under his breath, his eyes riveted on a sketch of Cassie sleeping, nude. "I'll bet he doesn't. Wouldn't want the guys to think he's some kind of pansy—"

"Tony," Cassie grabbed his arms, pulling his attention back to her more-or-less-clothed self. "Please. Promise me."

He looked down on her and gave a smile that made him look almost charming. "All right. For you, Cassie. I promise." Then he saw the iron staircase spiraling to the ceiling. "Where's that go?"

"Up to the roof."

"Anywhere to hide up there?" He was already climbing it, opening the door at the top. Cassie jogged up behind him. "Jesus," he breathed after he opened the door and inhaled the heady perfume that swirled over the roof.

The rooftop garden was Cassie's sanctuary, just as the studio was Drake's. She'd spent most of the spring resurrecting it. Cultivating roses, viburnum, Japanese maples, weeping almonds, juniper, and a variety of flowers.

She'd researched the Liberty Times building and found they used to hold concerts and dinner dances up here. Some of the best musicians of the twenties and thirties performed on the rooftop gazebo, bringing Pittsburgh its first taste of the Jazz revolution sweeping Harlem. Cassie used old photos to recreate the rooftop oasis, including the gazebo with its bandstand, slate dance floor, bistro tables and benches, wrought iron gliders, even a trellis covered with climbing roses arching over the paved path leading from the elevator.

Tony turned in a circle to appreciate the entire moonlight panorama. The facade in the front of the building blocked the view from the street and the trees that grew in the ravine behind shielded the roof further and muffled most of the city noises.

"It's like a dream. You can't even tell you're in the middle of a city."

Cassie smiled. Exactly the effect she'd been aiming for. Tonight the air was scented by night blooming jasmine and gardenias mingling with roses and oriental lilies.

Tony took a deep breath. "It's like heaven. What's that smell—the vanilla one?"

Cassie picked a small purple blossom for him. "Heliotrope," she told him. It was Drake's favorite so she'd placed containers of it around their favorite settee.

Tony drank in the sweet fragrance. "Sexy," he murmured and his eyes lit on her once more. Before Cassie could move, the burly ex-cop encircled her in his arms and kissed her.

Cassie felt heat wash over her but it was the warmth of embarrassment, not passion. She pushed him away. "Tony—" she started, but didn't know what to say.

"I know, I know—I'm sorry," he said, although his expression was unapologetic. "But now you know how I feel. If you ever come to your senses about Drake, well, I'll be waiting." His eyes narrowed in the moonlight. "Where is Drake, anyway? He didn't leave you here alone. Not with some crazy freak coming after him. Not even Drake would be that stupid!"

Cassie chewed her lip. "We thought it would be safer if he left," she finally said. "I couldn't leave. I had to meet with the DA about the Eamon case."

"Obviously he was wrong," Tony said, not bothering to hide the disdain in his voice. He held the door open for her and followed her down the stairs back into Drake's apartment. "Wait here and lock the door. Give me ten minutes to check the rest of the building." When he returned he was shaking his head.

"If you hadn't seen her and if the alarm hadn't gone off, there'd be no trace of anyone getting in. If it was Pamela's sister, she knew what she was doing." He sat on the couch while Cassie took the seat across from him. "Do you want me to call it in?"

"Would they be able to do anything?"

"Other than tear the place apart dusting for prints, I doubt it."

Cassie shook her head. It was bad enough that Tony knew Drake's secret, she wasn't going to allow more of his coworkers to pry into his private affairs. "She'd be too smart to leave any anyway."

"Just what I was thinking." He yawned. "So, the way I see it, either you come home with me or I take the couch here."

Cassie looked at him. "I don't need—"

"So it's the couch then," he said. He stretched his length along the leather surface making it very clear nothing short of a bulldozer would budge him. Cassie sighed and went into Drake's room. She grabbed a spare pillow and the gray and black striped comforter from the bed and took them to Tony.

"Good night, Cassie," he said with a smile.

Cassie rolled her eyes at stubborn men everywhere and closed the bedroom door behind her.

Chapter 15

DRAKE TRIED TO WAKE up, tried to stop the dream He opened his mouth to shout a warning, but no sound came. He watched helplessly while Hart screamed as the hostage taker pulled the trigger.

The gunshot sounded more like a sonic boom. It rocked him but he couldn't move. A sliver of rational thought reminded him it hadn't happened this way, that he had saved Hart. But it was quickly drowned out by the nightmare vision of what could have happened after Spanos froze. Hart's screams dwindled to a croaking gasp, her mouth filled with blood. Helpless to save her, her blood gushed out, covering her face. Drake shuddered and turned away—to see Pamela. God, why did it always come back to her?

She turned to him, his weapon in her hand. She raised the gun to her head and, this was the most horrible thing, the thing he had never told anyone about that night, she smiled at him. Just before she pulled the trigger, she smiled.

The scene played out in slow motion. He leapt toward her. The sound of the shot reverberated through the room, deafening him. He fell down beside her. He grabbed her arm, tried to find a pulse. He held her head in his lap, her blood covering him, saturating him with the smell of copper and salt, a rank smell that turned his stomach.

He looked down on her face. It no longer was Pamela. It was Hart.

Drake bolted from the realm of dreams. His breath came in gasps. His body shivered despite the sweat pouring from him. Damn, damn, damn. He hadn't dreamed of Pamela in months—not since Hart entered his life.

Now, somehow his screwed up mind mixed up Hart and Pamela. As if both women were doomed to die.

He couldn't save the one. Was his subconscious trying to tell him to give up any hope of protecting the other as well?

The air in the small room was heavy, too thick to breathe. He pushed his morbid thoughts aside. Hart was safe—as long as he kept his distance, and kept her out of the sights of his stalker. As long as he was out of her life, like King had suggested? No, no way. He couldn't accept that. This was only temporary. A few days and he'd find the creep who was doing this and it would all be over.

He hoped.

He pulled on a pair of shorts, crept downstairs, and walked out to the dock. The moon was hidden behind a haze, casting a faint glow over the lake. He sat on the edge of the dock and dangled his legs over the side.

The tide was high enough that cold water swelled around his ankles. He used to do this when he visited Nellie and Jacob as a child, sneak out of the house at night and no one would know.

His aunt's voice startled him. "I guess old habits are hard to break."

She eased herself down beside him. Drake noticed she was still fully dressed.

"I thought no one knew I came out here," he said.

"Of course we knew. Couldn't let you go falling into the lake, could we? What would your mom and dad say?" She settled against one of the railings. "So what was the fight about?"

"What makes you think there was a fight?"

"You've never once talked about bringing someone home for the family to meet. Now you've been with the same woman for almost six months and you come home without her?"

"Still a reporter after all these years, Nellie?"

"Like I said, old habits. What really happened?"

"I don't know. Sometimes she's just so stubborn. She never sees my side of things."

"Drake, you're a grown man who to my knowledge has never been shy of speaking his mind. But sometimes you have a habit of making your arguments in such a forceful manner that it puts people on the defensive."

"You make me sound like Captain Ahab. I listen to Hart, but she didn't see how important this was to me."

"And what was it that was more important to her?" Nellie asked softly.

Drake was silent, ashamed to tell her. What could he say? He'd never given Hart the chance to tell him? "That's beside the point. Sometimes I just feel smothered."

"Oh, I see. Cassie is the clingy, dependent kind?"

"Of course not. She's independent, resourceful." He rubbed his eyes. He was confused; he didn't know what to think.

"Is it Cassie smothering you, or yourself?"

Drake took a deep breath. Sometimes his aunt was too smart for his own good. "I think it's the whole idea of staying with one person. It's an obligation. It's frightening. I wake up in the morning and I see her there and I think what would happen if I ever lost her . . . and I panic. Then I start thinking maybe it would be better not to let things get that far. Just to end it quickly, cleanly. But I can't."

Nellie laughed. She patted his thigh and gave him a quick hug. "For someone who prides himself on seeing everything, sometimes you have the biggest blind spot." She hauled herself up and turned toward the house. "And don't stay out here all night. You need your rest."

DRAKE WOKE TO MURIEL and Nellie's voices floating through the open window as they worked in the garden below.

"Not as many tomatoes as last year," Nellie said.

"Why do you really think he didn't bring Cassie?" came his mother's voice. "Think it has anything to do with that other one from last year?"

Drake tensed. He hadn't told his mother about Pamela's HIV. He wanted to protect her from worrying. He moved closer to the window, but a creaking floorboard betrayed him.

"Come on down and enjoy the morning," Nellie called out. Her hearing was still as good as always. He never could get anything past her.

"Be right down," he yelled out the window. He pulled on a pair of khaki shorts and a T-shirt.

"What do you want for breakfast, Remy?" his mother asked. She never could understand his aversion to eating first thing in the morning.

"I'm fine, Mom. Besides, I need to head back to the city."
He winced at the look of confusion that crossed her face. She and Nellie exchanged a glance.

"Help your mother. I'm going in to start some laundry." Nellie left them.

Drake knelt beside his mother and began pulling weeds from

the extensive vegetable garden. His mother sat back on her heels and watched him.

"You okay, Mom?"

"I'm fine. When did you learn the difference between a weed and a plant?

Drake smiled. "I guess Hart taught me." An image of her flashed through his mind. "I really do need to get going. Now."

She ignored his last statement, her hand resting over top of his, holding him in place. "I thought it probably wasn't the other one, the one who killed herself with your gun. You weren't in love with her, were you?"

An uncomfortable pause stretched between them.

Muriel sighed. "You've never been easy to talk to—you take after your father. Laughing on the outside and bottling up everything else inside of you."

Drake stared at her. He thought of his mother as someone who would always depend on others. Deep down, he had been afraid that after his father died, she would cling to him. The idea had terrified him. Now for the first time, he realized she had an inner strength of her own.

"Why did she do that to you, this Pamela Reynolds? Was she in love with you?"

Drake took his time answering. "At the time I thought she did it because she was afraid to face me, to tell me the truth—" He paused and took his mother's hands in his and helped her to her feet. They began to walk toward the dock. "Mom, Pamela had AIDS. I didn't know until after she died."

Muriel opened then closed her mouth. The muscles in her face went slack. For the first time in his life, his mother looked her age.

"Are you all right?" she whispered.

"So far, I'm fine. I took their drug cocktail, and I've tested negative. My last test was last week. Then it'll just be the yearly screening the PD does."

"Oh my God." She clasped his hands. "I wish you had told me sooner."

"I didn't want to worry you."

She paused by the lawn chairs at the edge of the grass beside the dock and sat down. Drake joined her. "I don't think she loved you, Remy."

Drake nodded. When had his mother become so smart? He lied to himself for almost a year, telling himself Pamela did what she did because of some misguided idea of love. "I'm starting to believe that myself."

"Why do you think she did it?" Muriel asked.

"I think if she couldn't have me, and she didn't want me to be able to get close to another woman. It was her only weapon." It was the first time he'd ever voiced his suspicions about Pamela, but as soon as the words were out, he knew they were true.

"She was obsessed. How is Cassie taking all this?"

Drake looked away. That was his mother—straight to the heart of the matter. "Every time we get close I find myself thinking of Pamela, thinking of the consequences, thinking of my own death even—" He broke off.

"Let me tell you—" he continued, his voice stronger. "It's a real mood breaker." He laughed harshly. "Spontaneity is definitely out of the question." He took a deep breath and looked down at his mother.

"She's haunting you, Remy," she said softly.

"That's a good word for it. It's slowly driving me crazy. I look at Hart and all I want to do is touch her, hold her, make love to her—but then I have to stop, make sure that we have protection, think about what we're doing. And every time I do, it's Pamela I see in front of me. It's not fair to Hart. Sometimes I think I should just break it off with her . . ."

They were both silent for a minute, then Muriel took his hand. "Your father and I were married for thirty years before he died. There were plenty of bad times, but having him there helped me get through them. The worst pain I ever felt was when I lost him. I thought I was all alone, that I'd never make it without him there to help me. It was like I was half the person I had been. Nothing you do can ever replace that part of you."

Drake looked over at her. He couldn't believe his mother was talking to him this way.

"But then I came to realize that Mickey was still here. He was inside of me, with me always." She patted Drake's hand. "I talk to him almost every night. The point is, even knowing that pain and how awful it is, I wouldn't trade having Mickey Drake in my life for anything. I can't stand to see you passing up the most wonderful experience life has to offer."

Drake hung his hands between his knees and looked past her, his gaze sinking into the cerulean blue of the water. "You're such a romantic. Hart and I have a good thing going, I just don't want her to get hurt."

"Don't lie to me, Remy," she replied in a stern voice. "I don't know how Cassie puts up with you, but if you ask me and if she'll have you, I think you ought to marry her."

"You want me to marry her? You hardly even know her."

Muriel shook her head and laughed. "You younger generation, always trying to reinvent the wheel. You love her. Sounds like she loves you. Marriage is what two responsible adults—" She emphasized the last word. "Do when they care for each other. You're thirty-four years old. Time to grow up. You should feel lucky you've found someone to grow old with. I just wish your father and I could have had longer together. Not a day goes by I don't thank

God for the time we did have."

Drake looked at her. It was the longest speech he'd ever heard her make. Muriel stood up and brushed her hands on her slacks.

"I'm going in to help Nellie. You think about what I said."

He stared out over the lake. Marriage? It was a foreign concept to him. He might love Hart now, but a lifetime commitment?

Most of his friends had been married at one time or another. The vast majority were now happily divorced. But a few of them, like Jimmy and Denise, had remained devoted to one another.

If he did this, it would be for a lifetime, he promised himself. He'd had plenty of time to play the field. If he was going to commit to one person, it would be forever.

That thought made him shiver. He stood and walked out to the end of the dock, catching the breeze from the lake. Never make love to another woman? Monica Burns' face raced through his mind, but the spark of desire that tormented him yesterday was gone.

What if he asked Hart and she said no? After her past experience with unholy matrimony, she just might.

Even more terrifying—what if she said yes?

Chapter 16

THE NEXT MORNING AFTER she sent Tony on his way, Cassie searched through the clothing she'd left at Drake's house to find something to wear to the deposition. All she found were work clothes in need of washing, and a simple sleeveless ankle-length voile dress. It was pale green with tiny violets, and at least three-dozen buttons down the front.

Cassie smiled as she remembered the last time she'd worn this dress. A week ago Sunday. She'd come to Drake's after taking Gram Rosa's friend, Tessa, to Mass. She'd been hot and sweaty and feeling more than a little naughty. She hated going to Church—she had mainly done it for so many years out of habit, and a sense of debt to Rosa and Tessa. But Father Shuster's sermon on the ways of wickedness and corruption seemed directed solely at her. Which, of course, left her in a most rebellious mood.

Drake had been out for a run and despite the open windows, his apartment was hot and steamy. Cassie had made a pitcher of fresh squeezed lemonade, brimming with ice and lemon quarters, then slid out of all her clothes except the button front dress, covered with its tiny violets done in purple and indigo, and waited for Drake to return.

The first thing he saw when he entered was sunlight streaming through the thin cotton of her dress, silhouetting her body. The second was the tall glass of lemonade she ran over her cheek, beads of condensation streaming over the glass.

"Is that for me?" he asked hopefully, kicking his shoes and socks off and dropping his sweat soaked shirt on the couch. "Looks wonderful."

She smiled a wicked smile and took a small taste. "Oh it is," she assured him. Her fingers snagged an ice cube and ran it above the bodice of her dress.

"Just one problem, sugar—" She mimicked a southern accent as he approached. "There appears to be only one glass."

Drake arched an eyebrow, backing her up until she was against the table. "What are we going to do about that?" He licked the condensation the ice cube left in its wake.

Cassie carefully set the glass on the table out of reach. "First one to beg loses," she said, teasing him with the ice cube against his lips.

He grinned, nipping at her fingers as he sucked on the frozen water. "Deal." He moved his mouth to her top button, his tongue flicking her sweaty skin. She in turn reached around and rubbed the ice cube down his spine, her fingers slipping below his waistband to the sensitive spot at the small of his back.

"Only one rule," she whispered as his teeth clamped down on the small button, ready to yank it from her dress. He glanced up at that; they both knew rules weren't her forte. "You tear any buttons, you sew them back on."

Drake straightened, his hands sliding down to her hips. "No fair. There must be a hundred of them," he protested, his palms heating her skin through the thin fabric of the dress.

She wasn't swayed by his argument. Instead, her grin widened. "Maybe even a hundred and one."

"So we'll leave the clothes on," he told her, sliding the ice cube from her fingers before it could wreck his resolve. "I remember a certain lap dance you gave me once," he murmured as he slid the ice cube down her cleavage, his lips close behind. She shivered beneath his touch. "I've been wanting to pay you back for that."

His fingers moved the ice cube over one of her breasts, holding it there as her nipple swelled. Then he clamped his mouth over both the ice and her flesh, teasing her through the fabric of her dress, his tongue directing the ice in its movement.

She writhed beneath him, her fingers clamping around his biceps with a bruising grip. Relentless, he slid the ice cube down her body until it rested just beneath her belly button. His hand held it there, her dress staining with the melting water, as he nudged her hips up onto the table. He spread her knees apart and leaned forward until his pelvis and hers rubbed together, separated only by several thin layers of fabric.

Then he moved his hand down even lower.

In the end it was Cassie who had ripped the dress open, buttons showering them from every direction.

Drake took his victory drink and tortured her with it. He squeezed drops of lemon over her lips and chin, his tongue dancing over her skin, tasting the refreshing tartness. He sipped lemonade from the notch above her sternum, slurped it from her belly button, sucked it from her breasts, all the while using his fingers to bring her to climax after climax.

Afterwards, Cassie remembered sitting naked, sewing buttons back on her dress, all thirty-six minus two lost forever, while he sketched her. The perfect summer day.

Now Cassie bounded down the steps from Drake's apartment,

the memory of that lazy Sunday warming her. She lowered her head and sniffed at the fabric of her dress, disappointed to smell only laundry detergent. No hint of lemons or heat or passion. But still, every time the cloth caressed her skin, she felt Drake's hands. As if he was there with her, protecting her, helping her get through this ordeal.

Even if he wasn't.

Reality hit her as she punched the alarm code into the new system. That was the nice thing about fantasies. They wouldn't let you down like real people so often did.

It wasn't Drake's fault. He didn't even know she had the deposition today. Or what was going on with Mary's case.

Because he hadn't given her the chance to tell him. If he really did love her like he said he did, he'd be here when she needed him. Good thing she didn't need him, Cassie told herself as she stepped into the parking lot. Good thing she wasn't in love with him.

Just a bad case of hormones run amuck. That's all her and Drake were. And she could handle hormones.

—⋀⋀⋀⋀—

DRAKE HAULED HIS BAG out to the Mustang, still confused by his discussion with his mother. Could he ask Hart? It was the worst time possible.

Yet images of her laughing face, beaming, hell, even crying tears of joy in answer to his proposal filled his mind. Irresistible future gems of emotion he yearned to experience in real life.

He was so engrossed in fantasy he didn't hear Muriel call his name until she stood right beside him. "Remy."

"Sorry, Mom. What did you say?"

"I said be careful." She hugged him tight, so tight he lost his breath. He was surprised such a small person could squeeze so hard.

Then she broke away, wiping her eyes with her knuckles.

"And take this." She thrust a tiny black velvet box at him. One side was worn down to gray cardboard. "Your father used to rub it like a good luck charm. Took him three months of carrying it around before he worked up the courage to ask."

He opened the lid. Her sapphire engagement ring sparked in the morning sun.

She laid her hand on his and squeezed the lid shut again. "Don't you make Hart wait that long. She's not one to wait, Remy. You ask her."

"When? How?" Surely not while he was being stalked by some psycho-nut who wanted him dead.

"You'll know when the time is right." He must have looked worried because she reached her fingers to his brow, soothing it just like when he was a little boy. Only now she had to stand on tiptoe to do it. "You'll know." She kissed his cheek and returned to the house.

Drake slid the tiny box into his pocket. It felt warm, solid. Just like Hart. He drove away, his mind buzzing with possibilities, Hart at the center of them all.

He couldn't resist calling her. Her cell went to voice mail, so he tried her house, then his. To his surprise a man answered.

Spanos.

"Where's Hart?"

"Still in bed," Spanos replied. "You know how horny she gets in the morning. The way she came, over and over—"

"Fuck off, Spanos. What the hell are you doing there?"

"Cassie asked me to spend the night. Showed me all those fruity paintings you do—no wonder she needed a real man. Oh, she's calling me back to bed, gotta go."

The buzz of a broken connection filled the car. Drake swore, his chest constricting with anger. No way Hart let a Neanderthal like Spanos touch her.

But the testosterone fueled fool who lived inside Drake's mind whispered in opposition, remembering the way she'd smiled at Spanos yesterday morning, the way his own body had responded to Monica Burns' blatant advances.

No. Hart wasn't like that. Wasn't like him.

Or was she?

Why the hell was Spanos in Drake's apartment?

He tried Hart's cell again. No answer. Just as he was getting ready to try her home, a call came into his phone. Not Hart. Jimmy.

"What the hell's going on?" Drake snarled at his partner. "I just called my place and Spanos answered. Is Hart okay?"

"Is she with him?"

Drake's fury checked itself at Jimmy's worried tone. "He said she was. I didn't talk to her. Why?"

"Just got off the phone from a guy I know on the Gang Unit. Both the Rippers and Gangstas are gunning for Hart and some girl she saved yesterday. She needs to stay off the streets."

"Why the hell—" Without waiting for an answer, Drake pushed the accelerator, glad the back roads he'd taken were empty. "I'm two hours out. Can you get to her?"

"Spanos will keep her safe. I'm more concerned about the girl she helped, Athena Jackson."

"Why?"

"Turns out she's the chief suspect in a homicide of the head of the Gangstas, Rodney Hunsacker, gunned down two weeks ago. If we don't find her fast, there's going be war breaking out between the Rippers and the Gangstas."

"Why are the Rippers after her? Seems like they'd be pretty happy she did their work for them."

"Apparently she and Rodney were going to run away together. He convinced her to steal the Rippers' bankroll, but then dumped her."

"So she killed him and kept the money." Stupid girl. Did she really think she could outfox two of the most vicious gangs in Pittsburgh? "Call Spanos. Tell him to keep Hart at my place. I'm on my way."

He hung up and concentrated on the twisting mountain road. He'd left her. She was in danger and he'd abandoned her. Maybe that was why she'd asked Spanos for help.

The thought of the ex-cop alone all night with Hart twisted in his gut. He shifted his weight, the ring box in his pocket digging into his thigh, and forced the Mustang to go faster.

Chapter 17

JULIET NGUYEN, THE LIBERTY Center lawyer who represented Cassie in her malpractice case, was waiting in the King, King, and Ulrich law offices. Despite being a weekend, secretaries bustled about pushing carts laden with documents, associates huddled over computers or talked on phones, the hum of a copy machine filled the air.

"Thanks for coming, Juliet." Cassie shook the attorney's hand. She felt a little naked. The other woman wore a formal suit and carried both a large purse, as well as an official appearing attaché case.

Cassie had nothing but her car keys. She'd left her cell in the car, as usual. It was bad enough carrying a trauma radio inside the ER. She hated being tethered to a device when she was outside the hospital.

Of course, if Richard's malpractice suit went the wrong way, she might never see the inside of an ER again. At least not as a physician.

Before Juliet could answer, the large oak doors to the conference room opened. Alan King stood there, smiling in greeting as if they were overdue guests at a cocktail party. "Ladies, come inside, come inside."

The conference table was an immense slab of mahogany surrounded by elegant leather chairs. No glass or chrome. The entire room had an old world sense of grandeur with framed original oils and sculptures standing guard in the corners. At one end of the room a videographer set up his camera and recording equipment beside a court stenographer who already held her dictation cup to her face.

Alan guided Cassie to a seat at the end of the table. Juliet took the chair beside her. Before Alan sat down, six associates filed in and piled documents on the table top, then each took their seats. Alan remained standing, smiling over the proceedings in his elegant suit with its crisp linen shirt and red silk tie.

Cassie was a little surprised Richard wasn't here to watch her suffer through Alan's interrogation. Lately he acted as if he thought they might reconcile. Strange coming from the man who was simultaneously working to destroy her, and accused her of trying to kill him. But Cassie had long ago given up trying to understand either of the King brothers or their narcissistic actions.

Alan remained silent as his associates walked Cassie through the name, rank, and serial number of her CV, outlining her education and training. The junior lawyers fired their questions in random order. Cassie's gaze ping-ponged back and forth across the table as she braced herself against the next barrage.

"Tell us about the night you poisoned Dr. Richard King," one of the associates sang out, so fast Cassie wasn't sure which one. Although they all looked different: two women, four men of varying ethnicities, their voices were eerily similar, same tone, same volume, same quick-fire cadence.

"I didn't—"

Juliet silenced Cassie with a quick shake of her head.

"Objection." Juliet made a note.

Another attorney picked up the line of questioning. "You gave him a cup of coffee laced with fentephex, a deadly drug, didn't you?"

"It was meant for me." She'd come close to exposing the man behind several deaths at Three Rivers and he'd poisoned her coffee in an attempt to silence her forever.

"He took the cup from your hand. Your fingerprints as well as Dr. King's were found on it."

"It was my cup. Of course my prints were on it. But I'm not the one who put the fentephex in the cup." As they well knew. The police had their man; the case was closed.

"What are the effects of an overdose of fentephex, Dr. Hart?"

Finally something she didn't have to think twice about answering. "High fever, malignant hypertension, seizures, coma, larynospasm, muscle rigidity, rhabdomyolysis, cardiac failure, and cerebral edema."

"And you've seen people die from fentephex overdoses?"

"Yes, unfortunately."

"It's an agonizing death, isn't it, Doctor?"

"Yes. It's very difficult to treat. We had little to offer patients until I tried an experimental protocol using a pentobarbital coma."

"Patients suffer massive seizures, often resulting in a lack of oxygen, correct?"

"Yes."

"How long can a person go without oxygen before they suffer permanent damage?"

Cassie hesitated. "It depends. There are so many variables."

"Give us an average. Common medical thinking."

"Again, it's difficult to pinpoint." She opened her mouth to start to hazard a guess but Juliet kicked her below the table and Cassie shut up.

"Very well. Let's look at a specific patient. Dr. King. How long after he drank from your coffee cup, ingesting a massive overdose of fentephex, was he deprived of oxygen?"

"We were alone in my office and I had no resuscitation equipment," Cassie stammered. It wasn't the answer she'd rehearsed with Juliet, but right now all she could do was re-live the scene as it played out in her mind. As soon as Richard collapsed, she'd realized it was from fentephex. Although at the time she thought he'd taken it himself. He'd just gotten back from rehab and she'd been suspicious he was abusing drugs. Again.

"How long before you called for help?" This time the question came from Alan King. His voice filled the room even though he didn't raise it. Everyone else went quiet. "How long did you let him lie there, dying, convulsing, foaming at the mouth like a rabid dog before you did something to save the man who loved you?"

"Objection," Juliet snapped, her voice cracking like a whip.

Cassie ground her fingers against the tabletop, trying to keep a hold on her emotions. Guilt flooded through her. She remembered Richard's face, gasping for air but finding none. She remembered standing over him.

Remembered thinking he deserved it. That she would be safe with him dead.

It was only a second—no longer than a heartbeat. But for that single moment, she wanted him dead. She'd forgotten she was a doctor and remembered only the pain he caused her. And she hesitated. A second. One second.

Cassie blinked slowly, the faces of the associates blurring.

"What do you want from me?" her voice echoed from the elegant walls of the conference room. The stenographer looked up with a start. Juliet reached over to grab Cassie's wrist with a warning squeeze.

"We're all tired," Juliet said in her calm, lawyer's voice. "I suggest we finish this later."

King shrugged. "I'm finished."

He nodded to the stenographer and camera operator and they quietly left, followed by the associates who were all smiling as if they'd achieved some huge victory on a battlefield.

Cassie sat frozen, hands fisted on the sleek mahogany tabletop. Juliet packed her case, occasionally sliding her gaze over to where King stood at the other end of the table, waiting for a sneak attack. King moved to the doors as if to usher them out.

"Could we have the room for a moment?" he asked graciously as Juliet went through the door.

Juliet stopped and turned to Cassie, who still sat at the table. "I don't think that's a good idea."

Cassie welcomed the opportunity to give King a piece of her mind. "It's all right," she told Juliet. "I'll see you Monday."

King shut the door before Juliet could protest.

Now it was just him and Cassie in the enormous room—but it felt very crowded. As if an unseen audience had joined them.

Cassie stood. She refused to allow King to see how wobbly she was. Black spots raced across her vision until she took a few breaths to banish them. King escorted her through an interior door to another large room, this one furnished with leather couches, an elegantly appointed bar, fireplace, and club chairs.

"It's almost one." King reached for a baccarat decanter. Part of the churning in Cassie's gut was hunger. A small part. "I seem to recall you prefer Irish. Black Bush neat, correct?"

A genial host, King poured several fingers of liquid gold into a glass and placed it on the table between the two leather club chairs. "Sit down," he directed as he poured himself a generous helping of

Johnny Walker Blue.

Cassie would rather stand. He came out from behind the bar, placing him all too close for comfort, so she slid into the seat behind her and ignored the drink at her side.

Instead of moving to the other chair, King set his glass on the mantle. He leaned against the marble, directly in front of Cassie, staring down at her with a leer.

As she realized the disadvantage her position placed her in, she wished she'd kept to her feet.

"You were the only thing Richard ever had that I was jealous of." King surprised her with his nostalgic tone. He shrugged. "You grow up in a house like ours, you learn to be competitive in everything. As the eldest, I made certain one way or the other I always won. Poor Richard," he gave a mock sigh, "always with big brother's castoffs. I don't think there was a woman he slept with that I didn't—" he paused, searching for a word, "conquer first. Until you came along. And you were the ruin of him." He shook his head as if disappointed in her. And Richard.

Cassie finally understood how Richard came to be the way he was. It was more than just being spoiled by the power and money he had his entire life. Growing up in the shadow of his brother had also warped him.

"So," King continued with a smile, "what'll you give me to save your precious Liberty Center?"

Cassie stared up at him, confused. She bit her lip, certain he was setting her up for something. What was with all this quiet talk? She wanted to vent and rage at him, not discuss things calmly.

"C'mon now, Cassandra, I'm negotiating in good faith here. I'll make sure the Center gets all the funding it needs. Or I can save your medical license, and let you be a doctor again. Which will it be?" His gaze raked her body, a master surveying his possession.

This discussion had nothing to do with being civilized.

She fought to still the surge of panic that came when she looked into those predator eyes, so similar to Richard's.

"Of course, you'll need to go back to Richard. After all, that's the point of all this, isn't it? We have to give my little brother something in exchange for his pain and suffering." He waved his hand at the sumptuously appointed room. "The only question is how much you lose beforehand. If you agree to my terms, here and now, you can save the Liberty Center or your medical license. Your choice."

Cassie took a deep breath and met his eyes. In her mind she was far away, on Drake's roof, roses perfuming the air, Drake's arm curled around her. King noted her attention wavering and sweetened the pot.

"What about your boyfriend, Drake? Our firm has been in contact with Pamela Reynolds' family. What if I took care of that problem as well? Saved the Liberty Center and Drake? What would that be worth?"

Cassie yanked her attention back to the here and now. King was behind Pamela's sister stalking Drake? It made sense. His firm had the resources to do surveillance, to give her everything she needed to make Drake's life a living hell.

King's gaze narrowed. He had her now.

"What would you do to save everything important to you, Cassandra?" His voice was a seductive croon. "Would you leave Drake in order to protect him, to guarantee his future? Does he mean that much to you?"

Cassie sucked in her breath and bit her lip against her answer. But she saw from the gleam in his eyes he knew. If that was all it took to keep Drake safe, then yes, she'd walk away.

But she knew better. She knew the lawyer wanted more.

"So that's the deal then. Drake in exchange for your future." He took a sip of his drink, his gaze glowing with avarice. "Of course, before you return to Richard, you'll need to seal the deal. Give me a chance to see why my little brother is so very fascinated with you." His voice trailed off and the room filled with a heavy silence. "Do we have an agreement?"

Cassie took a deep breath. She couldn't—wouldn't—hurt Drake that way. And she couldn't trust the lawyer to keep his word even if she did. Alan loved toying with people. Shocking them into a reaction he could hold against them. She shook her head. "No deal."

His eyes flared with fury. Crossing the two steps needed to reach her, he leaned over her, his hands circling her wrists, trapping them against the wooden arms of the chair. His grip was bruising. The delicate bones of her wrists ground together, bringing tears to her eyes. She choked them back. Any revelation of pain or fear and he'd pounce like a hungry wolf. Just like his brother.

It took all her strength to meet his gaze. But she'd lasted almost three years with Richard and he couldn't break her. No way in hell Alan could do it in three minutes.

Abruptly he released her. He stalked back to the mantle where his drink waited. "Fine. Just remember this is a one-time offer. You walk out that door and everything is gone. Your career, your house, Drake's building, the clinic, his career, both your lives over."

Anger brought her to her feet but she held it in check. Turning her back on him, showing no fear, she stalked to the door. His voice caught her just as she placed her hand on the doorknob.

"What about Ronald Brickner?" he asked, his voice low and ominous. "What would you give to make certain he goes to jail before he rapes and kills another three-year-old?"

She paused. He was bluffing. There was no way he could influence a homicide trial. Was there? She dared a glance and saw his face held the same smug expression it had during her deposition.

"Could you bear that, Cassandra? To be responsible for letting a murderer, the man who raped and killed poor Mary Eamon, go free? That's what will happen if you don't agree to my deal. What will you do when he kills again? How many little girls will go through that hell because of you?"

A shudder ran through her body, fierce enough to rattle the doorknob in her hand.

"You can't be serious," she told him. His bland mask of indifference never wavered. He moved to the bar to freshen his drink, waving her out as if she were an inconsequential.

"See you Monday, Cassandra," he said as she fled from the room.

Chapter 18

BLINDED BY TEARS OF anger and frustration, Cassie fled the
law office. She swiped at her face with fisted hands. Rosa always
said she cried too easily, felt too much. Nothing wrong with feeling,
Rosa would say, as long as it doesn't get in the way of your doing.

What was she going to do? Cassie asked herself as she
approached the law firm's lobby. What the hell was she going to do?

The elevator's doors stood open, waiting for her. She had
the sudden fantasy that Drake would be waiting inside, ready to
wrap his arms around her, give her the comfort and strength she
so desperately needed. The thought frightened her . . . it came too
easily, without any hint of anger that she'd grown to depend on him
to that extent.

As if part of her had accepted he was a permanent part of her
life, and had surrendered to the fact that she wasn't strong enough to
do this on her own.

She struggled with the realization, shoving it down, drowning
it with a surge of fury. She could handle this. She wasn't going to
go crying to Drake. This was her fight and by God she'd finish it
herself!

This time it was the words of her grandfather, Padraic, that echoed through her mind. *Never start a fight, gal, but always, always finish it.*

She stepped into the elevator, head high, shoulders straight. She had no idea what she would do, but felt confident she could save the Liberty Center. And Drake. If Richard and his brother were behind Drake's stalker, maybe Jimmy and Drake could use that information. The doors slid shut, finally allowing her to drop her guard.

They immediately opened once more, revealing a man in a sleek black wheelchair. Richard.

"We need to talk." He wheeled inside the small box, blocking her escape.

Cassie whirled on her ex. "Did you come to gloat? To see me beg for mercy? Forget it, Richard. It isn't happening. I don't care what game you and Alan think you're playing, you're not going to win."

She pounded the button for the parking garage and turned away from him. The elevator lurched to a halt. He'd hit the emergency stop. Trying to control her, like old times. She spun to face him, fists balled at her sides.

"Tell me one thing, Richard. How many innocent people need to suffer before you get your revenge?" She faltered when she saw the look on his face. None of the smug satisfaction of his brother, and none of the sadistic delight in her pain she expected to see.

Instead, he hung his head in shame. When he looked up to meet her gaze she was surprised to see tears sliding down his cheeks. "I don't want revenge."

"What do you want?" she snapped, her patience with the King family long since spent.

"Forgiveness."

She backed away as far as she could. This wasn't Richard. Forgiveness? How could he possibly—

"Cassandra—" His voice was low, pleading. "I can't remember the difference between the fibula and the humerus, not anymore, but I remember a beautiful woman who loved me with all her heart. I remember dancing on the deck of a ship in the moonlight. I dream of—" He broke off. "Do you really want to know what I dream of, Cassandra?"

He was as lost in this as she was. She once loved this man. She was responsible for his life being stolen from him. Listening was the least she could do. She nodded, slowly, cautiously.

"I dream—" His voice grew wistful, his eyes never leaving hers as he spoke. "I dream of surgery. I see myself performing marvelous, technically complex operations—things I could have never done—" his voice caught, "before. Things I don't even have the words to describe, but in my mind I watch as my fingers dissect and probe and reattach muscle and ligaments and vessels. It's a wonder of precision and boldness that gives me this rush of adrenalin, of power and confidence I never had before—not even in the real operating room. But the best part, the very best part—" He reached across to take her hand in his. "Is when I come out of the OR, exhausted but triumphant, you're there, Cassandra. You're waiting for me. You tell me how brilliant I was, how no one else could have saved the patient. And I'm the happiest man in the world."

His voice trailed off and he looked away. "Pretty sappy isn't it?" he muttered.

Cassie leaned back on her heels, surprised. Before his coma, Richard wanted only to own her, control her, warp her into his idea of the perfect love.

Afterward he'd woken to his new life of disability, he'd been angry and bitter, wanting to take everything away from her, and bring her down to his level. He'd been obsessed with her, unable to accept the fact that they were no longer married, that she didn't belong to him.

But this . . . she didn't know what to say. Maybe he truly was a different man now. The old Richard would have never confessed such vulnerability to her. He would have gnawed on it, twisted it into something painful he could use on her like a weapon.

Instead of sharing it with her as a gift.

"Thank you," she finally said.

He cleared his throat. "I didn't—I never intended to tell you that." His words slurred a bit as he fought for control over his wayward muscles. "But we do need to talk." He straightened in his chair, looking at her once more, his hand tightening on hers. "Alan won't listen to me. He thinks I'm incompetent, weak, infatuated by you." He gave a small shrug. "I guess he's right. But I can't let him take everything away from you—your house, medicine, the clinic."

"I won't let him. I'll fight him. I'll quit the clinic, sell the house, use my savings, whatever it takes."

"You'll still lose," he said quietly. "Believe me, I know these people. I've fought them all my life. And lost. Even you can't win against them, Cassandra."

"What do you propose?"

He surprised her by smiling. "Just that. I'm proposing to you, Cassandra."

She watched in amazement as he slid his fingers into his shirt pocket and pulled out a delicate diamond ring. Her old engagement ring. Left behind with her wedding band that last horrible night when she'd fled his house, their house, beaten and bloody, running for her life.

"No, Richard—" Her voice shivered as memories pounded

through her. Maybe his damaged brain had forgotten what happened during their marriage, but she didn't have that luxury. She remembered it all. Every humiliating, painful second of it.

"You two are working together," she accused him. It was the only way she could make sense of her macabre day. "First, Alan humiliates me, then you—"

"No. Alan wants to punish you. I'm trying to save you." The look on Richard's face convinced her at least he was sincere, even if his brother was playing games with people's lives.

"Cassandra, please, hear me out. It doesn't have to be a real marriage. Separate bedrooms, separate houses if you want. But if you marry me, the family will stop their vendetta against you. Much as they'll hate the idea. You can save the clinic, Drake's career, your future."

Cassie looked down at the gleaming rock in his hand, stunned by his logic. He was right. But it was so very wrong.

When she looked into his face and saw the puppy dog look of devotion there, she knew in her gut she couldn't accept even if she wanted to. If she went through with this, this time she'd be the one battering and torturing. Because she could never return the affection he so obviously had for her.

She lowered herself so that she was at eye-level with him. "Richard, I can't—I don't—"

"Shhh." He pressed the ring into her palm, stopping her. The jewel scorched with cold. "You don't have to say anything. Just think about it. I'm here for you, if you need me."

He closed her fingers around the ring and released the elevator. They completed the short journey in silence. Cassie slowly regained her balance when they came to a stop. The doors opened and she started through them, then turned back to face the lost and lonely man in the wheelchair.

"Richard," she started, intending to give him her final answer.

"Just think on it, Cassandra. I promise it will be different this time."

The doors slid shut before she could respond.

Chapter 19

CASSIE CLENCHED THE DIAMOND, the faceted stone biting into her flesh. How had everything gone so wrong, so fast? Once she had a promising career, the promise of a relationship with Drake, and so much to look forward to. And now, everything was threatened.

She stuck the ring onto her finger. Her dress had no pockets and she couldn't risk losing a King family heirloom. The ring felt cold and heavy on her hand. Foreign.

She sat in her Subaru for a moment, trying to regain her equilibrium. Her hand brushed against the hem of her dress where the two buttons, forever lost somewhere in Drake's apartment, were missing. All she could think about was Drake. He would make it right. Help her find a way through this mess.

She needed to know he was safe, warn him about Alan King's possible involvement with Pamela's family, and let him know she was there for him on this awful anniversary.

And to apologize. She should have never let him leave without explaining herself. God, he must think she was heartless. A total bitch.

She started to call him on her cell phone but there was no reception in the underground parking garage. As soon as she got back to his place, she promised herself.

Maybe he would be waiting for her, safe and sound, at the Liberty Center. The hope kept her from cursing the slow traffic as she sped back to Drake's building.

But there was no sign of Drake's car as she pulled into the Liberty Center's parking lot. Tony's van was still there, parked on the far side of the construction dumpster at the back of the lot. She felt a twinge of guilt about all the work he was doing on his day off. Especially after staying up most of the night babysitting her.

Of course she hadn't asked him to stay. He was as bad as Drake, not giving her any choice in the matter, not believing she could take care of herself. Suddenly she found herself irritated at the ex-cop. Then she realized it wasn't Tony who was making her angry.

It was herself and these out of control emotions. She wasn't one to wallow self-pity. Or let other people run her life. Grow up, Hart, she chided herself. First she moped about Drake, feeling sorry for herself, and now she was upset the wrong man spent the night with her.

Time to do something, anything.

With fresh resolve, she got out of the car. Just in time to see Drake's Mustang make the turn onto Ravenna. He skidded into the parking lot, stopping at an angle, his car blocking hers as if worried she'd try to escape.

"Drake!" she called, not caring that her voice exposed every single one of her jumbled emotions. Her heart sped as she turned towards him. He jumped out of his car, arms spread, ready for her. His face glowed with a smile richer than the July sunshine.

DRAKE HAD PROMISED HIMSELF he'd play it cool. Make sure Hart was safe, then leave to track down his stalker. Then, and only then, would he tell Hart how he really felt. About her. About them. About their future.

Seeing her, in that dress, worry weighing her down, he'd practically rammed her car in his haste to get to her. So much for playing it cool.

"Drake," she called, her voice filled with anxiety and joy, breaking the single syllable into two.

Air shimmered from the scorching blacktop, casting rainbow shadows around her. God, she was beautiful. What kind of fool was he, leaving her?

A shot cracked through the air, slamming through the side of her Subaru.

Drake leapt across the space between them and tackled Hart. He covered her body with his, and he had his answer. The kind of fool who'd put the woman he loved in even greater danger by returning.

Gunfire peppered the air above them. The Subaru rocked as it took hit after hit. Glass rained over them. Metal pinged and groaned. He'd slammed Hart face down and knew the blacktop was scorching her—hell, it burned him and only his palms pressed against it—but he kept her pinned.

When it was safe to look, he scoured the horizon, searching the vacant buildings for the shooter. Somewhere in the few seconds that fractured his initial joy into panic, he'd drawn his gun, but it was useless. There was no one to aim at.

He heard a car in the distance. After that, silence.

"Are you okay?" Hart asked, her voice muffled by her hair.

He rolled off her, his gaze searching for danger. "Stay low, we're moving."

She drew her legs up into a crouch, ready to run at his

command. He held his gun high, but there was no movement from across the street. "Edge past your car, and hug the ground until you're behind the dumpster. I'll cover you. Go."

For once, she didn't argue. When they were both behind the dumpster's cover and no one tried any potshots, he allowed himself to relax long enough to check on her. Glass sparkled in her hair and tarry bits of blacktop speckled her skin along with a few scrapes, but otherwise she was fine.

"Got your cell?" he asked while gauging if the scene was safe enough for them to try for the door. Too exposed. Better to wait.

She shook her head. "In the car."

Of course it was. Hart never carried the damn thing when she needed it. He grabbed his and called Jimmy.

"I'm two minutes out, hold tight," Jimmy said.

Drake hunkered down, wishing he could hold Hart but needing his hands free. She seemed to understand. She said nothing, but slipped one hand behind his back, touching him without limiting his movement or field of vision. He kept vigil on the parking lot and the street, making note of the graffiti that wasn't there yesterday. Ugly red and black paint dripping with vile defaced Tagger's art. Death threats from both the Rippers and Gangstas.

"What the hell happened?" Tony Spanos appeared at the clinic's back door, ear buds dangling from his neck. "I look outside and—"

"Stay inside," Drake shouted. Useless bastard. Probably watching porn on his phone when Hart was out here getting shot at. No movement on the street. The shooter was long gone. Still, he didn't take any chances as he shepherded Hart inside.

"Did you call it in?" Spanos asked.

"Yes." As if Drake was an idiot.

"Who was it?"

Before Drake could tell the ex-cop what he really thought,

Jimmy Dolan arrived in a departmental sedan.

"Jeezit, anyone hurt?" he asked as he emerged from the car and joined them.

"No," Hart said.

"Hart was almost killed," Drake corrected.

Two patrol cars, sirens blasting, raced up. Jimmy went to mobilize the troops, getting them started searching for the shooter's perch.

"Third floor, fourth window in," Drake directed them to the empty warehouse across the street. Once the patrolmen radioed no sign of a shooter, he joined Jimmy outside. Hart followed, leaving Spanos inside.

Jimmy circled around his and Hart's cars—only Hart's had been hit. Two tires blown, it listed to one side and had bullet holes peppering its frame. The only glass that remained intact was in the passenger side mirror.

"Spanos?" Jimmy asked Drake in a low voice.

"It wasn't him," Hart answered before Drake could say anything. "Why are you two so against Tony? He's been getting threats, too." She looked from one man to the other. "You thought he was Drake's stalker, didn't you?"

"He fit the profile," Jimmy said.

"Everything pointed to him." Drake's gut told him Spanos was still number one on his suspect list.

Hart considered for a minute. "Someone broke in last night and he almost caught them. Maybe someone is framing him?"

Drake shrugged, unwilling to relinquish his prime suspect. He narrowed his eyes at Hart, wondering what else transpired during his brief absence. "Someone was here last night? In my building?"

"Inside your apartment. Tony scared them off." Hart looked sheepish.

"Before or after this graffiti went up?" Jimmy asked, using his phone to take pictures of the spray-painted tombstone with Hart's name scrawled in black, the letters dripping red teardrops of blood.

"Jesus, Hart, only you could get the two deadliest gangs in the city coming after you." Drake pulled her close. Any gangbanger could have done the shooting. Might not be Drake's stalker after all. But he wasn't taking Spanos off the suspect list.

"Not to mention Brickner." Hart said, hugging herself. Now that the danger was gone, she turned pale. It was the aftershock of adrenalin, Drake knew from firsthand experience. Every time he looked at her, he felt queasy himself. All he could see was Hart on the pavement, bleeding out.

Then her words made it past the images. "Ronald Brickner?" he said. "What's he got to do with this?"

Hart shrugged free of Drake's arm and spun to face him. "That's what I was trying to tell you last night, why I couldn't leave. He's out on bail."

"No way. What judge—?"

"They didn't have a choice. He's got a new lawyer who got most of the evidence thrown out. I spent most of last night going over my testimony with Lisa Dimeo."

Jimmy gave a low whistle. "So our list of suspects includes the members of not one, but two gangs, a self-confessed child killer, and a crazy stalker obsessed with Pamela Reynolds' death?"

"Tony thinks maybe her sister is the stalker."

"Yeah, I've been looking into her myself, but haven't tagged her yet."

"Alan King said his firm was in contact with her, if that helps." Hart looked down, scuffing her foot against the blacktop. "I had my deposition with him this morning."

Christ, Drake thought with chagrin. "I should have been here."

She wove her fingers in his. That was encouraging, after the heel he'd been. "You didn't know."

Jimmy finished taking pictures. "Let me call the gang guys and see what word on the street is about the shooting. I'll get CSU over here as well."

"And find Brickner," Drake put in, wondering if Hart would be safer with him guarding her or with him on the other side of the planet. Seemed like she was doing a good job of putting a target on herself without any help from him.

"Right. Then we'll start from the top."

DRAKE WENT THROUGH THE building checking to see if anything was missing while Cassie told Jimmy everything she knew. Then she returned to Drake's apartment to change her clothes. Her dress was ripped and tar had seared black blotches into the fabric. It was ruined.

Once she was alone, she finally felt able to breathe. First the deposition, then Richard. Could Richard have orchestrated all this? Sent someone to threaten her, hoping she would run to him?

She twisted the large diamond, watched the cold stone sparkle despite the late afternoon shadows gathering in Drake's bedroom. No. She didn't believe Richard capable of such subterfuge. Before his coma, definitely. He was a consummate actor—had fooled her for almost three years. But he wasn't the same man since the overdose. The tears he shed in the elevator over his lost dreams, those had been genuine, she was certain of it.

Maybe Alan?

No. Even Alan would never condone someone trying to kill her. It would take away his pleasure watching her pay for Richard's trauma.

How was she going to explain Richard's proposal to Drake? He was already upset. Not just about the shooting, but the fact someone invaded his privacy, his home, and now Tony knew the secret about his art. It also didn't help that she'd allowed Tony to spend the night. Not much choice at the time, but the look in Drake's eyes when she had tried to explain . . .

And now Richard wanted her to marry him again. Worse, it seemed like it might be the best way to protect Drake.

If the Kings were in contact with Pamela's sister, they could make her stop tormenting Drake. Richard would end the malpractice suit, and stop the threats against the Liberty Center. Maybe even convince Alan to see that Harold Brickner got what he deserved.

She shook her head. Never. She couldn't bear the thought of even a sham marriage to Richard King—no matter how much his stroke had changed him. It was as ludicrous as Alan's insane proposition.

Although it was amazing to think of Richard ever placing anyone else's welfare above his own.

Before she could take her thoughts further, Drake entered the bedroom behind her. How was she going to tell him that because of her, he might lose the Liberty Center and everything he worked for?

"The shooter left his casings. 5.56 millimeter rounds. Definitely not a standard gangbanger weapon." His voice was tight with fatigue and restrained anger. She knew if she turned to face him, she'd find his hands bunched into tight fists.

"So it wasn't the Rippers or the Gangstas."

"No." The word emerged with a soft sigh and she had a feeling she knew where this conversation was heading. With him leaving. Again.

She lowered her head, fumbling for the top button of her dress. He moved to stand behind her, his hands on her shoulders.

"You sure you're all right?"

She nodded, still facing away from him.

His hands caressed her arms as if assuring himself that she was truly unharmed. "I love this dress. Promise me you'll buy another just like it."

The memory of their passion the last time she'd worn this dress flashed through her mind. Was it only a week ago they had the perfect life? She wished she could go back in time, and somehow stop their world from spiraling out of control.

"I'm so sorry," he continued, his face lowered beside hers. "I never should have left last night. If anything had happened to you, I don't know what I would have done. I just felt so overwhelmed. I was afraid of what might happen if I stayed, that I might not be able to stop it . . ."

His voice trailed off and she knew he was thinking of his past failure to save Pamela. The other woman's ghost was an almost physical presence insinuating itself between them.

Cassie might be crazy enough to talk to her dead grandparents at times, but no way was she going to allow Drake to torture himself for something not his fault.

She turned within his embrace, and reached her hands up to caress his face. God, he looked so very tired. Why did he insist on taking this all on himself?

"You don't have to protect me. I'm not Pamela." There, she'd said the dreaded name aloud. "I can take care of myself. But I can do it a lot better if there are no secrets between us."

Her words came out sharper than she'd intended. It wasn't until then she realized how angry she was at him. For not telling her about the stalking, for leaving her last night, for returning now when it was obvious he was in no shape to deal with an obsessed maniac who might be trying to kill him..

She had the sudden feeling it might be Drake who needed protecting.

His crestfallen expression revealed the impact of her words His hands fell away from her as he stepped back out of her reach.

She followed his gaze and saw it centered on the gleaming diamond on her left hand.

"Secrets?" he said. "What the hell is that?"

Chapter 20

CASSIE COULDN'T HELP HERSELF. Drake's face was such a twisted mix of dismay and disbelief at the sight of Richard's ring, she broke down laughing. He stared at her in horror, not understanding how surreal her day had become, while she sank down onto the floor, uncontrollable laughter shaking her from head to toe.

"What's wrong?" Drake knelt on the floor beside her.

She gasped for air, waving her ring finger. "Richard—proposed—"

"King gave you this?" The fury returned.

Usually Drake had the consummate poker face, but Cassie had learned how to read him, while he in turn learned to let down his guard around her. She watched as suspicion edged his fury aside. "And you accepted it? Why?"

He thought she and Richard were—she laughed even harder at the thought. She shook her head because she couldn't swallow long enough to form words, she simply slid the ring off and tossed it aimlessly across the room. Priceless King family heirlooms be damned.

"No . . ." She wiped her tears with the back of her hand.

Drake finally got it. He started laughing himself, at first a deep chuckle, followed by a cathartic guffaw that rocked through them both as he gathered her onto his lap. "Of course not."

"You actually thought—me and Richard?"

"No. Yes. Maybe. I don't know what to think." His tone grew serious again. "I leave for one day and Tony Spanos is answering my own phone, you're wearing King's diamond . . ."

"You have no idea the day I've had." She sat up straight, took his hands in hers, wrapping them tight around her belly. This was what she'd been missing. This feeling of solidarity. All week she'd been searching for it. "After working with Lisa all night on Mary Eamon's case, I spent the morning with Alan, in a deposition."

"How can King ask you to marry him if he's going through with the damn malpractice case?"

She didn't tell him about Alan's ludicrous proposal. The attorney was just tormenting her, trying to manipulate her with meaningless threats. Or worse, manipulate Drake into reacting. But he deserved to know the Liberty Center was at risk. "Richard said he doesn't want it, but Alan and the rest of the family are after my blood. As well as everything I care about. Alan's trying to block the Center's funding."

"Bastard. Let him try."

"Alan's also been working with Pamela's family. He might be behind your stalker."

The idea obviously left a bad taste in Drake's mouth. "Jimmy thinks the sister might be involved. He tracked her down in LA but her landlord said she left a month ago, no forwarding address. No trace of her since."

"Maybe Alan flew her out here? Or maybe she has nothing to do with it, other than giving him enough details to set it in motion.

He's richer than God, and could hire someone to do his dirty work for him."

"What about King?" Drake never could bring himself to call Richard by his first name. "He has just as much money and even more reason to want me out of the picture." He jerked his chin towards the far corner of the room where the ring landed.

Cassie blew her breath out in frustration, hating she might have caused Drake's misery. "I don't think so."

"What's with the proposal?" His voice grew flinty and his hands went lax in hers. She tightened her grip on him.

"He thought it would solve our problems. A sham marriage to get Alan and his family to back down. It would save my career and the Center."

"And you said yes?" He tensed against her. Any other circumstances and she would have teased him, but this wasn't the time—or the topic.

"I said no. Emphatically. No. Never. Not in his wildest dreams. But he left me holding the ring and last thing I need is Alan adding the price of an heirloom diamond to the things he hates about me, so I—" She wiggled her ring finger.

"You sure?" His hands fell away from her. "It would solve everything. Even get you back your job. I know how much you miss it."

Cassie shook herself against a sudden chill. She twisted around on his lap to face him. "It would solve everything. Including saving the Liberty Center."

Their eyes met. His had darkened to the indigo of a summer's midnight—a sure sign he struggled to contain his emotions. She felt his breath enter and leave, faster than normal, more shallow. Like he was holding something in.

"It would keep you safe," he finally said. Then he looked away, the muscle at the corner of his jaw bunching as he waited for her answer.

"I can take care of myself," she whispered as she tried to kiss him, erase his fears. But he pushed her away, just as he had last night.

"I'm serious. King has a point. Much as I hate to admit it. You're not safe around me. Not now."

"That's ridiculous! You can't be serious."

He slid out from under her and stood, leaving her kneeling on the floor. "If King's family is behind all this, nothing will stop them. Nothing short of—"

"Of me giving in." She jumped to her feet. "I'm not going to do it. I won't let them win. I won't even let them think there's any chance of that."

"Just give me some time to find this actor," he pleaded. "Play along with King. Keep the ring for now. Tell him to tell his brother you're considering his proposal. Anything to keep you safe. Let me and Jimmy do our job without me worrying about you."

"I'm such a bother you want me to—" Anger clipped her words short. "No. I can't do it. Not to us. Not to Richard."

His hands closed into tight fists. "Then stay away from me. Until we can figure all this out. I don't care about the Center, don't care about any of this—" He glanced around the room. "But if something happened to you . . ."

She wanted to slap him, jolt him from his idiotic delusions. Then she tried to look at it from his point of view. In twenty-four hours her world had turned upside down and everything Drake held dear threatened along with it.

"For how long?" The words made her mouth go dry. She hugged herself, wishing they could turn back time and return to laughing on the floor.

"I don't know." He reached for her hand but she was too angry. She spun away.

A victim. He was treating her like a victim. The one thing he knew she hated most in the world.

His phone rang and he retreated to the other room to answer it.

Cassie stood in the center of the shadows, still hugging herself as if it was December instead of July. Hunger, fatigue, adrenalin, shock, she told herself as she failed to control her shaking. Fear.

"I have to go," he said from the doorway, not crossing the threshold. "I'll call you when . . ." His voice trailed off. "When I can."

His body leaned forward and she thought—she hoped—he was going to forget this insanity and come back to her. But his phone rang again and the moment was lost. A moment later she heard the door slam behind him.

The floor tilted below her. She sank down on the bed, dizzy and sick. Tried and failed to think of one thing she had left in her life she could control. She'd lost it all: her job at Three Rivers, her work at the Liberty Center, Mary Eamon's killer walked the streets, Alan King possibly manipulating a stalker to ruin Drake's life, and Drake. He thought she was helpless, defenseless, a victim . . .

She sank back onto the silver and black duvet and watched the ceiling spin above her, blurred by tears. There was one thing worse than being helpless, unable to control her life, she was discovering.

Being helpless and alone.

Chapter 21

"WHAT THE HELL JUST happened?" Drake asked himself as he steered the Mustang towards Monica Burns' apartment. He almost blew through a red light. Horns sounded all around him, adding to the cacophony in his mind. Had he really just told Hart she was better off with King?

"Idiot." He jerked the wheel to one side and pulled into a vacant parking space. He couldn't do his job, not with all these thoughts tangled inside him. He stepped out of the car and fought the urge to run back to Hart before it was too late.

His phone rang again. Jimmy, thank God. If Monica Burns called one more time asking why he wasn't at her side protecting her from the man she thought had followed her home, he'd shoot something.

He couldn't believe he'd been stupid enough to give her his private cell number—he never did that. Just goes to show how far off his game he was.

He answered. "What'cha got?"

"Got your apartment locks changed. Not Spanos' company, the same one that did Hart's house for you. CSU guys came up empty. Except some empty spray paint cans in the basement of your building. Doesn't match any of the death threat graffiti, though."

"Tagger." He'd suspected the boy had been staying in the basement but hadn't been able to catch him. "Nothing to worry about."

"Hart left. Went to the hospital to check on that baby from yesterday."

"Good." The word tasted like a copper penny. No, the copper of blood. "Safer that way."

"Not sure she agrees. You certain about this, partner?"

Usually Jimmy was the one person whose advice Drake listened to. But not this time. Not with Hart's life at stake. He couldn't risk his wanting her near interfering with his needing her safe.

"I'm sure." He paced a circle around the Mustang. "Walk me through this."

They did their best work when they challenged each other with theories. "Someone's using Spanos' name to access the photos needed to create the threatening letters. Which would either make him the stupidest crook in the world or—"

"Or he's pulling a double-blind. Thinks he's being clever."

"I take it you still like him for the stalker?"

"Yeah, but I don't think he's in it alone. Hart told you about her ex's brother and how he's been in contact with Pamela's family?"

"Not sure what that has to do with anything. Why would the stalker need Pamela's family? It's not like he's gonna get permission to use her death to drive you nuts. What's this actor really after?"

That was the question. After what Hart told him about Richard King's proposal, everything changed. "Maybe this whole game isn't about me."

"What, the world doesn't revolve around you? Since when?" Jimmy's attempt at levity fell flat.

"Maybe it's about driving a wedge between me and Hart. I leave for one night and shit happens."

"It was her car the shooter aimed at. So far the stalker hasn't done anything to hurt you."

"That's what doesn't make sense. If it's her ex behind all this, he'd never try to hurt her."

"Don't forget we've still got a gang war brewing. And neither side is very happy with Hart. Maybe they got their hands on an AR-15." It was the type of rifle used in the shooting—similar to what the SWAT team carried.

"But would they want to kill her?"

"The graffiti—"

"Yeah, but didn't you say they wanted to find Athena Jackson? If they thought Hart knew where she was, why would they try to kill her?"

"Maybe they wanted to scare her into leading them to Athena."

Drake stopped, leaned against the car, drumming his fingers on the hood. "Where'd you say Hart went?"

"To Three Rivers to check on Jackson's baby—oh shit."

Drake didn't bother with expletives. He grabbed the driver's door handle, and then immediately realized he couldn't go. Not without putting Hart in more danger.

He closed his eyes, palm burning from the sun-heated metal. "Hey partner—"

"Don't worry, I got her," Jimmy reassured him. "Least I can do if you're willing to deal with Monica Burns and keep her off my back."

Drake hung up, opened the car door, and got behind the steering wheel. He still wasn't ruling out homicide as a potential way to deal with Burns and her whining.

—᠕᠕᠕᠕—

CASSIE ENTERED THREE RIVERS through the ER, her usual route, only to be turned away by the security guard and sent to the main visitor's entrance. Talk about embarrassing. The triage nurse saw what happened, but pretended to be too busy to notice Cassie.

Made her wonder what her reception would be even if she did get her job back. Sure, she had Ed Castro on her side, but would that really sway the minds and hearts of everyone who believed the rumors she wanted Richard to die? Not to mention the other accusations she'd faced down. The rumors had time to grow and mutate in her absence, poisoning the staff against her.

Maybe life as a clinic doctor wouldn't be so bad, she thought as she signed in at the visitor's desk. And she'd be working regular hours, have more time with Drake.

The thought brought her up short. She never dreamed she'd give up the ER for anything. Or anyone. Here she was fantasizing about being at the clinic, waiting for Drake when he got home?

Could she really live that life? Drake would be happy if she did. Would she?

She got onto the elevator, musing about living a nine-to-five life with Drake and was surprised to find herself smiling. Until she remembered the reason why she was here alone.

The sight of the cooing babies lined up in the bassinettes beyond the nursery window cheered her. Baby Jane was under the warmer and on a monitor, still needing oxygen, which was to be expected for a preemie her age.

Cassie put a gown on and was washing up at the sink outside the nursery when a kid came in. Tagger's age, maybe a little older, wearing a red ball cap. Instead of stopping at the sink he barged right into the nursery.

"Hey, you can't—" A nurse followed him then stopped short. She backed up against the door, propping it open, eyes wide.

Cassie turned, soap dripping from her wet hands to see the kid holding a gun. His expression was a strange mix of emotionless smugness. Like he enjoyed holding that gun and terrifying the nurse, but didn't really care too much about what happened next.

"Where's Athena's baby?" he shouted.

The nurse jumped but didn't move, her mouth opening and closing like she was trying to force words out but couldn't. The kid had picked the right time. It was shift change, the other nurses were all in report.

"Don't just stand there, bitch! You want to be dead?" He jerked the gun at the nurse.

Cassie strode past her, eyes on the boy. "I'm Dr. Hart. Can I help you?"

"Yeah. Give me Athena Jackson's baby."

"Baby Jane's very unstable," Cassie lied. "She was born way too early, you know. She'll probably die if you take her out of here."

She hoped the kid wanted Jane alive. No such luck. He didn't even blink at the idea of the newborn dying. "Just give me the damn baby."

Time to try Plan B. She heard the door shut behind her and knew the nurse would be hitting the panic button, initiating a lockdown of the nursery.

The boy didn't realize it, but he was trapped. Now all Cassie had to do was make sure he didn't try to shoot his way out of here, using the babies for target practice.

"Baby Jane's over here, under this warmer." She led the boy to the far corner of the nursery where the babies needing warmers were stationed. Through the glass separating her and the nurses' station she saw the nurse use her keycard to open the door out to the hallway and let someone inside. Jimmy Dolan took the key card from the nurse and ushered her out.

Cassie had no idea how the detective had gotten here right when they needed him, but she was glad to see him. She positioned herself so the boy's attention was on Baby Jane while Jimmy exchanged his suit jacket for a lab coat.

"As you can see, she's got an oxygen monitor and temperature probe. This is an IV giving her fluids and antibiotics. She's hypothermic and suffering from bronchopulmonary dysplasia." Total lies, but the big words obviously impressed the kid who for the first time seemed interested in the baby.

"Is that bad?"

"Yes, it's very serious."

"What are all these?" He touched the tangle of monitor leads with the muzzle of his gun, the purple wires looking stark against the black of the pistol.

"They monitor the electrical impulses of her heart. And this—" She gestured to the tiny white cuff wrapped around Jane's thigh. "Monitors her blood pressure."

He hesitated then nodded, his decision made. "Take it all off. Now."

"But—"

"I said now." He pointed the gun at Cassie's heart. Beyond them, at the nurses' station, Jimmy stood at the door, ready to use the nurse's keycard to come inside.

Cassie just needed to distract the kid long enough. "Okay, okay. Whatever you say."

She took the pulse ox lead off first, knowing the monitor would alarm and give Jimmy a distraction.

A second later the monitor screeched. The boy jumped back. Jimmy slid through the door.

The boy raised his gun at the monitor. "Turn it off."

Cassie reached up to the monitor, putting her body between the boy and Baby Jane. She silenced the monitor but didn't shift her body, still using it as a shield.

"Drop it." Jimmy's voice sliced through the air.

Cassie dared to look over her shoulder to see Jimmy hold his gun at the back of the kid's skull while using his free hand to pull the boy back away from Baby Jane.

The boy let out a few choice expletives, but dropped his gun into Jimmy's waiting hand. Jimmy put the gun in his coat pocket and then twisted the boy's wrist, forcing him face down to the floor.

"Put your other hand out to your side," he ordered as he holstered his own gun and brought out a pair of handcuffs.

A few moments later, the boy was cuffed and searched, and hospital security guards swarmed over him. Jimmy stood and turned to Cassie. "The baby okay?"

She nodded, the aftermath of adrenalin making her mouth too dry to talk. Swallowed and tried again. "She's fine. Thanks to you."

"Thank Drake. He's the one who sent me."

Chapter 22

DRAKE PARKED THE MUSTANG in front of Burns' apartment. He couldn't believe he was doing this, but Jimmy already had his hands full, he couldn't ask him to take time to clean up a mess Drake created.

If only he'd done more to discourage Burns yesterday. She had all the markings of a cop groupie, and after Pamela, Drake was an expert on the kind of woman who needed to play the role of damsel in distress to his shining blue knight. He wanted no part of that.

Especially not when someone was after Hart. She was all he could think of—or wanted to think of. Was he wrong to send her away to keep her safe? It sure as hell felt wrong. Leaving Hart had left a taste of char in his mouth, as if everything bringing joy to his world had burned to ashes.

He barely had the energy to heave a sigh of frustration. It was this heat; it sucked the life from him.

The front door of Burns' building stood wide open as it had earlier. The woman was obviously a slow learner.

She waited for him on the landing. Her hair was pulled back into a loose, tousled knot and she looked even younger than before.

Younger and more vulnerable.

As he drew closer he noticed she was shivering despite the heat. "I thought I told you to lock the doors and wait with a neighbor."

"It's Saturday night. No one else is home. And I did lock the doors." She did a double take, looking past him down the stairs. "How did you get in without buzzing?"

"Front door was wide open."

Her mouth formed a small *oh* of dismay but no sounds came. He moved past her, into the apartment. "Tell me what happened."

"It's like I said on the phone. I was at the Giant Eagle and this guy, he was watching me, then I saw him again, and I didn't know what to do, so I ran home and called you." Her words emerged in a breathless gasp.

"What did he look like?" Drake asked when she paused for air.

"Normal. I don't know." She closed her eyes, concentrating. "Brown hair, or dark blonde. My age. I don't know how tall." Her eyes popped open. "I've seen him before, I know I have. I can't think where. Oh my God. How long has he been following me?"

"What happened after you got home?"

"I locked the door, just like you said. But when I went into the bathroom—" She latched onto his arm, fingernails digging in, and he didn't have the heart to disengage her. The kid was scared stiff. Together they walked into the bedroom and he could see why. Smeared on the dresser mirror in ragged red lipstick were the words: *Never Forget.*

"What does it mean?" she asked, her grip on him tightening. "I've never hurt anyone in my life. What doesn't he want me to forget? Why me? What does he want from me?" Her voice raised to an unpleasant shriek as panic overwhelmed her.

Drake sat her down on the bed. She collapsed like a rag doll, sobbing incoherently. He returned to the scene of the crime.

Never Forget. His stalker's mantra.

Conflicting scenarios swirled through Drake's mind. If the stalker was Spanos, the ex-cop could have gotten someone to pull Drake's case files and tracked down Burns. But Spanos had been at the Liberty Center all day. There was no way he could have done this.

Had his stalker followed him yesterday and decided Burns made an easy target? Maybe Drake enraged him by leaving the city last night, triggering the attacks on Hart and Burns. Were innocent women now being pulled into the bastard's sick game because Drake refused to play?

Then he thought of something. Maybe they were not so innocent women. At least one of them.

"How did you get my number?" he asked Burns.

She wiped tears from her eyes and looked up at him. "It's on your card. You said to call you day or night."

He could have sworn he'd given her a regular card without his private number. "Where's the card?"

She frowned, stood, and moved on unsteady legs to the living room. "Right here." She pointed to where a business card rested beside the phone. "Did I do something wrong? Why are you so upset?"

Drake ignored her, grabbing the austere white Pittsburgh Police Bureau card. He turned it over. There, in his own handwriting, was printed his private number.

He blew his breath out. Damn it, he was losing it. He never gave his private number out—not after Pamela, at any rate. He didn't even remember writing it on the back of the card. How could he forget that?

Five nights with no sleep, and days filled with worry. He was definitely off his game. Which meant the stalker was winning. "Get your things together. I need to get you out of here."

"Why? Do you think he's coming back? Am I in danger?" Her eyes grew wide and the trembling returned.

Drake wasted no time on reassurances; he had no idea what the answers to her questions were. Instead, he took her arm and led her back into the bedroom.

"Is there someone you could stay with?" he asked.

"No. I'm new here, and haven't had time to meet anyone yet." She gave a harsh, tight laugh. "Except you and Detective Dolan, of course."

"Pack some clothes. I know a place where you'll be safe."

THE BLARNEY STONE WAS crowded despite the fact it was not air-conditioned. It was Saturday evening in a hot Pittsburgh summer and everyone wanted a beer.

Thankfully, Andy Greally had an empty apartment above the bar and was willing to loan it to Burns for a few days. There was no safer place safer upstairs from a bunch of cops, Drake reasoned. Secretly, he hoped she'd find someone else to lean on instead of him.

While Burns settled in, he dialed Hart's cell. No answer. Right, it was in her Subaru, probably destroyed. He tried Jimmy.

"Dolan."

"Just me, checking in."

"Was she crying wolf?"

"No. I wish she had been." Drake told Jimmy about what happened at Burns' apartment.

"Think she could be involved? Or did we lead the stalker to her?"

"I don't know." Drake dragged his fingers through his hair. "I was even wondering if she could maybe be Pamela's sister."

"I had LAPD fax me a DMV photo. They don't look anything alike. Elizabeth Reynolds is five-six, weighs one-sixty, with brown hair and brown eyes."

One theory blown. Burns was about that tall but couldn't weigh more than one-fifteen, and had green eyes and blonde hair. "I'm stashing her at the Stone for the duration."

"Good move. You were right about the Rippers."

"What happened?"

"They sent a kid to the hospital. Guess they figured he'd get through security and up to the nursery easier. He wanted the baby."

"Shit. Was Hart there?" Drake prayed not.

"She's fine. Talked the kid down. She kept him from doing anything until I got here and took him down." Jimmy's nonchalant tone only increased Drake's frustration. Drake knew damn well how volatile a situation like that could be.

Helplessness tore at Drake's gut. Hart was in danger and all he could do was make it worse. "Where's she now?"

"I took her home and had patrol increase their presence on her street. She's locked up tight."

"But too easy to find."

"I offered to stay, but I got another call out. Besides, you know Hart—"

"Stubborn." Drake glanced around the crowd of off-duty cops. Laughing, enjoying watching the Buccs fight to hold onto a lead, without a care in the world. He used to be like them.

Before Pamela.

Never Forget. As if he could.

"She'll be fine," Jimmy said. "You're the one I'm worried about."

Maybe the best thing for everyone, especially Hart, would be to let the stalker catch him. Anything to end this. "Don't. Just keep Hart safe."

"You know I will."

"Thanks, Jimmy." Drake hung up, approached the bartender, Kenny, and ordered a shot of Jack Daniels and a beer.

He ignored Kenny's look of surprise and drank the shot in one quick gulp. It had been a long time since he'd had anything stronger than beer, not since last July and Pamela, but the sensuous warm feeling it left in its wake was the caress of a familiar lover.

"Another," he ordered.

Kenny poured the shot but held out his hand, palm up, before handing it to Drake. "You know the rules. Besides, you're out of practice."

Drake dumped his car keys into Kenny's palm. He poured the JD into the frosty mug of beer.

Carrying the beer, enjoying the cold heaviness of the mug in his hand, he wandered into the back room. There was a pool table and several old-fashioned pinball machines; Andy Greally refused to allow video game machines into his establishment.

Burns came through the rear door. She'd changed into a skimpy black dress that made every man's eyes go wide with appreciation. She ignored them all and approached Drake, offering him a cue stick.

"Wanna play?" she asked.

Drake took a long swallow from his beer then nodded, reaching out for the pool cue. What the hell? If he was going to make it easy for the stalker to find him, this would be the best place. Besides, he could keep an eye on Burns.

"Why don't you rack the balls?" she told him.

Drake set his beer on the counter and leaned his pool stick against the table. He quickly gathered the balls and was leaning over the table to position them when he felt her hand brush against his buttocks. He turned and looked at her but she was smiling and chalking her cue stick, leaning against the counter. He stood up and drank his beer as she broke and started shooting.

"I'll take stripes," she announced, leaning into her shot.

He couldn't help but think the same thing as every man in the room: How far would that dress inch up and what was she wearing underneath? He watched, fascinated, as she curled her fingers around the stick without gouging herself on her bright red talons. It was as if by changing her clothes, she'd changed into an entirely different woman.

"Could you help me with this shot?" she asked, leaning precariously far over the table.

Drake gulped the remainder of his beer and joined her. She gestured to her hair. "Just hold my hair up, will you? It keeps falling into my face."

He gathered the long silken threads into his hand and gently held it up off of her neck. She moved closer to him and curled one leg around the back of his, her foot stroking his calf. He caught his breath and realized her position gave him an excellent view of her ample cleavage. A view that answered the question as to what she was wearing under the dress: nothing that he could see.

She drew her arm back and shot, missing the ball she was aiming for. She stood, entirely too close for comfort, her body pressed against his.

"You can let go now," she said, and he let her hair fall from his hand. He held his hand awkwardly away from her, hovering over her shoulder, then backed away. The clinging victim had vanished, replaced by a woman used to bidding men to do her pleasure.

Which one was an act? Memories of Pamela buzzed through his brain, confusing him more than the alcohol. Pamela had as many personalities as she did outfits: drama queen one minute, soft-spoken schoolgirl the next.

Burns pivoted, now so close he could see the clumps of mascara deposited on the tips of her eyelashes. "Your turn," she whispered, her breath stirring the tiny hairs on his neck.

"I need a drink," he said, not realizing at first he'd said it out loud.

"Here, have mine." She took a step away from him and suddenly he could breathe again. She handed him a tall glass containing a tea-colored drink.

He took it, his hand slipping on the sweaty glass and drank it in quick gulps. The liquor burned on its way down but it was a good burning, a match to the heat beginning to ignite elsewhere.

Drake handed her the glass, empty except for a few ice cubes, and she smiled. "My, you were thirsty," she said, tilting the glass and placing one of the ice cubes into her mouth to suck on.

Reminding him of Hart. What the hell was he doing here?

"I'll buy you another." Drake's head buzzed and he felt like his feet weren't quite touching the ground. Jeezit, he was out of practice. Alcohol never affected him like this. He picked up his empty beer mug and took her glass.

"Don't be long," she pouted as he went out to the bar.

"Here you go, Kenny," Drake told the barman as he handed over the empty glasses. "Another of whatever the lady was drinking and club soda for me." It'd been a mistake to start drinking again— especially with Burns.

"Long Island iced tea coming up," Kenny said, placing the club soda in front of Drake. Drake drank it, hoping to dilute the effects of the alcohol in his system, his eyes on Burns as she bent over the jukebox, selecting a tune.

Why was it that all he could think of was Pamela?

"Hey, killer," came a sarcastic voice behind Drake.

Spanos came up beside him and whistled when Burns waved at Drake. "Now that's a fine piece of ass," he said in appreciation. "Did you visit Pamela's grave today? I see you're real broken up over the anniversary of her death."

"Why don't you just shut the hell up?" Drake forced the words through clenched jaws as he grabbed Burns' drink.

Spanos shoved Drake against the bar, splashing the Long Island iced tea down Drake's shirt. "You almost got Hart killed today, and now you're here trying to get into another woman's pants. No wonder Hart keeps coming to me for comfort. Did she tell you how I made her scream this morning?"

Drake pushed the ex-cop away. "You don't talk about Hart. You don't mention her name. Hear me?"

"You're a drunken piece of shit, Drake. It's not my fault you can't get it up long enough to please your woman."

"I'm not so drunk that I can't take you if you don't back off," Drake told him in a level voice, fighting to keep control.

"Let's see." Spanos stood up tall, chest expanded in challenge. Just like a freakin' gorilla, Drake thought. "Out back."

Spanos led the way to the alley behind the bar. The heat and humidity had turned the narrow space into a stench oven stinking of vomit, urine, and rotting food. Drake's stomach gave a heave and he tasted bile in the back of his mouth. This was not a good idea, the last sober remnant of his mind informed him before it fled for the hills.

The ex-cop threw the first punch, a slow motion roadhouse that Drake ducked easily.

Drake didn't have Spanos' reach or muscle mass, so he made up for it with sheer passion. Letting all the pent up rage and frustration that had built over the past week boil to the surface, he lunged at

Spanos, breaking under the ex-cop's guard to head-butt him in the belly. Spanos went down, taking several trashcans with him.

As Drake straightened, Spanos grabbed his ankle and brought him down as well. Spanos jumped up, landed a kick to Drake's ribs that connected a little better than Drake would have liked. He heaved his weight against Spanos leg, grabbing the other one as well, and Spanos was back down. Drake rolled on top of him, hauled off, and planted a right hook to the Spanos' jaw that hurt like a sonofabitch but felt oh so good.

It wasn't a knock-out punch, but it got Spanos' attention. The rush of anger and adrenalin sent the alcohol spiking through Drake's blood and he sent a left into Spanos' gut. Then he hesitated.

Hart. She'd hate this. Hate him for it.

But Spanos deserved it. On so many levels. Drake pulled his elbow back for the finishing blow.

Spanos raised his hands in surrender. The blood haze filling Drake's head almost blinded him but he managed to check his motion before striking the ex-cop. Heaving in a ragged breath, Drake climbed off Spanos.

"You're not worth it."

Sucking blood from his knuckles, Drake staggered down the alley. He'd done his job; Burns was safe for the night. He patted his pockets. No car keys. But he found the ring box that had been in there since this morning. Then he began humming. *Don't need no cars, don't need no keys.*

He knew exactly what he did need and it was only a short walk away.

Hart. She was all he needed.

⎯⎮⎪⎮⎪⎮⎪⎯

DRAKE WALKED TO HART'S house on Gettysburg Street. He

hesitated at the door—should he ring the bell? That seemed too impersonal, so he compromised by knocking briefly before letting himself inside and re-setting the alarm code, leaning forward so his nose was an inch from the keypad as he stabbed the tiny buttons.

It took him two tries. Just as he finished, Hart came down the stairs in her bathrobe, toweling her wet hair. She startled when she saw him.

"You scared me," she told him, dropping the towel onto the sofa. "What are you doing here?"

Drake looked at her—was her nervousness because she was guilty of something? Or was he reading into her actions because he felt guilty about letting Burns flirt with him?

"Why? Were you expecting Spanos?" The words came out harsher than he intended.

She stared at him, inhaled, made a face, then straightened and crossed her arms. "You're drunk."

"Or maybe Richard King?" Damn, he hadn't meant to say any of that. But once he let his jealousy and anger grab hold of him—aided by the alcohol—there was no stopping it.

"I can't believe you have the gall to come in here and accuse me—in my own house!"

"Please. Just tell me nothing happened, okay, Cassie?"

"Drake, nothing did happen!" Then she looked at him and chuckled.

"What's so funny?" he asked, his head splitting from the noise.

"You are. I never took you for the jealous type. I can't believe you thought Tony and I—"

"So nothing happened?" Drake was beginning to feel foolish. How had he gotten into this, anyway?

"No, of course not."

"Oh, good, nothing happened with me either." He caught her

puzzled look and rushed on, "I mean, not that anything would have happened, but she was gorgeous, but nothing did happen—"

"Drake, I really am in no mood to listen to this." The laugher vanished from her voice.

"No really. I thought of you and it was like splashing cold water on my face and waking from a dream."

"Just the effect I strive to have on men," she snapped.

"No, I don't mean it like that." He scrubbed his hands over his face and through his hair. God, he hated this feeling of being disconnected. Like the alcohol created a thick fog. A fog he had to cut through if he was going to make her understand.

Drake sighed and lowered his palms onto her shoulders. At first she glared down at his hands. She hated to be restrained, to feel confined. But he needed the physical contact; it grounded him, and helped clear his mind.

"What I meant was, once I thought of you, nothing else mattered. I didn't care what that woman looked like. I didn't care what anyone in the bar thought of me. I just wanted to see you." He paused and spoke slowly, straining to enunciate each word to make his thoughts clear. "I only cared about you."

Her glare softened but her shoulders still tensed under his hands.

"Drake." She took a step backwards, shrugging his hands off of her shoulders. "I'm exhausted and you're drunk. Too drunk to drive home. You can have the couch." She grabbed her towel and turned to leave.

"No, wait." Drake fumbled in his pants pockets for the velvet ring box.

Hart put a hand on his back and propelled him towards the couch.

"No," she said when he started to protest. "Not another word.

Or one of us is going to say something we'll both regret." With that she was gone up the stairs, the sound of the bedroom door shutting echoed after her.

Drake stood there, confused for a moment as his hand closed around the ring box. He held it up before him, then stumbled to the bottom of the steps.

"Come back, Hart. I have to ask you something," he shouted.

"Go to sleep, Drake, before I get really mad."

Drake collapsed onto the sofa.

This night wasn't going exactly how he had planned.

Chapter 23

CASSIE WOKE AS THE sunlight streaming through the bedroom windows hit her face. She yawned and almost rolled over to go back to sleep until she remembered Drake downstairs. She'd checked on him several times during the night, making sure he didn't throw up and aspirate, but she really, really was in no mood to coddle his hangover. Or fight anymore.

She showered and threw on some work clothes, then after seeing Drake sleeping peacefully—nice someone had gotten a good night's sleep around here—she left for the clinic. After missing all day yesterday and Friday, they were terribly behind schedule.

She was outside and halfway down the porch steps when she remembered she didn't have a car any more. It was hazy, hot, and humid again; at least eighty-five degrees already and only a quarter past nine. She sighed and began walking, wondering what the hell she was going to tell the insurance company when she called them about her car. Excuse me, am I covered for semi-automatic weapons' damage?

The car was ten years old, but damn, she loved it. And she hated the thought of change.

She almost tripped on the curb before crossing Fifth Avenue. Change. Drake was a huge change in her life, drawing her out of her self-imposed hermitage, making her care about someone again. After Richard she never thought that'd ever happen.

So why was she fighting it? Fresh mown grass tickled her nose as she strolled down Walnut. An early morning jogger passed by. She reached College and still had no answer. Other than plain old fashioned fear.

Loving Richard nearly killed her. Could she risk loving Drake?

The morning sun sparked from the broken glass littering the Liberty Center's parking lot and she still hadn't decided.

No new graffiti. It had to be a good sign. Still, she approached the building cautiously, wondering if it had been a good idea to come here alone. She'd been so focused on avoiding Drake, she'd forgotten she had to also worry about whoever shot at them yesterday. But the street was quiet. No movement other than a stray cat pawing at a sewer grate.

"Doc Cassie—" An urgent whisper called to her from the shadows of an empty building. Cassie froze. It was the same building the shooter used yesterday. But the voice was that of a girl. She turned and saw Athena standing there. "I gotta talk to you."

Athena looked pale and hungry, but otherwise in good shape. Cassie stepped into the shadows to join the girl. "Are you okay? No pain, no dizziness?"

"No, no." Athena waved away Cassie's concerns. "How's my baby? She doing okay?"

"She's just fine. A fighter. Like her mom."

"Good. You make sure she gets a good home with a real mama who can take care of her." Her sentence was punctuated by a rumble from her stomach.

"When's the last time you ate?" Cassie asked.

Athena shrugged. "Had me some bananas and grapes at the Whole Foods over in East Liberty yesterday before they kicked me out."

Cassie took her hand. "Let's get you some proper food. Come on inside."

Athena peered past Cassie's shoulder, scrutinizing the Liberty Center. "I don't know. There's something bad happened there last night."

"What?"

"I was hiding in that cubby hole in the basement beside the elevator, you know?"

"Near the loading dock?"

"Yeah. And a car pulled up. Man and woman. I could hear their voices."

"Could you see them?" Cassie couldn't help but remember what Drake had said about being with a woman last night. She glanced at the parking lot. Drake's Mustang was there, parked crooked, between the dumpster and the side door. "What did they look like?"

Athena shook her head. "Couldn't see nothing. Just heard them. They went inside and the elevator started running—you know how loud it is."

Drake wouldn't take the elevator. Unless he was too drunk to stumble up the steps?

"Then came the shot."

Cassie whipped around to stare at Athena. "A shot?"

"Yes'm. Just one. Not sure if it was inside or out. Sounded strange, like it was close but not too close. Echoey-like. Then the elevator came back down and the man left. But not his car. Just him walking."

Not Drake. Couldn't have been Drake. But— "A man and a woman and only the man left?"

Athena nodded. "I got out of there then, thought the cops might be coming. But they never did. No one did."

"Did the woman leave?"

"Not that I saw." She shrugged. "Could've. I guess. If that man didn't kill her dead with that shot. Maybe she was shooting at him to get him to leave."

"We need to call the police."

"Not me." Athena moved to push past Cassie.

Right. The girl was a homicide suspect. Cassie blocked her way. "I'll do it. What time did this happen?"

Athena shrugged. "Don't got a watch. But it was late, real late. Past midnight at least."

Definitely not Drake. He was asleep on her couch by then. Someone else in his car—with whom?

"Here." Cassie slid a twenty from the pouch on her keychain that held her driver's license and credit card. "Get something to eat. But take a bus, go over to Monroeville or someplace where the Rippers and Gangstas won't be looking for you. Somewhere safe."

"No ma'am. Gotta stay close to Baby Jane. Until she finds a proper home. Safe and sound." She edged a glare at Cassie. "Don't you be sending her with any of my sorry-ass family. You find her a real home. Until then, I'm not going anywhere."

Cassie thought the girl might want to say more. "If you gave the Rippers back their money, that might help."

"I don't got none of their money. Wouldn't take it if I had the chance, no how. That's blood money, pure and evil."

"So you didn't steal their bank roll? Did you kill Rodney Hunsacker?"

Athena blinked fast and looked away. Her shoulders slumped as if she might cry. Cassie wanted to hug her but knew the teen would never allow it. Too proud. "Rodney died trying to save me and Baby

Jane. So, yeah, I guess I killed him. He'd be alive if it wasn't for me, that's for sure." She sniffed hard and wiped her face with her palms. "I gotta go."

"Athena." Cassie wasn't sure what to say. "If you need anything—if there's anything I can do—"

"Don't worry. I'll get word to you. I'm not about to let them win."

"Wait. If you didn't steal from the Rippers or kill Rodney, why are they after you?"

The teen's gaze hardened to steel as she gripped Cassie's shoulders and stared into her eyes. "Baby Jane. You keep her safe no matter what. Promise?"

"Of course. I promise. Come with me. I'll find you someplace safe."

A van turned the corner. Athena jerked away. "No. Only I can fix this." She fled into the shadows between buildings before Cassie could stop her.

The van pulled into the Liberty Center parking lot and Cassie saw it was Tony. She ran across the street to him.

"Beautiful day, isn't it?" he greeted her. His mood quickly dampened when she told him what Athena had told her about hearing a gunshot. He reached into his van and emerged with a pistol. "Wait here."

"No. I'm not letting you go in there alone. Shouldn't we call the police?"

"Gunshots happen around here all the time. What if it was a woman Drake brought back to his place—do you want to embarrass him by having the police wake her up?"

"It wasn't Drake—"

"Cassie." Tony sighed as if breaking bad news. "I was at The Stone last night. Drake had some young chick all over him. She was drunk as hell, could barely walk. And he left with her." He rested his free hand on her shoulder. "I'm sorry. But it's the truth."

She remembered the reek of liquor and perfume that smothered Drake's clothes. Remembered how confused he'd been. Maybe he'd been with another woman, but he hadn't brought her here. She marched towards the door. "I'm not staying out here alone. So if you want to protect me, come along."

Tony hustled after her, going through the door first after she opened it. "The alarm's off," he noted.

"They turned it off while the police were here yesterday. But I thought I turned it back on again." Then she brightened. "Drake doesn't have the alarm code so it couldn't have been him coming here last night."

"If the alarm was even on," Tony reminded her. "Wait here. Do you have your cell?"

"No. It was in my car."

"Here. Take mine. If I shout, you run and call 911."

She stayed by the door in the stairwell while he checked the first two floors. "Nothing," he said. "Only Drake's place left." He ran up the stairs, rattled the doorknob. "It's locked, and the key you gave me isn't working."

Had she given him a key to Drake's place? She must have. "Drake had the locks changed yesterday. I don't have a key yet."

Tony came back downstairs. "Guess he must want his privacy. I wouldn't worry. Athena probably heard wrong."

"She said they used the elevator." Cassie glanced suspiciously at the wrought iron door of the old-fashioned elevator.

"So? We checked everywhere except Drake's place." He glanced around. "Where the hell is he, anyway? Does he know you're here alone?"

Cassie wasn't about to tell him that Drake was passed out on her couch. Instead she reached past him to punch the elevator call button. "There's one other place. The elevator goes up to the roof."

The doors opened. Tony shrugged and joined her inside. When they reached the roof, the scent of jasmine and roses filled the elevator car. Tony slid the wrought iron gate back. "Not much chance of a killer lurking in the middle of your rose bushes, but stay close, okay?"

She fought the urge to roll her eyes. It was getting pretty old, all these men trying to protect her. Handling Drake was hard enough, but now Richard and Tony?

The roof was eerily silent. Usually, this time of day there were birds chirping and the faint noise of the city. Today the air felt still and heavy. As if it were holding its breath.

As soon as she and Tony stepped forward, she saw why.

A young woman in a black dress hiked up past her waist lay on the ground face up, arms and legs sprawled. Her face was demolished. Gray matter mixed with blood created an unholy halo around her blond hair.

Cassie's initial impulse was to rush forward, and check for signs of life. After a single step she realized how futile that was.

Crows had already torn away chunks of flesh. A dozen of them perched on the other side of the roof, watching over their meal. Tony shouted at them but they didn't move.

She and Tony stayed on one side of the body, unwilling to contaminate the crime scene, as Tony called it in, while the murder of crows stared at them from the other side.

Tony hung up the phone and turned to Cassie. "This doesn't look good for Drake. That's the girl I saw him with last night."

"How can you tell?" She doubted the woman's own mother could identify her. Then it hit her. The girl's wounds looked a lot like Pamela Reynold's.

"I recognize the necklace she's wearing. And the dress."

"Could it have been suicide?"

He glanced around the scene. "No gun. Someone shot her in the face, though. Point blank range. Maybe they were trying to make it look like suicide." He turned to her. "You need to stay away from Drake. If he did this—"

"He didn't." Her voice was firm, certain. At that moment, she realized her heart was sure as well. "I know Drake didn't do this. He couldn't have."

—⋀⋀⋀⋀⋀—

DRAKE WOKE TO THE scratch of a tongue licking his face and the smell of rancid tuna. He opened one eye and stared directly into a yellow cat's eye. Hennessey.

"Go away," Drake muttered, closing his eye once more.

Hennessey responded with a bat of her paw to Drake's nose before she turned in a circle. Her tail swatted Drake across the face and then she leaned back, resting her hindquarters against Drake's face, and giving him a mouthful of fur.

"All right, all right," he told the cat, sitting up and yielding the sofa pillow to her. Which was what she wanted in the first place, of course.

It was a big mistake to move. Drake's head roared, protesting the sudden shift in position. He opened his eyes only to have them seared by the bright sunlight coming in the bay window. God, he'd never had a hangover hit him this hard before. He shut his eyes again but now the roaring was accompanied by waves of nausea.

He compromised. He slit his eyes open and gingerly looked around, taking in his surroundings. Hennessey sat in her accustomed place on the sofa and regarded him with amusement.

Hennessey was Hart's cat. Drake concentrated on simple, basic facts—trying to slice through the cotton wool that enveloped his brain. That was good. The sofa he found himself on was also Hart's. He strained to remember how he came to be there. He remembered drinking. He could still taste stale beer and whiskey. He must have passed out on Hart's couch.

That was bad. He was covered by Rosa's velvet crazy quilt. Hart's most precious possession. That was good. But he was still fully clothed; she hadn't undressed him. He saw the red plastic bucket placed at the foot of the sofa. That couldn't be good.

Drake groaned and ran his fingers through his hair. Why couldn't he remember? Even his hair hurt. It hurt to swallow, it hurt to breath, hurt to think.

Gingerly, he rocked onto his feet and stood. The room spun. He grabbed the couch for support but he remained upright. So far so good. Now which way to go? Coffee or bathroom?

He lurched toward the powder room beneath the staircase.

Leaning against the basin, he splashed water on his face. Drake's memory began to return. He'd been at the Stone, drinking—why was he drinking, he never drank anymore—oh yeah, Hart and King were getting married. Had to celebrate that, didn't he?

And there was a girl, wasn't there? Spanos had been there, too, or was that a bad dream? The bruise blossoming on his chest and the soreness that came every time he moved brought that into focus. Drunk, brawling with Spanos—he was lucky Hart had let him have the couch. What he deserved was a good kick in the ass.

A shower could wait. First, he needed to apologize to Hart. He moved back out into the hall and up the steps. Her bedroom door was half open, a good sign. Hart never closed doors unless she was seriously upset.

He knocked and pushed the door the rest of the way open.

Hart's bed was empty, the snarled bunch of sheets giving silent testimony to her own restless night.

Going down the steps hurt worse than going up, but he ignored the pain as he prowled through her house. First floor empty, except for the fat cat sitting beside an empty food bowl. Drake didn't take the bait; Hennessey had conned him too many times in the past. Now he knew better. Hart fed the cat once a day, just as the vet had directed her, and usually at night before she went to bed. If the bowl was empty it was because the cat had scarfed it all.

Drake opened the cellar door. No sounds of Hart pounding her heavy bag, no clank of weights, not even the rumble of the washer or dryer.

She was gone.

The trilling of his cell phone echoed through the empty house. He dashed into the living room, grabbed the phone from the end table where it sat alongside his weapon.

"Drake here."

"Where are you?" Jimmy's voice was harsh and way too loud for a Sunday morning.

Drake winced and held the phone farther away. "At Hart's. Why are you shouting?"

"Stay there. Kwon's on her way."

"Kwon? What the hell—"

"Where'd you leave your car last night, DJ?"

He stopped to consider the answer. He remembered staggering away from the Stone after the fight with Spanos, but he didn't remember driving anywhere. Probably good thing, drunk as he was. "Parked at the Stone. I think."

"You think?" Jimmy's voice barked out of the small phone. "You'd damned well better be sure before Kwon gets there."

What the hell was going on? This wasn't Jimmy—his partner

got quieter the busier, more tired he was. Even after a weekend on call for the squad, he'd never be this upset. And what the hell did his car have to do with anything? Surely he hadn't driven it, and hit someone?

His stomach roiled at the idea. Then he had a clear image of Kenny, the bartender, taking his keys and hanging them on the rack behind the bar.

"It's definitely at the Stone," he told Jimmy. "Ask Kenny, he cut me off and took my keys."

"Was that before or after you and Spanos fought over that Burns woman?"

Aw hell, Jimmy already knew about that. No wonder he was pissed. Drake screwed up royally, and might even be hauled up on charges with Spanos now a civilian. Which wouldn't reflect well on his partner. "Before. Is Spanos pressing charges?"

"Who the hell cares? This isn't about some barroom brawl, kid. This is about murder."

Chapter 24

JANET KWON WAS NONE too happy about being woken on her Sunday off to play chauffeur to Drake. Jimmy caught the case, since he was the detective on call for the weekend, but as soon as he realized Drake was involved, he turfed it to the next detective in rotation, Webster, and called in Janet along with her partner, Eric Summers, for backup.

"Let's get this fucking right before Internal Affairs fucks it up," Janet parodied Jimmy's Marine drill-instructor voice. "And before Miller ships us all off to fucking Siberia."

Of course, Kwon wasn't the only unhappy police officer today. The head of the Major Crimes Squad, Commander Sarah Miller, and the guys from Internal Affairs called in on their day off weren't too thrilled either. Not to mention the Assistant Chief, the press officer, or the union rep Jimmy called to protect Drake's rights, and who would be meeting Drake at headquarters for a talk with IAD.

It was only made worse by the fact that Drake knew with certainty the black humor that would accompany this routine of violent death.

"Jimmy was sure it was Monica Burns?"

"Found her purse, and Spanos ID'd her from last night at the Stone." Kwon cut him a glare assigning him to a special hell for cops who went out and got drunk with vulnerable victims.

"It wasn't like that." A weak protest, mainly because he was too busy beating himself up for being an idiot. He'd been upset he'd almost gotten Hart killed, angry at Burns, angrier at the stalker turning his life upside down, but it was just downright stupidity that had made him take that first drink. He knew better.

"Not what I heard."

"What'd you hear?"

She hesitated. She couldn't tell him anything relevant to the case, of course. Technically he was a suspect—although he thought that wouldn't last long. Jimmy would see through the bullshit and keep things on track, even if he did have to do it from the sidelines.

"Heard you clocked Tony Spanos. Good."

Drake smiled at that. His knuckles were red and sore as hell, but damn, it was worth it, putting that bastard down. "Yep."

If only Spanos was the actor. That would wrap everything up in a nice, neat package. But Drake knew it wouldn't be that easy.

The only good thing was that Isaiah Steward was on call this weekend for the ME. The assistant medical examiner was the best in the business, nobody could match him for thoroughness or persistence.

Gee, so much to look forward to, Drake thought as Kwon escorted him into Internal Affair's interview room where Hansen, his union lawyer, waited.

The room was twice the size as the one in their own station house. It was obvious this was where high profile suspects came to be interviewed. The chairs were upholstered instead of rickety refugees from a backyard patio and there was a sophisticated video recording set up on the far end. No expense spared in the pursuit of corrupt cops. Drake's squad merely handled crimes against persons, minor things like homicide, assault, kidnapping and rape.

The IA guys kept them waiting, par for the course. Hansen didn't seem to mind, except for moving his chair as far away as possible from the reek of liquor wafting from Drake's dirty clothing. The union paid the lawyer by the hour. The clock ran even as Hansen pulled the Sunday crossword puzzle from his briefcase.

Drake settled in, his drumming fingers the only outward sign of his impatience. Hansen looked up in annoyance at the *ratatattat* of the Stone's *Sympathy for the Devil*, so Drake kept it up, shifting into Jim Morrison and *LA Woman* and adding an accompanying humming. Didn't want to disappoint his fans.

Drake was familiar with IA's routine. It was almost comforting in its predictability. Last year after Pamela's death, he'd been kept waiting. Next came a monotonous repetition of questions interspersed with personal commentary and insults. Even though Drake had been cleared of any wrongdoing and he was the last person to defend corrupt cops, he fully appreciated why IA was nicknamed the rat squad.

Their routine didn't change today. Even the faces remained the same: Justin Sandosky and Carlos Ventura, two politically savvy detectives who didn't have the street smarts of a Liberty Avenue whore.

"Drake?" Sandosky said loudly from outside the open door of the interview room. "That can't be Detective Rembrandt Michael Drake, the sorry assed punk we almost nailed last year, can it? Surely some other woman didn't accidentally get shot with his gun?"

"Now, now," Ventura put in, "accidents do happen. Over and over again, even."

"Especially if you're a drunken piece of shit like Drake,"

Sandosky finished. They sauntered into the room, each with a cup of coffee in his hand. "Why, hello Drake. Didn't realize you were already in here," Sandosky said in a saccharine tone as he and Ventura sat down at the large conference table.

Hansen took his cue, carefully folded his newspaper, and slid it into his briefcase. "Let the record show," he began as the video officer appeared and switched the equipment on. "That my client is here voluntarily to answer any reasonable questions placed to him. He understands his rights and has agreed to cooperate fully to the best of his knowledge and ability."

"Yeah, right," Ventura muttered under his breath. "Glad my track record with women isn't as bad as yours, Drake."

Drake held his tongue, turning away from the camera to give the IA detective an eat-shit-and-die smile. The only challenge with these two would be to see if Drake could worm the information he wanted from them before they ran out of jibes. Drake worried these two excuses for detectives probably hadn't even noted the important details about the crime scene and so might not have the answers Drake needed.

If they didn't, Isaiah and Jimmy would, Drake told himself. He just had to get through this and buy them some time. He gritted his teeth with impatience as the pair from IA began to fire their questions in what they thought was an intimidating style designed to wear their subject down.

Drake was worn down as he went through the routine questions about his movements last night. But it was from hunger and lack of sleep more than anything. Being passed out drunk most of the night and half of the day didn't make up for missing real sleep. This was definitely the worst hangover of his life. He had to navigate his mind around gaping holes in his memory while fighting a raging headache.

He answered the questions automatically. Thankfully they were predictable, most of his energy focused on using the clues they gave him to re-create the crime scene in his mind.

Why the roof? When the actor couldn't get into Drake's apartment, why not just kill her on the steps, or one of the lower floors. Unless they needed to use the elevator?

Drake's mind skidded to a halt, causing his automatic answers to the IA detective's questions to falter. Richard King. He'd gotten into the clinic before. And he'd have to use the elevator.

Ventura pounced on Drake's hesitation. "So you don't remember what time you left the Blarney Stone?" he demanded in a dramatic tone as if he was unmasking the fatal flaw in Drake's diabolic scheme.

"It hasn't changed since the past two times I told you," Drake repeated. "I left a little after nine. The bartender and Spanos can confirm it."

"Yeah, well, we're checking that out," Ventura muttered, upset to be upstaged by Drake's calm attitude.

"I need a break," Drake told them, getting to his feet. "Where's the john?"

"We're not done here," Sandosky protested.

"We'll tell you when you can leave," Ventura added.

Drake ignored them and left the room. Behind him, he heard Hansen reminding the IA detectives Drake was there of his own volition and could terminate the interview anytime he wanted.

The men's room was down the hall. After using the facilities he washed his hands and face and then held his fingers under the cold water, trying to keep the swelling down.

King was a maniac. No matter what Hart said about him trying to redeem himself9, Drake knew better. But no one would suspect a man confined to a wheelchair of stalking Drake or killing Monica

Burns.

And Burns herself. Her behavior last night had been so erratic. Like she'd do anything to keep Drake there with her.

Drake left the men's room. Ventura waited in the corridor and fell into step beside Drake as he proceeded towards the interview room. But instead of going inside, Drake kept going down the hall towards the Internal Affairs Division office.

"Where the hell are you going, Drake?" the IA detective demanded. Drake ignored him, entering the office, and perching himself on the corner of a desk as he picked up the phone.

"Hey, that's my phone! What the fuck you think you're doing?"

Drake just placed a finger to his lips as he dialed Hart's number. No answer at her house. Shit. He reached for the phone to dial Jimmy's cell number when Ventura grabbed his arm.

"Enough of this bullshit! There's nothing that says I've got to let you make any phone calls."

"Assaulting a suspect—that's something Internal Affairs will need to investigate," Drake said, easily wrenching his arm out of Ventura's pudgy grasp.

"Fuck you, Drake," Ventura shot back, revealing his rapier sharp wit.

As Drake dialed Jimmy, his gaze roamed Ventura's desk. A framed family portrait occupied center stage. He picked up the photo. Ventura smiling so wide his eyes almost disappeared into his cheeks. His arm was around the shoulders of a sullen faced teenaged girl with lanky brown hair and a bad case of acne. Beside them stood a round-faced woman wearing thick-lensed glasses with hair so yellow it had to be a dye job gone bad.

"Nice of you to take a picture with your dear old mom," Drake said as Ventura snatched the photo from his grasp. "Is that sweet young thing your wife, Ventura? Didn't know you had it in you."

The other detective's face turned crimson with anger and Drake was surprised he didn't throw a punch in Drake's direction. Before Ventura could send any wayward synapses in the direction of his fist, Drake turned his back on him, listening as Jimmy came on the line.

Background noise that could only be coming from an autopsy in progress accompanied Jimmy. Drake didn't want to know what favors Jimmy had called in order to be present at the post mortem, or to get it started so fast. He was certain he'd hear about them sooner or later when it was time to collect. "Dolan."

Ventura grabbed the extension on the other desk in the office, listening in. Drake didn't care.

"It's Drake. Along with Detective Ventura from IAD. I need you to do something for me," Drake told Jimmy. "Find Hart and get her somewhere safe."

"I think she's still with Summers, going over her statement. But I'll check."

"Tell her to stay away from King."

Jimmy knew about Richard King, and Drake's many reasons for hating the man. "Really? Think he might be a player in all this?"

"Not sure. Just one more thing to look into." Drake asked, frustrated he couldn't say more with IAD listening in. Who knew how they'd use King against him? But he was confident Jimmy would fill in the blanks. "What'd they get from Spanos?"

"Dunno," Jimmy replied. "Webster has him. Thought I'd be more useful down here."

"Right." Drake paused. He wanted to thank Jimmy for watching his back, but not with Ventura on the line. "Anything on the tox screen?"

"Like what?"

Ventura leaned forward, waiting for Drake to incriminate

himself. Hell with it. "Like maybe rohypnol?" Another thought penetrated the haze that permeated Drake's brain. "Or it may be in her personal possessions?"

"You think she used it on someone else or someone gave it to her?" Jimmy asked.

Drake shook his head in frustration and immediately regretted the new headache the movement unleashed. "I don't know."

Rohypnol and other drugs like it only lasted a few hours after ingestion and were almost impossible to detect, so it was too late for Drake to be tested. But maybe the autopsy could still pick it up.

"I'll have Steward check for it and call the guys to look for anything suspicious in her belongings."

"Thanks. Tell Hart I'll call her."

"What makes you think she'll want to talk to you?" Jimmy asked.

Drake knew it was a jibe, Jimmy's way of pretending Hart had nothing more to worry about than their fight last night.

"Just find her, Jimmy. Okay?" Drake told his partner, in no mood for any more banter and not caring his tone had an edge of desperation to it.

"Don't worry, partner. I'm on it." Jimmy hung up.

"So who's this King?" Ventura asked, moving back down the hall, at Drake's heels like a pet terrier. "And what's with the rohypnol? You saying you drugged Burns? That's pretty sick, even for a loser like you."

Drake ignored him and wearily resumed the tedious answering of questions. Sparring with the IAD guys, buying time for Jimmy to find the answers they needed just wasn't fun anymore. When Ventura unveiled the crime scene photos of Burns' face and body in all their blood glory, all Drake could see was Hart.

Chapter 25

SPENDING THE DAY BEING interviewed and questioned and sitting, waiting for more interviewing and questioning and sitting, left Cassie more exhausted than an entire day of hanging drywall in the clinic. Much less worrying about Drake and what he was going through.

Thankfully, they finally sent her home around six o'clock. When she got there, her answering machine was blinking fast enough to induce seizures. Messages from reporters, Tony asking if she was okay, Lisa Dimeo reminding her about testifying in the morning—like she could forget the fate of Mary Eamon's killer rested in her hands—and a final one from Richard.

Richard. Jimmy Dolan passed Drake's message to her about not trusting him. As if her ex and his proposal were the most important things on Drake's mind. More important than being framed for murder.

She punched the button to hear his message. "Cassandra. It's me. I just heard. I wanted to make sure you were safe. If you want, you can stay with me. No strings. We need to talk. I'm worried about you. Alan, he—well, never mind, we can discuss that later.

Just call me. Let me know you're all right. I love you."

The dial tone flat lined. She raised the handset, and hesitated. Then she called Drake. His phone went straight to voice mail. She hung up without leaving a message. What would she say? Ask him what really happened in the bar last night with Monica Burns? Yell at him for getting drunk and fighting with Tony? Or beg him to come back so they could work everything out?

Maybe the first two. Definitely the last.

She showered, fed the cat, and he still hadn't called. Could they have actually arrested him? Maybe he was in a detention cell somewhere?

She sank down onto the sofa, pulling Gram Rosa's quilt around her. It was hot enough she wore only shorts and a tank top, but she needed the comfort the generations-old hand sewn heirloom offered. Having Drake's arms around her would have been better. But if he was being detained then at least he was safe.

That thought took her into sleep.

CASSIE WASN'T SURE WHAT woke her. She sat up on the couch, disoriented, surprised she wasn't in her own bed. The cat screeched from somewhere in the rear of the house.

"Hennessey?" Cassie called. Had she forgotten to feed the poor thing? She wrapped the quilt around her and walked towards the kitchen. Then she stopped.

A thin beam of light danced through the air. Someone was outside the kitchen window.

The cat raced past her. Cassie tiptoed towards the phone halfway between her and the kitchen. Before she could reach it, glass crashed, showering over the kitchen floor. Followed by something bright and on fire, flying through the air where the window had been.

Cassie turned and raced towards the front door, but only made it as far as the living room when the explosion hit.

She felt it more than heard it. A wall of air more solid than steel slapped her body. The strange, rock hard wind sucked the breath from her lungs and her ears roared with pressure.

Cassie slammed into the couch. When she opened her eyes the room was lit by tendrils of flame racing along the heavily polished hard wood floors and up her bookcases and drapes and onto the ceiling. She looked in the direction of the kitchen. It was like looking into the mouth of hell.

Cassie dropped to the floor, holding the heavy quilt around her body. Glass crackled as shards flew through the air like shrapnel. Tendrils of flame rushed over to her, licking at her flesh and Rosa's quilt.

Thick, black smoke filled the air. A new wall of flames broke out behind her as the fire found the rag rug. She crawled towards the door, eyes squinted shut, filled with smoke and tears. Her lungs burned as she held her breath against the searing air.

Move, move, move, was her mantra, keeping in time to the pounding in her ears as she scooted across the floor.

She didn't have far to go, less than eight feet. But it was like swimming through black tar. She hoped she still headed in the right direction as she pressed her body as low to the floor as possible.

Finally, she hit the glass of the sidelight, felt her way up to the doorknob, and fell through the opening to the porch outside.

She lay there like a freshly hooked trout in a fisherman's creel, gasping for air. Flames, fed by the new oxygen source, sped after her, shooting through the open door, reaching out towards her.

Coughing, Cassie pulled her feet under her and ran. Fire sparked on the lawn as flames rained down from the roof. She dodged these, zigzagging down the porch steps. Her neighbors, Mr. and Mrs. Ferraro, appeared on their porch across the street.

"Roll, roll," Mr. Ferraro shouted in what seemed to Cassie like a foreign language. He met her in the middle of the street, hauled her down onto the asphalt, and began to tumble her body.

It wasn't until then that Cassie realized she was on fire.

Chapter 26

DRAKE WAS STILL TRADING barbs with the IAD detectives
at 9:30 pm. He figured the longer he kept these two goofballs tied
up, the more freedom Jimmy and the real detectives would have to
do their jobs. Maybe even actually find the actor who shot Burns
instead of making assumptions without any evidence.

Which was what Ventura and Sandosky were doing. And had
been doing for the past five hours. Hansen kept looking at his watch
like he was late for the symphony, but Drake didn't care.

"So you still claim you have no knowledge of the victim's
movements after you vacated the bar?" Ventura asked, trying to
impress Drake with his vocabulary.

"No."

"Witnesses state she left with you."

"No. I was with Spanos in the alley behind it, then I left alone."

"How about her movements in the bar?" Sandosky cut in. "Do
you remember those?"

"I was only with her for twenty minutes or so—"

"According to the bartender, it was an hour. During that time
you drank a beer, a Long Island iced tea, and a total of two shots of

whiskey."

Drake looked up at that. It had been a long time since he'd had that much to drink in one sitting. Probably since last year and Pamela. He grimaced. Think he'd grow up and learn one day. But it wasn't enough to explain his hangover symptoms this morning. The more he thought about it, the more convinced he was that Burns had drugged him.

He replayed the bits and pieces of the night that he could remember. He saw her handing him his beer. Then her drink.

She could have easily slipped something into either. But why? Surely not to set him up for her own murder.

And who the hell shot her?

"And your only alibi is Dr. Hart?" Sandosky interrupted Drake's chaotic thoughts.

"I slept on her couch."

"But she can't verify this?"

"She wasn't watching over me all night long, but she could tell you what time I arrived at her house. Anything more and you'd have to ask her—I was dead to the world."

They looked up at that. Poor choice of words. This was definitely wearing thin.

The two detectives exchanged glances, sensing he was close to breaking. More from irritation than their cutting-edge interviewing techniques, but they didn't know that. "Do you have a backup gun registered to you?"

"You know I do. Two, in fact. The Glock on my ankle right now and a Baretta nine millimeter."

"Where is the nine millimeter?"

"Secured in a lockbox bolted to the trunk of my car. Per department regulations." Too late, he saw where they were going. And he had no choice but go along for the ride if he wanted to know what they knew.

Ventura smiled and it wasn't a pretty sight. "Would it surprise you to learn we found your gun in a storm drain across the street from your apartment building?"

"Or that it's the same weapon used to kill Monica Burns?" Sandosky added.

Shit. But it made sense. Whoever took his car would have had keys to the trunk and lock box. It was only damn luck he'd had the locks changed on his apartment and Jimmy had the only keys—otherwise the frame would have been air tight and Burns would have been killed there.

So. Someone at the Stone—like Spanos. Or someone who followed Drake there. Which could have been anyone. Or someone Burns called after she drugged him. She must not have realized that she was also being set up as a victim. Damnit, all this and back to square one.

"What? No comment? Detective, did we hit a sore spot?" Sandosky asked.

The door opened and Janet Kwon entered. "Drake, Jimmy just called. Something's happened to Hart."

Drake was on his feet before she could say anything more.

"Where are you going, Drake? We're not done yet!"

"We can finish later," Drake told them.

"My client is here of his own volition," Hansen reminded the IA team.

"If he leaves now it's without his badge and gun," Ventura said.

Drake spun on his heel to glare at the excuse for a police officer in front of him. They didn't have the authority to suspend him, not without going through their superiors, but he didn't care.

All he cared about right now was Hart. Drake flipped his badge onto the table then removed his Glock from its holster, spinning it across to Ventura, followed by his Baby Glock from his ankle holster. The IA detective was startled and fumbled at the guns like he'd never held one before.

"Let's go," he told Kwon, stalking from the interview room.

"Is she all right?" Drake asked once the elevator doors had closed behind them and there were no prying ears or video cameras.

"I don't know. There were a bunch of 9-1-1 calls on the scanner for fire and EMS to her neighborhood. Then Jimmy called and said to get you over there, so here I am."

Drake digested this, trying to ignore the knot in his stomach. Too little information. It might not even be her, he told himself. Don't waste energy on worry until you know for certain what's going on.

That's what his mind was saying. The rest of his body surged with adrenalin, ready to fly to Hart's side.

Kwon was smart enough to know this, handing him the car keys to her departmental Intrepid without him even asking. Drake appreciated that; anyone else would have wasted precious moments arguing with him.

As they sped through the light Sunday night traffic, Kwon tried to raise Jimmy on his cell. "No answer," she told him. Drake clamped his jaw tight and hit the accelerator.

⎯⎰⎱⎰⎱⎰⎱⎯

"KEEP THAT OXYGEN ON now," the paramedic told Cassie before glancing away from her to the spectacle of the fire. He wasn't the only one fascinated. The entire neighborhood turned out to watch the firefighters in their futile attempt to save her house.

Cassie clamped the oxygen mask back on her face, then let it drop once more as soon as his back was turned. They were just annoyed because she had refused transport. Medics got touchy about things like that.

She shivered despite the summer heat. She was lucky. A few minor cuts and burns, but Gram Rosa's quilt had taken the brunt of the damage. The lining was seared, but the carefully pieced quilt top had been next to Cassie's body and had sustained only minor cosmetic damage. The quilt now resided safe at hand in a red plastic biohazard bag.

"Everyone back," a fireman called. The crowd looked up in anticipation as the roof bucked then twisted, finally wrenching free from the feeble bonds that tied it to the earth. There was the sound of a deep sigh, as if the roof were trying to take flight. It collapsed inward; sending a new shower of sparks and flames into the night sky.

Cassie worried about Hennessey while a few of the onlookers clapped and cheered, the ones who brought their own beer and chairs.

Most of Cassie's neighbors shook their heads and looked over at her with expressions of relief. Relief that she hadn't been seriously injured, but most of all that it had happened to her and not them.

Watching her home burn was almost as bad as watching her father die all over again. His furniture and books and collection of records—all fodder for the flames. Her mother had died when Cassie was born and the only memory she had of her was a portrait Drake painted based on the photos jammed into albums on her bookshelves. The same bookshelves the fire devoured so eagerly as it chased after Cassie.

Gone also were any trace of Padraic and Rosa—except for Rosa's quilt. Gram Rosa's quilt saved her life when she escaped from the Nazis. Cassie wasn't surprised this seemingly frail piece of silk and velvet had been the sole survivor of the current holocaust that had overtaken her family.

Just as she was. The sole surviving Hart, the last person alive with any of Rosa Costello's blood. At least, the only one living on American soil.

All alone. And what to do next? Out of a job, out of money, out of a home. Out of options.

Cassie watched as the brick walls teetered then fell. She wanted to cry, but the tears had been seared from her by the heat and smoke.

She wanted to scream in anger and frustration but her throat was burnt raw and the only sound she could make was a small croak.

She wanted to hit something, to strike back at the human who so callously took everything she had except her life.

But there was no one there.

Naked as a newborn. She'd lost her job, her home, and the few mementos of her past. Whoever had done this had stripped her clean of all encumbrances.

Except Drake.

He would be the most painful piece of herself to shed. But necessary.

Cassie closed her eyes against the glare of headlights and the dancing flames. Very necessary. Because it was the only way to keep him safe.

Whoever had done this had intended to terrorize her. But what Cassie felt wasn't fear.

Cassie was angry. And willing to do anything to protect the only important thing left in her life: Drake.

Her eyes flicked open and she scrutinized the crowd gawking at the death throes of her house. *He* was out there somewhere, she was certain.

As she watched, she slid her hand inside the bag and stroked the

soft velvet and silk. The quilt had the blood of a Nazi soldier soaked
into one of the pieces, a soldier killed by her grandmother's own
hand.

She shrugged off the oxygen mask and stood up, moving in
a circle, her shadow cavorting in the strange light cast by the fire.
Come and get me, she broadcast the invitation with her gaze as she
looked upon the strangers gathered around the corpse of her home,
of her life.

Come out, come out, whoever you are.

—ᐟᜈᜈᜈᜈᜈ—

SHE WAS WEAVING HER way around the EMS vehicles when
Jimmy Dolan and Ed Castro, her old boss at Three Rivers, appeared
from down the block. Their worried expressions did the asking for
them.

"I'm fine," she told both men. "I can't find Hennessey, though."
She said the last with a one-shouldered shrug, knowing it sounded
pathetic after losing everything else, but she couldn't help it. The
thought of Hennessey caught inside the house—

"I'll go look," Ed volunteered while Jimmy wrapped his arm
around her shoulder and guided her back to the ambulance.

"You sure you don't need to go to the ER, get checked out?" he
asked. "The medics said you refused treatment."

Cassie ignored him, riveted by the death throes of her house.
"It's a total loss, isn't it?" she asked, her voice still hoarse but
gaining in strength.

Jimmy nodded and squeezed her hand. "I'm sorry."

The final flames were doused and the firefighters began the
messy work of unearthing any smoldering embers that might cause
further problems.

Cassie couldn't bear to watch any longer.

She strode away from the ruins of her home and found Ed Castro searching the neighbor's forsythia for Hennessey. If the cat got out, she would be fine. And if she didn't—she couldn't bear watching the firemen unearth Hennessey's remains. She rubbed a knuckle over her eyes. Still no tears, but it wasn't for lack of trying. "Got room on the couch?"

"Always. Are you done here?"

"Yes. I'm finished."

Chapter 27

DRAKE ARRIVED JUST IN time to see Hart drive off with Ed
Castro. He ran after her, but then stopped and let her go, his insides
feeling as charred as the blackened timbers that were all that
remained of her house. What would he do if he caught her? It would
break him to have to let her go again.

Jimmy arrived. "Where's Hart?"

"She left," Drake faced his partner. "What've you got for me on
Burns?"

Jimmy took a small notebook from his back pocket and leafed
through it.

"No useable prints or trace evidence."

"Any idea how he got inside?"

"That's what bothers me—no signs of forced entry at all."

"So we've got an intruder who goes through locked doors and
alarm systems without a trace."

"Like a fucking ghost."

"Or a cat," Drake put in, spotting movement from beneath
a parked fire chief's car. "Gimme a hand here," he told Jimmy,
crawling under the rear bumper, making tiny clucking noises with

his tongue.

"Jimmy, go around. She's trying to run away," he called out as the quivering ball of fur moved away from his arms. Jimmy's feet moved towards the front of the vehicle. Drake slapped his hands on the pavement, startling the skittish cat right into Jimmy's waiting arms.

"What have we here?" Jimmy asked, his big leathery hands embracing Hennessy, quieting her struggles easily. "Shhh. It's okay."

Drake smiled to see his partner clucking over the traumatized feline like a mother hen.

"Her name is Hennessy, right?" Jimmy asked as the cat tried to burrow inside his lightweight suit jacket.

"Yeah. It's a miracle she made it out alive." Drake reached out a hand to stroke the cat's head, the only part of her still exposed. "Good to see you girl."

"Miracle anyone made it out alive," Jimmy told him. "Arson says it was some kind of incendiary device. If Hart had been upstairs asleep—"

Drake dropped his hand and turned away. He couldn't think of that. Hart asleep in bed when the house caught on fire—he blocked out the image.

"Guess there's nothing more we can do here," he said, noting the firemen stowing their hoses and lighting their cigarettes, a sure sign they'd moved into cleanup mode.

Drake realized he had nowhere to go. His apartment building was a homicide scene, Hart's place gone. For the first time in years he was unsettled, a vagrant in his own town. It was an unsettling feeling, rocking his equilibrium.

"Get in," Jimmy told him. "Denise has the sofa bed made up already."

Trust Jimmy to be three steps ahead of him. Drake hadn't even realized his temporary lack of shelter until just now. He slid into the passenger seat of Jimmy's Intrepid. Jimmy plopped the sodden load of wet cat onto Drake's lap. Hennessy looked up at Drake with one disdainful amber eye, then curled up into a ball.

Drake called Ed's home. He and Hart hadn't arrived yet, so he left a message with Ed's wife that Hennessey was safe at Jimmy's house. When he hung up he realized he felt a strange sense of relief he hadn't been able to talk with Hart. She'd lost everything because of him. How the hell would he ever face her again?

He couldn't. Not until they locked this actor away for good.

"What else on Burns?" Drake asked.

Jimmy was silent for a moment, studying the four lanes of empty highway as they sped down 376. "Miller gave it to Webster," he told Drake. Drake guessed Miller wasn't too happy about having anything to do with the case but she was wise not to leave it solely with the Internal Affairs buffoons.

"And?" Drake prompted.

Jimmy shrugged. "Not much to go on except you were one of the last people to see her alive, she was killed above your apartment after what appears to have been consensual sex, and the murder weapon was your gun."

"Don't hold your punches," Drake muttered. The media would crucify him by morning. Not like his name was unknown to journalists. They had a field day after Pamela's death.

"You asked for it," Jimmy said. "And, just to warn you, you'd better be careful what you say around Denise. She's not too happy with the idea of you getting drunk and messing around with that girl. Even if nothing happened."

"Is that because she likes Hart or because she's disappointed in me?" Drake asked. Annoying Jimmy was one thing, but you didn't

mess with Denise. Drake learned that the hard way when he first
partnered with Jimmy four years ago.

"A little of both."

Great. It'd be like having his mother looking over his shoulder.
Drake thought of how happy Mom and Nellie had been when he left
them at the Lake. Was it only last night?

"Shit," Drake cursed, unsettling the cat in his lap as he sat
upright.

"What?"

"I've got to call my mom. Was there anything on the news?"

"How the hell should I know? I was stuck at the morgue."

"Right. What'd he have to say?"

"Usual. Wait until all the tests are in and I'll send you my final
report," Jimmy did a fair imitation of the medical examiner's tenor.
"There was one thing, though. Seems Burns didn't have long to live.
Advanced cancer with metastases everywhere: liver, lymph nodes,
even her brain. Steward thought it probably started in the ovaries.
He said there were signs she already had at least one course of
treatment, so it must have been extremely aggressive."

"Jesus, the poor kid was only, what, twenty-six?"

"Twenty-four."

Drake felt bad about the way he'd treated Burns. He'd done his
job, even gone above and beyond. But he thought of her as a nut
job, not a woman who deserved his respect. Just one more way he
acted like an idiot this week.

"How about time of death?" he asked.

"Based on witnesses and the state of the body, estimated
between midnight and six am. Hart talked to a street kid who told
her there was a shot sometime after midnight but couldn't narrow it
further and we've no confirmation. She also alibied you."

Drake hated the thought of Hart having to face those IA

assholes. Not to mention the fun the gossips at the House would have dissecting his sex life.

"But the brass won't be satisfied until they have Steward's final results. Another witness besides Hart would help. Not to mention the rumors you may have hired someone—"

"To kill a woman I had never laid eyes on before yesterday?" Drake scoffed.

"Relax. I think it was Spanos who started that one. Let the Keystone Cops have fun tracking down rumors."

They pulled into Jimmy's garage. Drake held Hennessy while Jimmy carefully emptied his Glock, checking the chamber twice. He locked the gun in the safe high above his tool bench. With six-year-old twins on the loose, he took no chances.

"Webster's set a meeting for tomorrow morning," Jimmy told him, placing the full clip into the glove compartment of his car and locking it as well. "Said they'd call you when they needed you."

Drake shot a glance over at his partner but Jimmy wasn't looking. That hurt, like he was an outsider. Or worse, a victim. But Drake had no shield, no gun, no standing whatsoever in this case.

He was worse than an outsider. He was an outcast.

With these thoughts, Drake trudged inside Jimmy's house, diligently wiping his feet clean of the soot and ashes before moving in to take position on the family room sofa bed Denise had made up for him.

—╲╱╲╱╲╱╲—

ED'S WIFE, NATALIE, HAD the guest room ready when they arrived, along with the good news about Hennessey.

"How's Tagger?" Cassie asked as she and Natalie rummaged through Natalie's closet for spare clothes to replace the tattered and singed tank top and shorts. Unfortunately, Natalie was barely four-eleven, so the best they came up with was an old T-shirt of Ed's to use as a nightshirt.

"He's good. Finding his comfort zone." Natalie sighed and opened dresser drawers in her quest to dress Cassie.

The real challenge would be tomorrow morning. Cassie was due in court at eight, leaving no time for shopping. Natalie improvised an outfit from a pair of Ed's scrubs with a drawstring waistband and rolled up cuffs, a smock top that looked more like a cropped top on Cassie, and, since Natalie's feet were also smaller than Cassie's, a pair of Ed's sandals with the straps pulled as tight as the Velcro would allow.

"But your hair…" Natalie brushed her hands over Cassie's long, dark curls. The slight touch left a cascade of burnt hair fluttering down to the carpet. "I'm so sorry."

Cassie couldn't bear sympathy. Not when it'd be so easy to slide down the path to self-pity. "Don't be. Just get me a pair of scissors and I'll take care of it after I wash up." She stifled a yawn.

"Let's get you to bed."

Cassie soaked for a long time in the guest bath. Her entire body was raw and bruised, but although patches of skin were lobster red and a few blisters had popped up, none of the burns were serious. The worst pain came from the multiple lacerations and abrasions from flying debris. Too shallow to bother with band-aids, too many to count, she tried her best to ignore them.

All in all, she would not recommend the experience, she thought, as she tried to wash the sour smell of smoke from her hair and ended up breaking off large clumps.

She slipped into the cotton robe Natalie lent her and sat in front of the bedroom mirror, trying to decide where to cut her hair so it wouldn't make her look like a freak.

"What happened?" Tagger's whisper came from the doorway.

The boy looked less gaunt, but just as scared as when they'd been in the alley, gunshots flying. Was that just two days ago?

"This is why they tell you not to play with matches," she joked. He frowned, his face twisting in distrust.

"Athena okay?" He shuffled in to stand beside her, his hand without the cast lifting lengths of hair and appraising it.

"I saw her this morning and she was doing fine." Not as fine as she'd be if she'd let Cassie take her somewhere, but she wasn't about to tell Tagger that. "The Gangstas are still looking for her. They say she killed your brother."

He straightened. "That's a lie. She didn't kill Rodney."

"Do you know who did?"

He nodded.

"Tagger, it's important. Why are the Rippers and GGs after Athena?"

He blew his breath out. "She said not to tell. Said they might hurt Baby Jane."

"You can tell me. I'll make sure nothing happens to Baby Jane."

It was silent as he studied his cast, as if it held the answers. "She and Rodney were in love. Rodney was trying to save her."

That's what Athena had said. "Is Rodney Baby Jane's father?"

He shook his head. "Lucien, head of the Rippers is. He's Athena's uncle."

That explained a lot. Baby Jane's DNA would prove incest if Athena disclosed the sexual assault. Lucien probably sent that young Ripper to take the baby. To him, Jane was merely evidence. "Lucien had Rodney killed?"

Tagger's eyes sparked. "Did it himself. Rodney was going to take Athena away but Lucien caught them, and shot them both. Athena got away, so he made it look like she killed Rodney."

"That way the Gangstas would be looking for her, and want to kill her?"

"Yeah. And then he told the Rippers that she stole the money, but it was really him. So now they're after her, too."

Wow. And Cassie thought she had problems. Damnit, she should have found a way to get Athena off the streets. "Why doesn't she run away? Why was she camped out in the Rippers' territory?"

"I heard them talking. Rodney stole Lucien's phone and there was a movie on there. Lucien and Athena." Tagger made a face. "Rodney hid it somewhere in the Stackhouse, but he died before he told Athena where."

"So she keeps going back to find it."

"Figures it's the only way anyone would believe her."

It wasn't. But there was no reason for Athena to believe the system might work in her favor. Cassie gave Tagger a hug, and wished Athena was there as well.

"Want to help me cut my hair?"

Tagger nodded, and supervised as she cut the tangled curls. The end result was pretty awful, but better than shedding chunks of burnt hair every time she moved. Finally, she got Tagger to go back to his bed and she was able to slip between the cool, clean sheets herself.

She woke several times during the night, propelled from sleep by the smell of burning flesh and the searing pain of flames devouring her. Each time she woke she found new injuries, and would fight to find a comfortable position.

As the pink streaks of dawn crept through the large windows, she finally rolled onto her belly and slept, one arm fitfully flailing at her side, searching in vain for Drake.

Chapter 28

DRAKE WOKE WITH A heavy weight on his chest. "Move it, Hennessy," he mumbled, attempting to roll over. His tongue was glued to the roof of his mouth, and seemed to be coated with fur.

The weight shifted and giggled. Drake opened one eye in time to see a handful of damp Cheerios arch over his head and land on the oversized sweatpants Jimmy lent him. More giggles ensued.

A tow headed six-year-old bounced on his chest, smiling in delight. "Uncle Drake's up!" she called out.

Drake cringed. Uncle Drake was definitely not up. Uncle Drake was down, down, down in a deep pit that echoed with the noise of Bridget's voice.

If Bridget was sitting on his chest, the thought slowly penetrated into the quagmire of Drake's brain, then Colton couldn't be far. Drake opened both eyes and rolled them back as far as he could.

There was the second of the twins, pelting stale breakfast cereal at him. Drake kept both eyes opened. A purple dinosaur danced on the TV across from him. He growled deep in his throat and let the noise rumble up. This produced more giggles of delight as Drake sat up and shouted, "I'm going to get you!"

Both twins scampered out of reach, giving Drake a chance to sit up straight. His back protested, as did his neck and shoulders. Got to find someone with a real spare bed, he thought.

Then he smelled the sweat and smoke emanating from his clothes piled beside the couch. Hart. She'd lost more than a bed. She'd lost everything.

And he'd almost lost her.

Drake ran his fingers through his hair, trying to garner the courage to open his eyes again. Monica Burns was dead, Hart was God knew where. How was he going to fix all this?

"Go outside and play. Leave DJ alone, you two." Denise's voice, and the smell of coffee accompanying it, brought Drake back to his senses.

Four feet pounded past, their noise sending shock waves through Drake's bruised brain. He gingerly opened his eyes again.

"Coffee, toast, and three Advil." Denise set the offerings onto the end table and took the chair beside him. "I seem to recall that was the hangover recipe you preferred."

She had the mother's tone of disappointment and scorn down pat, Drake thought, buying time by gulping down the ibuprofen.

"It's not what you think," he told her, his voice emerging as a rusty creak.

"Right." She didn't sound convinced. "I put some of Jimmy's clothes in the bathroom for you. Just a T-shirt and some running shorts. Unless you want to go around holding up your pants all day, you'll have to wash these." She kicked the pile of filthy clothes with her foot.

"I'd rather burn them," Drake told her.

"The mall opens soon, you can always buy new ones." She took a sip of her own coffee and looked at him appraisingly. "I'd appreciate it if you don't get Jimmy mixed up in whatever you've done this time."

Drake set his coffee down. "Denise, believe me. I haven't done anything—"

He stopped when her glance edged down to his liquor soaked shirt. "All right, I'm guilty. I had a few drinks too many and played a game of pool with a pretty girl. Maybe I flirted a little—believe me, I was tempted to do more, but I didn't. I went back to Hart's and told her everything. I even—" He ignored the buzzing in his head as he bent over and fumbled with his slacks. Damn it, he couldn't have lost it. Then his fingers closed on the tiny velvet box.

He gave the box to Denise. "I wanted to ask Hart to marry me."

The enormity of what he had lost in the last forty-eight hours hit him. For a second he craved a drink, but then he forced that thought aside.

Denise looked at him with skepticism as she opened the box, then her eyes widened. "You're serious, aren't you?"

"Of course, that was before she found a girl murdered with my gun, and her house was fire bombed." He shrugged and took the box back. He didn't have anywhere to put it, so he just held onto it, his sweat slicking the velvet.

"DJ, I'm sorry," Denise told him. "When Jimmy told me you were in a jam—"

"You thought of Pamela," Drake finished for her.

She nodded.

"Can't say I blame you." He looked at the toast, but his stomach rebelled against the thought of food.

Denise got to her feet and picked up their cups. "Go take a shower. Leave your dirty clothes and I'll wash them." She dangled the rancid polo shirt by one finger. "Well, your pants anyway. You can always wear one of Jimmy's shirts, it'll just be baggy."

"Thanks, Denise. Where is Jimmy?"

She looked at him, puzzled. "At work. Of course."

Then it really hit Drake. It was Monday morning and he had nowhere to go. No badge, no gun, no job.

And no Hart.

—⎺⏷⎺⏷⎺⏷⎺⏷⎺—

NATALIE LENT CASSIE HER car and she made it to the courthouse just in time. Except she had no photo ID to show the guard as she went through the metal detector, so he had to call Lisa Dimeo, the assistant DA in charge of the Mary Eamon case, down to escort her to Judge Flory's courtroom.

"What on earth are you wearing?" Lisa Dimeo, asked. "You can't go into court looking like that!"

Ronald Brickner and his family passed through the security entrance and stood staring at her. At first he frowned, as if surprised to see her—or maybe surprised by how different she looked than the last time they'd met. But then he smiled. A quirky smile that made his eyes glint and made her want to take a shower, as if he'd contaminated her. His mother gave his elbow a sharp tug and they both turned their backs on her, heading towards the elevators.

Cassie's silence gave Lisa further time to scrutinize her. "My God, what happened?" her tone had softened a bit, but not much.

"Someone firebombed my house last night."

At first Lisa looked at Cassie as if she had suggested the dog ate her homework. Then she glared at Brickner. They took the stairs up to the second floor courtroom.

"You don't think it could have been Brickner, do you?" she asked. She seemed eager to add witness tampering to the charges against the child killer.

Cassie shrugged. She hadn't thought of Brickner. It could be. It could also be the Rippers, the Gangstas, Drake's stalker, or someone hired by Alan King. Or maybe there was someone else out there with a grudge against her. She wouldn't rule it out. "I don't know who did it. The police are investigating."

Lisa gave Cassie another appraising glance. Cassie felt ridiculous beside the tall willowy blonde in her tailored suit and three inch heels. Appearing before Judge Flory looking like Bozo the clown on a bad hair day would only mean more unwanted attention.

"Don't worry," Lisa assured her after taking a second look. "We can use this to our advantage." She reached up and pulled off the ball cap Cassie had used to cover her mangled hair. "That's better."

Cassie sincerely doubted it, but she followed Lisa into the courtroom. Since this was a pretrial motion hearing, the courtroom was empty except for the essential personnel, lawyers, Brickner, his mother and wife, and Cassie.

Then she saw who sat beside Brickner at the defense table. Alan King. He smirked at her like she was the prize at the bottom of a cereal box.

She plopped into her seat, unable to stop staring at him. He'd said he'd be seeing her today. She should have realized he'd meant it as a threat.

After Judge Flory dispensed with some preliminaries, he nodded to Lisa. "I'll hear Dr. Hart now."

Cassie stood up. She was always nervous about testifying. She hated the double and triple negatives the lawyers used, trying to trip you and twist what you were saying.

Today was worse than usual. Rivulets of sweat made the cotton top cling to her like a clammy second skin and the lesser-burned parts of her body all itched simultaneously.

She squirmed her way onto the witness stand, and gave her

particulars to the court reporter. Judge Flory hadn't noticed her yet; he and his secretary were discussing a scheduling conflict. After Lisa approached Cassie, he turned his attention to the witness stand. And stared. His face grew red and his mouth dropped open. Lisa began to ask Cassie her first question, but the judge interrupted her. "Dr. Hart," he snapped. "Have you ever testified in a court of law before?" his tone was one of admonishment.

Cassie turned in her seat to look at him. "Yes sir," she said, feeling her face heat with an embarrassed flush. She looked over at the defense table and saw Brickner and King both shaking with restrained laughter.

"Is this what you would consider proper deportment for such grave proceedings? Your appearance is deplorable. Did we interrupt your week at the beach," he asked sarcastically, "if so, the court sincerely apologizes."

"I apologize, your honor," she said meekly.

"I could cite you for contempt," he told her.

Cassie looked to Lisa for help. The ADA saw her cue. "Your honor, Dr. Hart was the victim of a serious crime last night. Her house was set on fire by an unknown party and she barely escaped with her life."

Judge Flory straightened at that and regarded Cassie once more, still with no sympathy. "Is that true, Dr. Hart?"

"Yes sir."

"Have the police any idea who may have started this fire?"

"No sir. At least not that they've told me."

"Your honor may recall hearing about Dr. Hart's car being destroyed by automatic gunfire two days ago."

The judge nodded. "That was you?"

"Yes sir," Cassie replied.

"In light of these threats against our witness' life, the state asks Mr. Brickner's bond be revoked immediately. We would also request a continuance "

Alan leapt to his feet, objecting to Lisa's "unwarranted curtailing of his client's freedoms", and a legal brawl ensued.

Cassie watched the verbal jousting, but didn't really care. Her entire body alternated between itching and throbbing pain, her eyelids sagged with the strain of staying awake, and her head was pounding.

She just wanted this all to be over with one way or the other. Just let her tell Mary's story, and the facts would speak for themselves.

But the lawyers kept squabbling. Judge Flory leaned back, enjoying the legal antics, rewarding points to Lisa first, then Alan, as if this was about keeping score and not a little girl's murder.

Cassie took the opportunity to reach under her pant leg and scratch at a particularly bothersome patch of peeling skin. Ahh. Then there was silence and everyone was looking at her again. She edged her fingers back from under her pant leg and tried to look alert.

Lisa Dimeo led her through her credentials and the events surrounding Mary's care in the ER with efficient, well thought out questions. Several times Cassie noted the district attorney hesitated, as if waiting for objections from the defense which never materialized. Lisa cast several quick glances at the defense table but did not break her smooth rhythm as she drew the evidence of Ronald Brickner's confession from Cassie.

"Thank you, Dr. Hart," she concluded. "No further questions."

Cassie straightened in her seat, preparing for the defense's cross-examination. She watched as Alan ignored the stacks of paperwork in front of him and instead kept his gaze fixed on hers. And she realized what his tactics were. By not objecting to her testimony he reduced the horror of Mary's death to a cold recitation of facts, depersonalized her from a little girl to a gory list of medical facts.

Now all he had to do was destroy the credibility of the witness who presented those facts.

He sauntered over to the lectern and adjusted the microphone. "Good morning, Dr. Hart," he began in his melodious speech. "My name is Alan King. I'd like to thank you for coming here this morning."

It was a move Cassie had seen before when she testified. Force a potential hostile witness to be grateful for the opportunity to have her character shredded in public.

"You're welcome," she replied in a neutral tone.

"Dr. Hart, you've testified in how many abuse trials?"

"Eighteen," Cassie replied. Lisa had already asked this, but the ADA didn't object.

Cassie looked away from Alan to his client and Brickner's mother. Both smiled at her.

"Pardon?" she asked. It was a mistake to let her focus waver and Alan had pounced on it.

"Excuse me, doctor, I thought we had your full attention. I asked if you clearly remembered the events surrounding Mary Eamon's death." Alan kept his tone gracious but Cassie caught the frown Lisa threw her way.

"Yes, of course I do."

"But, correct me if I am wrong, Doctor, but you weren't actually present when Mary died, were you?"

Cassie flushed, embarrassed at being led into such a simple trap. Two minutes of questioning and Alan already had her contradicting herself.

"I was present at the events that immediately preceded her

death," Cassie emphasized the positive.

"But not actually at her death, correct?"

"Yes," Cassie grudgingly conceded the point.

"What were you doing while Mary Eamon's lay dying in the operating room at Three Rivers Medical Center?" he asked, implying the only reason Mary died was because she'd been delivered to the hands of incompetent surgeons.

Cassie forced herself to remain neutral, and chose her words carefully. Even though there wasn't a jury present, this was all on record. "I was speaking to the family, informing them about Mary's injuries and how serious they were."

"And you told them there was a good chance she might not survive. You already knew that after your resuscitation, did you not, Dr. Hart?"

Christ, now he was trying to blame her for Mary's death. "Yes. She had arrested in the ER but we brought her back."

"And while she was under your care in the emergency room did you perform any procedures that were temporally related to Mary's heart stopping?"

Cassie had no choice but to explain about the paracentesis. "But without releasing the pressure we would not have been able to get oxygen into her lungs and she would have arrested from that."

"I see," he nodded, making his disbelief evident. "And have you performed this procedure before under these circumstances, Dr. Hart?"

"I've performed paracentesis before on several occasions."

"But, under these circumstances, Doctor?" he persisted.

Cassie opened her mouth to snap that they didn't get many three year olds with their intestines ripped apart, but caught Lisa's warning glance and snapped her mouth shut. "No two cases are exactly alike," she allowed.

"So you've never done this procedure which led to Mary Eamon's cardiac arrest under these particular circumstances before?" His voice rose, implying he was incredulous that such an incompetent physician be allowed to practice.

Cassie took a deep breath to collect her thoughts. "I hope never to see these particular circumstances again."

"Your honor, the witness is unresponsive," Alan addressed the bench.

"Dr. Hart, please answer the question," Judge Flory instructed.

"Have you ever performed a paracentesis in these exact circumstances before, yes or no?" Alan repeated his question as if Cassie was a recalcitrant child. He pivoted so that his back was to the judge and leered at her.

Cassie couldn't restrain the glare she shot at the defense attorney. "No, but every case—"

"Thank you Doctor," Alan interrupted her. "And did you tell Mary's family your performance of the paracentesis led to her cardiac arrest?"

Cassie frowned. "No, that wasn't relevant—"

"I'm certain it was relevant to them, Dr. Hart," Alan shot back. "I'm certain her family wanted to know that their child was receiving the best possible medical care!" His tone of indignation filled the courtroom.

"Objection!" Lisa raised her voice to be heard over Alan.

"Sustained. Counselor, is there a question somewhere in there?"

"I apologize, Your Honor, my emotions got the better of me," Alan replied in a contrite tone and looked down to consult his notes.

Which left Cassie on the hot seat. Just as Alan cleared his throat to ask another question, Cassie noted a movement in the rear of the gallery. The bailiff held the door open to allow Richard to roll his wheelchair inside. Richard gave her an encouraging smile—at least she thought it was encouraging. Maybe he was waiting for his brother to decimate her and he thought he'd come to her rescue.

"Your honor, would you please instruct the witness to answer?" Cassie heard Alan's voice from a distance.

"Dr. Hart, please answer the question," Judge Flory sounded annoyed.

Cassie tore her attention from Richard. "Could you repeat the question, please?"

Alan rolled his eyes and sighed. "I asked if your competence had ever come in question prior to the Mary Eamon case?"

"No, of course not." Cassie was on sure footing here.

"And since then?" he flung the question out off-handedly, a casual inquiry, ticking off an item on his legal pad.

When Cassie didn't answer immediately, Alan waited a beat then raised his head as if surprised. "Dr. Hart?"

Cassie knew what he was doing, but there was nothing she could do. "Yes."

Alan did a double take as if this was a surprise to him. "Yes, your medical competence has been questioned since Mary's death? By whom? When did this happen?"

"I am currently involved in a malpractice suit," Cassie admitted.

"I see. And are you still caring for patients while this malpractice suit—" He made the last word sound like an epithet. "Proceeds?"

"No."

"And why is that?"

Cassie swallowed hard. "I was suspended from my duties."

"Suspended. That's pretty serious, right?"

"Yes."

"Let's get back to your previous experience. I believe you told the judge you testified in abuse cases before. Correct?"

"Yes."

"And what would you testify to?"

"The medical history, any actions—"

"Let's just stick to the medical history. That's based on questions you ask the patient's family, correct?"

"Yes." Cassie wondered where Alan was headed.

"And it becomes part of the medical record?"

"Yes."

"So when you wrote that my client and I quote, 'confessed to repeatedly punching the patient in the abdominal area as well as paddling her,' that was for the purposes of documenting her physical injuries?"

"Of course." Cassie frowned, trying to see where the trap lay. She glanced at Lisa who shrugged.

"But all this documentation took place after Mary died, correct?"

"Yes. As soon as I had a chance to dictate my part of her chart."

"*After* you learned that she died from a perforated intestine?"

"Yes."

"Dr. Hart, what is one of the most common complications of an abdominal paracentesis? The procedure you performed on Mary that sent her into cardiac arrest."

Cassie jerked upright. Alan leaned back against the defense table, containing his smile just barely.

"Intestinal perforation," she finally said. "But—"

"Your honor," Alan interrupted, "given that the medical examiner's report and other forensic evidence has been suppressed, I move for dismissal on the grounds Dr. Hart just admitted her own experimental procedure could have been the cause of death."

"Objection!" Lisa was on her feet. "Your honor, this is ridiculous."

"Then I move for suppression of Dr. Hart's testimony on the grounds it's self-serving in that it may be covering her own medical incompetence at the expense of my client."

Judge Flory leaned forward. "Silence," he thundered. "Ms. Dimeo are there other medical experts who could testify to the cause of the victim's injuries?"

Lisa glanced at Cassie, who nodded vigorously. Kurtis Waite, the pediatric surgeon, could tell them it wasn't Cassie who caused Mary's death. He could tell them about the festering length of dead intestine and how painful it would have been. Lisa drew in her breath. "Yes, of course, your honor. However, they aren't present here this morning."

"Very well. Before I rule on Dr. Hart's testimony or Mr. King's motions, I'd like to hear from them. Get them here tomorrow at nine o'clock sharp. Until then, bail is continued."

They stood as the judge exited. Cassie slumped against the side of the witness box, stunned. Ronald Brickner walked free another day. Because of her.

No wonder Mary haunted her nightmares.

Chapter 29

DRAKE FELT BETTER AFTER a shower and shave and clean clothes. He'd even come up with a plan for the day. At least the start of one. Hart was testifying this morning, so she'd be safe at the courthouse behind walls of security, but after that, he wanted to be free to watch over her.

"I've a big favor to ask," he told Denise after he returned to the family room and found her already at her computer, juggling spreadsheets. She worked from home, so he had the feeling she'd rather have him gone anyway. "Can I borrow the minivan?"

"My van?" Her voice was edged with disapproval. Maybe this wouldn't be so easy after all. "No. Take Jimmy's car."

When Denise was pregnant with the twins, Jimmy traded his sports car in for the safest vehicle in the safest color he could find: a Volvo station wagon painted canary yellow.

"I need something that will blend in."

"Are you implying that my minivan is boring?"

"Why would anyone think a gray—"

"Champagne."

"Champagne minivan is boring? I'm just saying it won't stick out like the banana mobile, that's all."

"Who are you worried will spot it?"

"Hart." And whoever was targeting her. "I want to stay close, keep an eye on her, but she won't like it."

"So you want to use my minivan to spy on your girlfriend?"

"Well—" Put that way and it didn't sound so good. "Someone's got to keep her safe."

To his surprise she jumped up from her computer and gave him a hug. "DJ, that's the most romantic thing I ever heard." Then she let him go and gave him the van's keys. "If it comes back with one scratch, one ding, so much as a scuff—"

"Don't worry," he assured her, already halfway out the door.

To his surprise, the Sienna handled better than his Mustang. Not as much power, but good suspension and decent acceleration. And damn comfortable once he unearthed the toys stuck between the cushions of the driver's seat. First stop was Wal-Mart, to grab clothing, snacks, and other essentials for the duration. Who knew how long he'd be living from the van?

He called the courthouse. According to Judge Flory's secretary, Hart was still on the stand. He sweet-talked her into letting him know when Hart left. Then he called Jimmy.

"Webster been through Burns' apartment?" If he couldn't work the case against him, he could use the time while Hart was busy in court working his original case: Burns' burglary.

"Yeah, didn't find anything. At least nothing interesting to him. Who knew if a crack detective with keen intuitive skills took a look? I'll meet you there in twenty. You can watch me in action."

"Since officially, I won't even be there."

"Right."

Drake hung up. Jimmy was waiting for him when he pulled up at Burns' apartment house.

"Denise let you use her van?" Jimmy gave a low whistle. "She doesn't ever let me drive it. What'cha do to my wife, DJ?"

"Wouldn't you like to know?" Drake waggled his eyebrow, feeling almost back to normal for the first time in days. "What've you got?"

"Copy of the file on Burns. Thought you'd like to take a look."

Jimmy was putting everything on the line here: job, pension, future. Drake didn't know what to say. So he said nothing except, "Thanks."

Jimmy nodded, realizing there was more behind the word, and they headed inside to Burns' apartment.

The crime scene guys and other detectives had not left it neat or tidy. Fingerprint covered the doorknobs, windows, and light switches, as well as other strategic locations. But Drake wasn't interested in forensics. He wanted to learn more about the woman herself. It bothered him the strange way she'd shifted personalities Saturday night at the Stone.

He went directly to her personal papers, now strewn across the kitchen table. "What was her job?"

"Didn't have one. Told her neighbors she was an acting student but there's no history of her being enrolled anywhere."

"She said she was new in town. Where'd she come from?"

"The landlord lives downstairs, but was gone for the weekend. We can check on the way out, see what she listed on her rental application."

Drake nodded as he leafed through her bank statements. They only went back two months. Each month there was a cash deposit for five thousand dollars. Burns' rent and living expenses added up to only a fraction of that. "Be nice to know where the money was coming from."

"A nice, even number. Maybe a trust?"

"Then why deposit it herself? Why not direct deposit?"

"Maybe she doesn't trust computers." Jimmy shrugged. They didn't find anything else of interest in Burns' papers, so he flipped open the binder. "I wanted to ask you. The guys found your card here in the apartment."

"Yeah. I gave it to her that first day. Why?"

"But they found a second card in her wallet. Did you give her another that night when you took her over to the Stone?"

Drake thought hard. "No. She already had one with my cell—but what's weird is I don't remember giving her my cell number at all. But she showed me the card and there it was, in my own handwriting."

"Maybe you didn't. Maybe you gave her the first card, the one without your cell number on it. Maybe someone else, someone who knew about your stalker, gave her that card. Who was the last person you gave a card with your cell phone written on it?"

"Hart. She has it programmed into her cell, but you know her, she never carries the damn thing. So she put it in that little wallet she carries on her keychain."

"That went in the fire so we can't check it." Jimmy blew out his breath. "Damn, I thought we were on to something."

"Anyone who knows Hart could have taken it from her wallet. It doesn't exactly narrow our field of suspects."

"Anyone else you gave your cell to?"

"A few people, like the Trevasians—"

"The couple with the kids who were being threatened a few months ago?"

"Yeah. But they aren't involved in this." Drake thought hard. "That's it, that's all I can remember."

"Okay. Let's see if we can find the landlord." Jimmy led the way down to the ground floor apartment. From the smells of cabbages and cigars concentrated in the hallway outside the door, Drake expected an overweight Polish guy. Instead, it was a young woman in her mid-twenties with a baby on her hip.

"Can I help you?"

Jimmy explained why they were there and showed her his credentials. Good thing she didn't ask to see Drake's, since he didn't have any.

"Oh, of course. We were at my mom's for the weekend and didn't hear about it until we got home last night. It's so awful to think about. That poor girl." She led them into the kitchen and secured the baby in a high chair where it happily played with a bowl of dry Cheerios.

"Did Monica express any concerns about her safety?" Jimmy asked. He sat at the kitchen table while the landlord, Gail MacAfee, searched for Burns' rental application.

"No, of course not. This is a very safe building."

"What about after the break in?" Drake asked.

MacAfee whirled around. "What break in?"

"The one Thursday night."

"We were here until Saturday morning. There was no break in I know about."

Jimmy and Drake exchanged glances. "Monica never mentioned it?"

"No."

"Did she mention being followed? Or being afraid?"

"No. She never said a word. Not that she ever left the place much. I think maybe she was sick, or not feeling too good. The only time I saw her come or go was to get groceries. She never even had any visitors."

Hard to attract a stalker when you never left the apartment, Drake thought.

"Found it. Here you go." MacAfee laid a folder in front of them. "I remember now. Instead of just first and last month's rent, they paid six months up front. Said they weren't sure when they'd get their checking set up here. Since they were moving from LA, I guess it made for complications."

"They?" Jimmy asked.

"Well, the lease and application were taken out by the one. But her roommate, Monica, arrived here first. Sounded like they were starving actresses, and when they couldn't break into Hollywood from out in LA, they thought they'd come here, since Pittsburgh is making so many movies these days."

"Did you meet the woman who signed the lease?"

"No. We did everything by fax and phone. But it's all there, even a copy of her driver's license."

Drake shuffled the papers until he found the lease application. Signed by Elizabeth Reynolds.

He glanced at the blurry copy of the drivers' license. It was dated six years ago and showed a brunette with short, dark hair, thick glasses, and a good fifty pounds heavier than Monica Burns.

"She lost weight with the cancer treatment." Drake showed Jimmy the license. "Dyed her hair, colored contacts—"

Jimmy gave a low whistle. "I missed it. But you're right."

They'd finally found Pamela's missing sister.

Chapter 30

CASSIE SPENT THE NEXT hour going over the medical facts
with Lisa Dimeo so the lawyer would have everything she'd need
to make sure Curtis Waite's testimony would be enough to nail
Brickner. Then she finally left the ADA. Lisa seemed happy to
dissociate herself from the mess Cassie had made of things. Or
maybe it was just Cassie projecting her own feelings—she couldn't
believe that because of her, Brickner might get off.

"Cassandra." Richard wheeled up to her in the courthouse lobby
when Cassie passed the security perimeter. "Now do you see what
lengths Alan will go to make you pay for what happened to me? You
need to consider my proposal. I can't control him—I never could.
The only time I was ever able to stand up to Alan was with you at
my side."

His words emerged so fast they slammed at Cassie, physically
backing her into a corner while she absorbed them. Richard was
right. His plan would solve everything. For him.

Her natural instinct to fix every problem was the only thing that
had made her consider his crazy proposal for more than a moment
in the first place. But she finally realized she wasn't the solution

here. She wasn't even the problem.

She was just the rope in a dangerous tug-o-war.

"Go home, Richard." She wanted to tell him exactly what she thought of a man who'd let a child-killer go free to get his way—much less the sociopathic brother who orchestrated it. "Leave me alone."

"But Cassandra—"

She walked away as fast as she could. The wheels on his chair squealed as he raced to keep up with her. They passed a crowd of people in line for the security checkpoint. She didn't care that they stared at her appearance, or the man following her. All she wanted was to be left alone. She ran down the steps, leaving Richard behind.

When she emerged out onto Grant Street, the sunlight was blinding. No clouds to be seen, but the humidity was still palpable, making the air feel clingy, like walking through gauze.

Two men approached her. One was broad shouldered and looked like an ex-college lineman gone to seed. The other was tall and thin, perfect type casting for Ichabod Crane in a production of the headless horseman.

With their ill-fitting suits and impervious manner, they had to be cops. The two men flanked her, ignoring the other people trying to crowd past on the narrow sidewalk.

"Dr. Hart?" Ichabod asked.

"Who are you?" She stopped, still in sight of the courthouse and the security guards inside. She wasn't taking any chances.

He seemed taken aback she would challenge him so soon. "I'm Detective Ventura and this is Detective Sandosky. We'd like to invite you to our office to answer some questions."

"Could I see some ID?" she asked. They exchanged glances and shrugged. Obviously she wasn't what they expected. Cassie took her time scrutinizing their credentials.

"You're a hard woman to track down," Sandosky, the paunchy ex-linebacker told her as he pocketed his ID.

Cassie shrugged. "What is this about?"

"Our car is right at the curb, we could get out of this heat," Ventura said, aiming at politeness but missing by a mile.

Cassie kept her feet firmly planted and waited for them to answer her question.

"It's about the death of Monica Burns," Sandosky finally allowed.

"You're from IAD." They nodded. "Let's go," she told them, leading the way to their white Dodge. They seemed discomfited when she beat them there. She stood waiting beside the front passenger door for them to unlock it. They exchanged looks as Ventura unlocked the door and moved to the driver's side while Sandosky maneuvered into the back seat.

The clatter of the blasting AC precluded any discussion as they zipped across the river to police headquarters. Not that Cassie was in any mood to chat.

The detectives escorted her up to a conference room with comfortable chairs and a video camera at one end. She waited with Ventura while Sandosky left for a minute, returning with coffee and a woman who silently began to fiddle with the video equipment.

She sipped on her coffee and waited for the detectives to make the first move. She wondered how much of her taxpayer's money was being used for the comfortable surroundings and expensive equipment. Not to mention the videographer's salary. She'd visited Drake at his station house and knew the detectives on the major crimes squad had nothing to compare with this.

"Just as a formality, Doctor," Ventura began. "I'd like to read you your rights as well as a release for the recording of this interview. Once I'm done, if you would please acknowledge your agreement and sign these releases?"

He slid a stack of papers in front of Cassie along with a felt tip pen. Cassie signed and initialed where he indicated as he read her Miranda rights. She thought they were being melodramatic. She knew they didn't have to read her the Miranda warnings unless they were questioning her as a suspect.

Which, of course she wasn't. Just one more intimidation ploy. She wasn't going to let it rattle her. Just like she wasn't going to let them hound Drake for a murder he didn't commit.

"Dr. Hart," Sandosky began the official questioning. "Have you ever seen this woman before?"

He slid a photo face down in front of her. Cassie flipped it over and froze. It was the crime scene photo, showing the young woman from the roof, a close up of her face demolished by the gunshot wound.

Cassie swallowed hard. Stay calm, she told herself. "I doubt if anyone could recognize this woman in the condition she is in," she told them, using her best clinical voice. She kept her face composed as she visualized Drake viewing the same photo. God, what visions of Pamela's death it must have brought back.

She idly picked at the peeling skin on her arm, then stopped as she realized that the movement would be picked up on the video. Sandosky slid another photo to her, this one face up.

"Try this."

Cassie glanced at the photo. It was a blown up bus pass photo of a young blonde with soft green eyes and a wide, toothy smile. "Sorry, I don't know her."

"Are you certain?"

Cassie looked again, then shook her head. "I never saw her before."

Sandosky and Ventura exchanged glances. "Do you have any knowledge of Detective Drake's whereabouts from approximately midnight to six am Sunday morning?"

"Yes. Detective Drake came to my house at about nine-thirty Saturday night," she told them.

"About?"

"He'd been there maybe ten minutes when I looked at a clock and it was a quarter to ten."

"And he stayed with you the rest of the night?"

"He was drunk. We argued briefly about his being drunk, and then I let him sleep on the couch. He was still asleep when I left the next morning around nine."

"Is there any possibility he may have left your house without your knowledge?"

Cassie shook her head, suppressing a smile. Finally she understood why she was here. "I have an alarm system on all the doors and windows. It would record any opening or closing of a door, as well as if it was deactivated."

"But didn't your house burn down last night? How can we verify this?"

Cassie frowned, she hadn't thought of that. "The alarm company will have a record. It will also show the exact time Detective Drake arrived, if that helps. Would you like me to call them for you?"

Half an hour and several phone calls later, the detectives were pouring over the data from the alarm company.

"Why the hell didn't Drake tell us about this yesterday?" Ventura asked his partner.

Cassie almost felt sorry for them. "Because he didn't have what he needed from you guys."

"What do you mean?"

"Drake didn't get to go to the crime scene himself. So he had to string you guys along, long enough to show him the crime scene photos."

"Sonofabitch."

"Except we never showed him the crime scene photos."

"We were about to. When Kwon showed up." They both stared at Cassie and she realized she was the reason Drake abandoned his plan.

This was why she had to stay clear of him—he could have ended up in real trouble because she got in the way. He'd been right all along.

DRAKE MADE IT TO the courthouse just in time to see Ventura and Sandosky pick up Hart. For once he was happy to see the IAD detectives. Hart was more in danger of being bored to death than anything else while with them.

He was about to follow when he noticed someone else watching Hart leave. Richard King.

It was time he had a little chat with the weasel. He left the van and took a brisk stroll down Grant Street, following King to where his BMW was parked in a handicapped space. He timed it so he reached the car just as King did.

"We need to talk."

To his surprise, King didn't appear upset or threatened at all. Instead he said, "You're right."

With practiced movements he transferred to the driver's seat, folded his chair, then slid it into the rear of the sports car where the back seat had been removed.

"You seem to be adapting well," Drake observed, noting that not only did King have plenty of upper body strength—enough to hold a woman down long enough to shoot her—but he also had regained partial use of his legs.

"Rehab. Does wonders. I can't wait until the day I show Cassandra I can walk again. She'll be so proud."

Definitely a no-no hitting a guy sitting in a handicapped spot, not to mention the fact that Drake was already suspended, but damn, it was hard to resist wiping the self-satisfied smile from King's face.

"Is that why you're doing all this? You think that's how you'll win Hart back, by ruining me?"

"What are you talking about?"

"Monica Burns. Or should I say, Elizabeth Reynolds."

King's expression didn't waver. He waited for Drake to explain.

"Don't play games with me, King. Whoever killed Burns might be after Hart."

"She's not in danger. Not really."

"What the hell are you talking about? You know her car got shot up and her house torched. She almost died."

King glanced inside the car as if thinking about leaving without answering. Drake took that option off the table by jogging around to the other side and hopping into the passenger seat. "Talk."

"It's not what you think. I want what's best for Cassandra. That's all."

Only King's idea of what was best for Hart verged on psychotic. Crazy bastard had cost her her job at Three Rivers, what more did he want?

"What did you do?"

"Guardian Security. They're not setting up the Liberty Center's security as a charitable contribution. I'm paying them. And Tony Spanos. I asked him to keep an eye on Cassandra. I didn't like her working there on her own. He's been watching her and reporting to me."

Spanos. That explained why the ex-cop always hung around, getting underfoot. It didn't take him off the suspect list, though.

"Did Spanos give you keys and security codes to the building?" he asked, remembering how he'd found King inside the Center the other night.

"Yes."

"How long has Spanos been working for you?"

"Two months."

The same time Burns received the cash deposits and moved here from LA. "And that's when you hired Elizabeth Reynolds to move out here and harass me?"

"I don't know anyone named Elizabeth Reynolds."

"Right. How about Monica Burns?"

"Her either. Believe me, Detective, Hart has never been in any danger from me. It's you who keeps her in that bad neighborhood, in the middle of a gang war. I'm trying to save her."

"Well, then, I suggest you call off Spanos and stay the hell away, because neither of you are doing a very good job of protecting her."

An ugly smirk flit over King's face. The kind of look that was gone in a flash but left a bad taste in Drake's mouth.

King started the engine. "Spanos told me how you were flirting with that girl. He said you were the last one to see her alive. And where were you when Cassandra's house was firebombed? If you want to see who's responsible for the danger Cassandra is in, look in the mirror."

Drake got out of the car and watched King drive away. He hated the smug bastard, knew he was behind at least part of this mess, but he couldn't get King's last words out of his head.

DRAKE SPENT THE REST of the day following Hart, first from
the Police Headquarters on the North Side, back to the car she was
using, then out to Monroeville where she shopped at the same Wal-
Mart he'd been at this morning, and finally to a small motel off
Route 22.

He snuck a peek through the window of her room and saw she
was napping. She looked so vulnerable, it took everything he had
not to pound the door down and take her away. To the Lake, to the
far side of the world, he didn't care.

But then Jimmy called. "We can't find any ties between King—
either of the brothers—and Elizabeth Reynolds. I'm hitting a brick
wall."

"How about between Spanos and Reynolds?"

"Other than both of them being at the Stone with you on
Saturday, nothing there either. But we're still working on getting her
LA phone records, they might have something."

"Call me if you get anything."

"Denise wants to know when she'll get her van back."

Drake looked around the already littered space. Stakeouts were
messy. "As soon as I get a chance to get it detailed."

"Better make it sooner rather than later. She hates driving my
car."

"Mine should be released. You can let her drive it."

"No way. If anyone's driving the Mustang, it will be me."

Drake hung up and ate some beef jerky and cheese for dinner.
Hart went over to the small cafe attached to the motel, but didn't
return to her room after dinner. Instead she got into her car.

As he followed her back to the city, keeping an eye to make
sure he was the only one following her, he realized she was taking
precautions as well. Instead of her usual carefully assertive driving,
she was varying her speed erratically, making turns without

signaling, circling around a block.

She did a good job, and even lost him at one point. But by then it didn't matter. He knew where she was going.

Back home.

Chapter 31

CASSIE PARKED AROUND THE block from her house. Or what remained of it. She took the flashlight from the car's glove compartment and flicked it on. Her shoes squished in mud and ashes as she headed down the alley.

The garden gate hung open, wrenched half off of its hinges. She ducked under yellow hazard tape. The carefully tended landscaping was now torn to shreds by fire truck tracks, footprints, and rivulets left behind by rushing water.

She didn't try to go through the structure. It seemed to lean threateningly towards her, the remaining walls ready to tumble over at any minute. The bright moonlight cast eerie shadows through the timbers and brickwork left standing. Like some kind of wild animal with its fangs bared; that was what her home had become.

Creeping around, she managed not to trip over any debris. Her bedroom furniture had tumbled out—or been blown out—and lay splintered, clothing strewn about and trampled on. The headboard Padraic had carved with such painstaking care had split in two. The way the scorch marks marred the red oak, it looked like it had been struck by lightning. The wrath of God.

It was the least of her worries, she told herself, as she cast a tearful eye about the remains of her garden. Glass and shattered paving tiles littered the area where the patio used to be. Her cast aluminum glider lay upside down in the rhododendrons. So much sweat had gone into remodeling the patio and reviving the garden, now all gone in one fell swoop.

"Thought I might find you here."

Cassie turned at Drake's voice. Where else was she to go? This was her home. Always before, she'd run here for solace when life became overwhelming. Sheltered by quiet memories, safe from the outside world, here she could find her balance, regain her perspective. She hoped to find something—anything—she could save of the only home she'd ever had.

But there was nothing left. She breathed in and her mouth filled with the bitter taste of sodden ashes. Where would she go now?

Drake's hand landed on her shoulder, an answer, an offer. She shrugged it away. He had his own troubles to deal with. She couldn't lean on him, not if it meant leading him into danger.

"Go away." She turned her face into the darkness so he couldn't see how much it cost her.

"I'm here to help."

How? Build her a new house? Catch the person trying to kill her? Get a child killer off the streets where she put him? Because that's what she needed.

She took a deep breath and turned to Drake. A crease of worry lined his forehead and his eyes were dark with exhaustion.

"I don't need you," she lied. She wished he hadn't come. This was so hard. "Leave me alone."

"Never."

The word slipped out so easily, so calmly, she wondered if he even realized he'd said it out loud. It came as a gentle whisper on the breeze, came and gone so quickly she might have imagined it. She wished she had, it would make this so much easier.

"Not before I do what I wanted to do Saturday night," he said, moving close so she could clearly make out his features, his eyes burning bright in the moonlight.

"Sorry, I'm all out of booze," she told him, gesturing at the shambles around her.

"That's not funny. This is what I came to give you when I came home from the Lake." He pulled something dark from his pants pocket and laid it in his palm.

Cassie stared at the sapphire ring sparkling amidst the black velvet. This wasn't happening, she told herself. It was all a bad dream. Please God, she didn't have the strength for this.

The last thing in the world she wanted to do was to hurt Drake.

Her gaze focused on the blackened remains of the last thirty years of her life. Thirty years in one place and now it was gone. She didn't even know where she'd spend the next thirty hours.

"Come with me," Drake persisted. "We can start over. Together."

Right. And lead whoever wanted to kill her straight to Drake. A swirl of ashes spilled across her feet, the wind dancing them over the debris.

If he only knew how hard it was for her, him being here. Every person she'd ever loved had left her to stand alone—you think she'd have gotten the hang of it by now. But this was harder. This time she was the one setting love free, and, God forgive her, she didn't want to let it go.

"Damn it, Hart! Why won't you let me take care of you? What are you afraid of? Why won't you allow yourself to be happy?"

The words hit her with a force that bowed her head. Drake's hands were on her shoulders, yanking her back upright, face to face with him, refusing her any quarter, any room to hide.

His eyes darkened to a deep indigo from their emotion. Then he pulled her back to him until she could feel the beating of his heart echoing hers. He laid his head on hers, his strong arms wrapping around her body like strands of a cocoon. Protecting, insulating, promising a brighter future.

"I love you! Why isn't that enough?" he demanded. "Do you still not trust me? Not believe that I'm not like King? I won't hurt you, not ever, I promise—" his voice trailed off and Cassie was horrified to see tears spill from his eyes.

"I love you," he finished in a choked voice.

Trust him? She did, with all her heart. Because when he left he would be taking the best part of her with him.

It took all of her strength to meet his gaze. "Please leave me alone," she said, forcing her voice to remain steady although the rest of her body was trembling.

He stared at her a long moment. "I came here tonight to ask you to marry me." He held the ring box up in the flat of his palm. "Is that your answer?"

She slapped his arm away. The box went flying into the ashes of her home. Pain seared through her and she felt like she was being torn in two. But it was only a feeling. She knew how to ignore feelings, lock them away until it was safe.

Drake's glare didn't help. She turned her back to him.

"Go. Now." The last came out with a force Cassie didn't know she could command. That one syllable stole all her remaining strength. She grabbed the trunk of a sugar maple to keep from turning back to him, or collapsing.

Her breath rattled through her constricted lungs and she almost surrendered. She wanted to turn back to him, when she heard his footsteps crackle on the broken glass and he was gone.

Cassie turned. Drake's shadow was the last she saw of him. She stood alone. Once more.

Her knees buckled and she fell to the ground. She closed her eyes against her silent tears and remembered the last time she woke with Drake in her bed. Remembered that feeling of utter contentment as she lay against him, his heartbeat echoing in her ear, the weight of his arms resting comfortably around her. She etched every detail of that moment into her brain, to cherish it always—the one perfect moment of peace, of release, of contentment—of love. Of knowing her home didn't have to be made of brick or mortar as long as Drake was near.

And now both were gone.

Cassie wept alone as ashes swirled around her.

When she finished sobbing and opened her eyes, she saw the sapphire glinting from the ashes at her knees.

It looked so hopeful, shining like a beacon. It was bright as Drake's eyes, a memory she would cherish for the rest of her life.

She squeezed the ring in her hand, tears splashing onto ashes, turning them into mud. Her insides felt empty as if they too had burned away to nothing—except for the memory of Drake, the look in his eyes, the feeling in his voice.

What had she done?

DRAKE STOOD GUARD AT Hart's garden gate. The sound of her crying was the most painful sound he had ever endured. His legs wanted to propel him back into the garden. He wanted nothing more than to lift her up and carry her away from everything.

But he knew that would be the worst thing he could do, so he restrained his impulses and listened, motionless.

He always sensed Hart had a place in her heart bound by grief, a place not even the fiercest love could penetrate. Not quickly, at least. But Drake hoped with time and patience, he could chip away at the stony barrier that separated them.

Now he knew he had, at least to some degree, been successful in his endeavors. Of course the timing couldn't have been worse.

The garden grew silent. Hart slowly rose to her feet, moving like an old woman carrying a burden too heavy for her. Drake looked to see that no one was nearby, and quietly moved across the street to where he'd left the minivan.

Chapter 32

DRAKE SQUIRMED, STRETCHING HIS legs out against the dashboard. Something poked into his back; he reached a hand around and withdrew a Matchbox car. Jeff Gordon, courtesy of Bridget. Her brother was strictly a Rusty Wallace man. He ran the small racecar up and down his jeans, flipped it off the curve of his knee, and crashed it over the dash until the amusement wore thin.

Yawning, he reached over and changed the radio station once more, and craned his head out the window trying for any hint of air not contaminated by his woefully unwashed body. Despite wearing the shirt borrowed from Jimmy and new jeans, the scent of Jack Daniels still surrounded him like a fog. It was seeping from his pores, in his sweat. He had a roommate in college like that. He would binge all weekend and still smell of Southern Comfort on Wednesday.

To this day Drake couldn't stand that smell. No wonder Hart wanted nothing to do with him if she thought he'd end up the same as her ex. Drunk, worthless, good for nothing.

Unable to protect her. Capable only of hurting her.

He cringed. There was more to it than that. Thus his non-covert surveillance of her motel room. He wasn't undercover here. He was advertising to anyone intending to harm her they'd have to go through him first.

An invitation to try some target practice. With him as the target.

His eyes constantly scanned the mirrors and the terrain of the almost empty parking lot. There was no sign of anyone taking him up on his invitation. Despite the Slipknot screaming from the radio, his eyelids began to droop. He was half-tempted to play another volume of Jungle Jams—at least the children's stories kept him awake.

He tensed, the Matchbox abandoned and his gun in his hand, as the door to Hart's room opened. She emerged, dressed in tank top and shorts, and walked directly to the minivan.

"If you wear down the battery," she said, leaning in the driver's window, her tone casual, " Denise is gonna kill you."

He reached a hand across to the ignition and turned it off. "Wouldn't want that." He was half-tempted to slide across, back into the driver's seat in order to be closer to her. Which was ridiculous, of course. The entire point of this exercise was to get her out of the range of fire, not in the middle of the kill zone. "Happy? Why don't you go back inside?"

"I know what you're doing. It's not going to work—"

"You thought it was a good enough plan to send me away earlier tonight," he countered.

To his surprise, she looked down. "Yeah, but I was wrong."

He inched closer, afraid he'd scare her off.

"We've both been fools, Drake. Pushing each other away to try to keep each other safe. Exactly what whoever is behind this wants. Time to regroup."

She arched an eyebrow at him. "Besides, I've got air conditioning and—" She wrinkled her nose. "A shower inside."

She pivoted and strode back toward the room. Drake watched her, his gaze locked on the sinuous muscles of her naked legs. He'd have to be an idiot to refuse an invitation like that.

He grabbed the keys and ran to join her as she reached the door. She paused, and looked up at him. The yellow light beside the door etched her face in shadows as if the events of the past few days had sucked the life from her. He remembered last night, how close he'd come to losing her, and couldn't resist.

He took her by her shoulders, pinned her against the still-closed door, and kissed her deeply, trying to breathe life back into her, to share his energy. What little he had left, he offered to her. She responded immediately, her hands reaching up to his shoulders, pulling her up into his embrace.

They were sitting targets, but for a few seconds the rest of the world vanished for Drake. There was only the woman before him. The woman he needed so desperately, the thought of forsaking all others seemed a tiny sacrifice. Not if he had Hart by his side.

They broke long enough to catch their breaths. Hart leaned her weight against his chest. He reached behind her to open the door, swept her into his arms, and carried her inside the dark room, kicking the door shut behind them.

The bang echoed through the room, then there was silence except for the friendly hum of the air conditioner and the sound of their breathing. Cool air brushed over his sweat-covered body with a tingle. Hart made no protest as he cradled her against him, standing still, absorbing every sensation.

She felt light; she'd lost weight these past few days. The thought angered him. He should have been here to look after her, should have taken better care of her. From now on he would.

He crushed her to his chest, lips brushing against the brittle remnants of her once luxurious hair. A small gasp escaped her and he immediately relaxed his hold on her, lowered her back to the ground.

"I'm sorry," his voice emerged a hoarse whisper. "Did I hurt you?"

In answer, she took his hand and led him into the bathroom. He blinked against the glare of the light. He caught his breath when he saw her, for the first time in light bright enough that he could begin to catalogue the changes in her appearance.

She seemed oblivious to the scrapes and cuts that covered her arms and legs, the peeling skin of superficial burns, the haphazard appearance of her hair, chunks of it broken off. Instead, she raised his shirt, tracing her fingers along his ribs, the bruises from the few blows Spanos had landed.

Christ, she was worried about him? He pushed her hands aside, turned her so he could continue to evaluate her injuries, cursing himself again when he raised her top and she flinched as the fabric brushed against a large patch of angry, red, peeling skin. With her back to him, she raised her head and watched him in the mirror.

"Guess neither of us are a pretty sight," she said, a wry smile twisting her face.

How could she joke at a time like this? His hands fisted at his sides and adrenalin roared through him with the need to find whoever had done this to her, to pummel them into the ground, to make them pay for every second of pain they had caused her.

She turned within his arms, her hands feathering to his, slowly forcing his fists open with their gentle insistence. "Why didn't you tell me you were hurt when you came to my house Saturday night?"

He stiffened. Spanos hadn't hurt him. A few lucky punches, that was all.

"Should've seen the other guy," he muttered. Damn, if only he hadn't had so much to drink and started the fight with Spanos, she might not have been angry with him and they might've been together last night. He might have been able to save her house instead of being trapped in an interrogation room half way across the city while she lost everything. While he almost lost her.

His breath tore through him in a ragged gasp and he pulled her to him once more. "Christ, I'm sorry, I'm so sorry . . ."

She held him for a few minutes while he pretended that those weren't really tears burning his eyes. She smelled of smoke, felt hot, as if the fire she had escaped still smoldered inside her. Her arms wrapped around his chest, softly stroking his pain away. Finally he could breathe again, and his anger banished until he could confront the person responsible for all this. Then nothing would stop him.

He stepped back. He relaxed his death grip on her shoulders and gave her space. She looked up at him and he saw the remnants of tears on her cheeks. But she was smiling.

"There are three things I want," she said.

Ahh, he knew that devilish smile, and could guess what one of those things was. "Three?"

"You smell. I want you to take a shower."

"No problem." He tugged her shirt over her head. "If you join me."

She returned the favor by shimmying out of her shorts, standing naked before him. One of the things he loved about her. She was never inhibited about nudity, in fact, somehow she seemed to appear more regal naked than when cloaked by clothing. Even now, with her disheveled hair and ravaged skin.

"The second thing?"

Her fingers tugged the belt from his pants, and then feathered their way down, teasing him. Her smile widened as he sucked in his breath. "No condoms. Nothing between us anymore. You've paid enough for Pamela. We aren't going to let her come between us again."

She removed her hand, looked up at him, waiting for his answer. He closed his eyes for a second, searching for any remnants of Pamela's ghost. And found none. He gazed down at her, brushed a kiss against her forehead, relishing the sense of freedom that filled him. "Done. And the last?"

She sighed, giving him the shy and wistful look of a child. "Would you hold me tonight? I know it's crazy, but I can't sleep without you . . ."

Good God, had things deteriorated so far that she had to ask? He yearned to give her such simple comfort. The thought of cradling her to sleep was more arousing than any erotic images of the sex that might come before.

He raised her hand to his lips. "Your wish is my command."

DRAKE KEPT THE WATER temperature lukewarm. Worried about her burns, no doubt. His concern both touched and irritated Cassie, and she realized she was still upset about what happened Saturday night. If he hadn't been such a jerk, getting drunk at the first sign of trouble . . .

Reaching a hand past Drake's glistening body, she cranked the temperature up higher. It stung against her tender skin, but somehow the pain felt good. A reminder that despite everything, she was still alive.

She had to admit it, she was angry with herself for not recognizing his deteriorating moods were because of Pamela. She'd purposely not researched the issue, too painful to think about, but that denial left her in the dark. Stupid. If she'd at least found out the date, maybe she could have stopped all of this, whisked him away from here before things got this far.

"It wouldn't have done any good," she said, her words echoing in time with the water as his fingers massaged shampoo ever so gently over her sore scalp.

He paused for a moment, shielding her eyes with one hand as he tilted her face up with the other.

"Even if you'd known Monica was Pamela's sister," she continued, "even if I'd left with you Friday night, even if you'd been with me last night—it wouldn't have done any good."

He frowned at her words, and then eased her eyes closed as he rinsed her hair. "Why do you say that?"

"Because it's not you they're after—whoever they are," she told him, the realization making her gut clench. "It's me."

She felt his body stiffen against hers. His fingers stroked down her hair, then along her cheekbones, over her shoulders, drawing her close for a long moment.

"But you already figured that out, didn't you?" She drew back from his warm comfort, and gave him a searching stare.

That was Drake, so much better at seeing the big picture than she was. She was always too busy rushing in to act on a problem, to solve things before they escalated. Another reason why they needed to stay together. Why she'd been so very wrong to send him away earlier tonight. "That's why you followed me here."

He nodded. "Too many coincidences: the Brickner trial, the stalking, even your malpractice case. Everything designed to separate us. At first I thought it was to target me, and thought staying away was for the best, a way to keep you safe."

"But all it did was keep us from seeing there's a puppet master out there, orchestrating all of this for his own private amusement."

He lifted a handful of charred hair, his eyes darkening with anger. "I'm not finding any of this funny."

She shivered at the tone of his voice. Drake pivoted so she

could share more of the warmth of the water and reached for conditioner, turning her so she couldn't see his expression. But she felt his fury in the tension of his fingers, the way he held his body rigid as if expecting an attack.

He was intent on placing himself between her and danger. Damn it, wasn't that what had gotten them into this in the first place?

"I'm sorry about earlier," she said. "In the garden."

"Wrong time, wrong place." His voice was light, but his fingers hitched in their rhythm.

He rinsed the conditioner from her hair, and she turned back to him. His fingers kept stroking her hair as if he couldn't bear the idea of not touching her.

"That was part of it. But I can't stand you thinking I need you to protect me. That I can't take care of myself."

His brow furrowed in irritation. He dropped his hands, and then spread them wide as if to emphasize how poorly she'd done taking care of herself.

Cassie stood her ground. She hadn't done so bad. She was still alive and ready to kick butt, wasn't she? Or at least she would be after a good night's rest.

"Drake, either we're in this together or—"

"Or what?" he demanded, ignoring the stream of water sluicing into his face as he leaned forward. "I love you. It's my job to protect you, to keep you safe."

She shook her head. Couldn't he see? That's exactly what Richard had promised her, how he had seduced her to relinquish control. Drake wasn't Richard, but she still couldn't enter a relationship based on his need to place himself between her and the dangers of the world beyond.

"That's not love, that's a bodyguard," she snapped.

His hands returned to her shoulders, holding her in place as his mouth ravished hers. He plunged into the kiss, leaving her breathless, yearning for more. A small sound caught in her throat, and she circled her leg around his, arching her pelvis closer to his.

"Would a bodyguard know how to do this?" he growled, his voice low and throaty. His sexy voice, rough as gravel, and capable of arousing her with a mere whisper.

He abandoned her mouth, left her gasping. His lips trailed down her exposed throat to capture her breast. Once more a wave of pleasure swamped her, leaving her trembling in his grasp. He pivoted them both so that her back was to the wall. She dug her fingers into the strong muscles of his arms, urging him to not stop, never stop. His hand slid down to her hip, then moved between her legs, knowing exactly where to touch her to bring her to instant climax.

Cassie banged her head against the tile as she arched back and cried out. She eased her leg higher, stroking against the back of his in encouragement. But he stopped. She looked up. His eyes were narrowed in concern.

"What's wrong?"

"We can't," he said, leaning away from her. "I don't want to hurt you."

"That's what I'm talking about. I'm not a baby. I know what I'm doing. And I accept the consequences of my actions." She feathered her hand down his chest, stroked his erection until it was his turn to utter a moan. "All of my actions."

He inched closer, but not close enough. She hooked her ankle behind his once more and pulled him to her, her flesh skimming, taunting his. She rubbed her pelvis against him until a small, feral noise escaped from his clenched jaws. They were both breathing hard, saying nothing as their gazes locked. She felt him against her belly and wanted him inside her, now. She needed to feel him. To feel alive. She was desperate for him to touch that place that only he could find, the place where she was free and safe and beyond the reach of the ordinary world.

She wanted what only Drake could give her.

Her fingers slid around to the small of his back to tantalize him. She watched as his eyes darkened. He arched back, signaling his surrender. With a primal grunt, he planted his feet, raised her up, and entered her.

She fisted her fingers in his hair, tugging as he cupped her buttocks in his large, capable hands. Her back slid against the soap slicked tiles as he thrust into her, each stroke sending a fresh wave of heat and fire through her. His head fell forward, his lips parting in an animal snarl of excitement. One hand left her to brace against the wall as her lips closed over his.

They moved together. Their passion rose, cresting beyond anything Cassie had ever imagined. Mutual need and animal desire drove them on until she could no longer separate any of her senses, all five mingling in an explosion of water tasting of vanilla and salty sweat, smelling of musk and sex and lavender, the pounding of their mingled pulses driving through her brain as her entire universe contracted to the sight of his eyes searching her soul.

She held on, her grip bruising as he thrust inside of her, pushing her over the brink into a world that existed solely for the two of them. She cried out his name, the water mingling with her tears as he filled her, completed her.

Finally the laws of physics and biology forced them into a thundering final climax that left them both shaking. Cassie lowered her feet back to the ground and sank against the stolid wall of tile. Drake stood, both arms braced against the wall, trembling.

"Jesus, Hart," he whispered, his head collapsing onto her

shoulder. "What you do to me."

He let out a deep, satisfied sigh. She wanted to tell him that the feeling was mutual, but was too exhausted to force the words out. Instead she clung to him, her body pressed against his, vibrating in harmony, the aftershocks of pleasure still rippling through her.

He turned his head to face her. "If we're done arguing, can we go to bed now?"

"Yes," was all she had the strength to say.

Yes to everything, to whatever he wanted. He could have all of her. He already did, she realized with dismay, tainted by a small undercurrent of joy. This was dangerous territory. She needed to tread lightly.

Which was impossible for her to do whenever Drake was around.

Chapter 33

THERE WAS SOMETHING PRIMAL and erotic about having a woman trust you enough to sleep within your arms, Drake thought. More than erotic. Soul-stirring. Knowing how hard it was for Hart to trust at all, to give up any control, it made him feel powerful, a better man. He remembered what she'd said earlier, about not being able to sleep without him and wondered if she had any idea that the same was true for him.

Finally, Drake allowed his exhaustion to overtake him and he fell into the realms of a deep sleep, free from nightmares for the first time in a week. Instead, he dreamed of Hart. Dreamed of saving her, of being strong enough to banish her fears—past, present and future. Dreamed of the ways she would reward him, with her body, with her love.

When he woke, bright sunshine streamed through the small slit in the curtains. Hart nestled against him, curled into him, one hand fisted at his chest, one leg flung over his. There was nothing more in this world that he wanted than to wake like this every day for the rest of his life.

The clock on the bedside table read 12:22. The growling

emanating from Hart's stomach confirmed the time. She never skipped breakfast. He drew his breath in, trying not to laugh. Amazing how good sex—hell, great sex—and fourteen hours of sleep could revive a man, change his outlook.

He felt Hart's breathing change its rhythm, felt her slowly ease into wakefulness. He feathered his fingers down her back, loving the way shivers raced over her muscles as if his touch brought them to life. Her fingers stroked his chest, quickly followed by her lips against his nipple. A teasing bite that only increased his arousal.

She opened her eyes, and looked up at him with wicked intentions as her hips met his. He watched the familiar crimson flush climb from her neck into her face, saw her eyes widen with pleasure.

A soft mewing sound vibrated from her and into him as he fought to keep control. Cascades of color shimmered in his vision. Every breath was filled with the scent of springtime rain, of damp earth, cleansing air, bright sunshine.

She arched her neck back, and Drake felt her go over the edge. He rolled her onto her back, her legs circled around his waist. Finally he could hold on no longer, and followed her, his vision exploding in a cascade of light as the climax engulfed him.

He collapsed into her arms. They had had sex numerous times over the past week. But nothing compared to the exquisite ecstasy of this, of making love.

They lay there for several long, quiet moments until the rumbling in Hart's stomach became insistent. With a laugh, he rolled off her.

"Time to get up," he said.

She closed her eyes. "I just want to lay here, to feel like this, forever."

Another grumble from her stomach betrayed her. She blew her

breath out, and opened her eyes. "I can't imagine a better way to wake up."

Knowing Hart was not a morning person, he accepted the compliment. He traced a finger around her breast. "If we were married, we could wake like that every day."

"We don't need to be married to do that," she said, her tone reminding him he was pushing his luck.

He didn't care; he was feeling lucky today. He stretched his body out, watching in delight as her gaze roamed over him. Feeling lucky, indeed.

"Maybe I'm going to save myself for marriage." He grinned, batted her hand away as she teased her fingers down his abdomen. "No more sex unless you make me an honest man. Marry me."

Her hand fell away, her forehead creased. He'd pushed the joke too far. Except it was no joke for him. She rolled away from him, and walked to the bathroom.

He followed her, but she had closed the door. Even he knew not to push that limit.

There were reasons she painstakingly built the barriers around her heart over the years. Impatient as he was to destroy them, he knew he had to take care. She knew how he felt, that was what was important now.

That, and finding the bastard intent on destroying their lives.

$$\sim\!\!\wedge\!\!\wedge\!\!\wedge\!\!\wedge\!\!\sim$$

"I'M SORRY ABOUT LAST night," he said, once they finished their lunch at the Eat n Park. "You were right. We're in this together."

"Together, as in equals?"

He remembered his dreams from last night. Dreams of Hart trapped in a cave, being smothered by Richard King, locked in a dungeon. Dreams where he had saved her from King. He sighed. Maybe that's how he wished it was, but the truth was Hart had saved herself.

He'd like to think if he knew her back then he would have been able to rescue her. But she wouldn't be the woman she was today if not for King. A woman who refused to bow to circumstances or superior strength, a woman who stood her ground.

If he tried to take that away from her, he was no better than King.

"Yes," he exhaled the word. "Partners. Whatever comes."

Her face flushed slightly as she nodded her approval at his words. "I like the sound of that." She reached her hand out to take his. "Now, who's on your list of potential suspects?"

"Same two I began with: Spanos and King."

She frowned at that. "But isn't Tony in the clear? He chased the intruder out and he was inside the Center when the shooting happened."

"He could have done the shooting and returned to the Center while we took cover behind the dumpster. We couldn't see the front door," he reminded her.

"You think he's that good of an actor? Tony?"

"Yeah. I guess. So that leaves us with King."

"I can see Alan paying Elizabeth Reynolds to harass you. And trying to ruin my life with the malpractice case and helping Brickner get off. But a shooting and firebombing? Not his style."

"Actually, I meant your ex, Richard King. He's not as helpless or weak as he appears."

She waved her hand as if King wasn't even worth discussing. "I already told him no. He knows we're never getting back together. So what's the point of escalating things? The shooting and firebomb could have just as easily driven me into your arms. Why risk it?"

"He's desperate. Sees you as his only hope. He's obsessed with you."

She rolled her eyes.

"Maybe King and Spanos together. Your ex told me he's the one who's paying Guardian Security to install the alarm system on the Center. And he hired Spanos to watch over you."

That made her bristle. "You mean all this time Tony's been working for Richard? I thought he—" Her voice trailed off.

"Thought what? He was doing it out of the goodness of his heart?"

For some reason that made her flush. She looked away for a moment, then said, "What about Brickner? Maybe all this was a ploy to discredit me and get him off?"

"You really think he'd go to the trouble of hunting down Elizabeth Reynolds and convince her to move halfway across the country even though she's dying—" He stopped. "She's the key. Maybe it wasn't murder after all. Maybe it was suicide."

"Then how did your gun end up in the dumpster?"

"She had help to clean up after her. Someone who wanted to destroy me just as much as she did."

"Then we're back to you being the target, not me."

"No. We're back to us being the target. You and me together. Start thinking of it that way and it all makes sense in a perverted sort of way."

"Maybe. But it still doesn't tell us who is behind it."

"Flip a coin. Spanos or King. Can't think of anyone else who would want to destroy us."

She shuddered, and he regretted his flippancy. After all, a woman was dead and Hart almost killed. Serious business.

"Do you really think either Tony or Richard would want to kill me? A few seconds either way and I wouldn't have made it out of my house. Or if I'd been asleep upstairs—"

Now it was his turn to shiver. "Don't even say it. Maybe the firebombing and the shooting were gang related?"

"What good am I dead to them?"

"You'd serve as a warning to Athena."

"A warning that would just send her further into hiding. That's not what Lucien wants. He wants that recording to make sure no one knows Baby Jane is his."

"Too late now. You already told CYS. Nothing will stop their investigation."

"But he doesn't know that."

He frowned. Too many variables. His phone rang. Jimmy. "Hart there?"

"Yeah, why?"

"So you guys kissed and made up? About time. Does this mean you'll be bringing Denise her van back anytime soon? She's driving me crazy."

"We're fine, Jimmy. How about you and the search for the person or persons who are trying to kill Hart, and who framed me for Elizabeth Reynolds' murder?"

"Yeah, not so good. That's not why I called. Tell Hart to be on the lookout for Ronald Brickner. Seems he was a no show in court today. Judge revoked his bond, so he's now officially a fugitive. Might make him desperate enough to do something stupid."

"Okay, thanks."

"Oh, and Miller says to come by and pick up your badge and gun. IAD dropped all charges against you—pending the conclusion of their investigation, anyway."

He brightened at that. "Will do."

"Good news?" Hart asked when he hung up.

"Yeah. IAD is giving me my badge and gun back. I just have to go pick them up."

"That's great."

He didn't like walking around unarmed, especially not with Hart to protect. It was like walking around naked. "We'll go together. I don't want to let you out of my sight."

"I'll meet you at the Center. I need to return Natalie's car and I want to check on Tagger."

Seemed safe enough. The station house was just down the street, so he'd probably beat her there anyway. "Will Tammy be at the Center?"

"Yes. And we're expecting a delivery of drywall, so there should be some nice, hunky guys around as well." She wrinkled her nose at him. "You can't babysit me. I have a life to live."

He sighed. "I know."

WHEN CASSIE REACHED ED'S house, Natalie was just getting ready to leave. "Perfect timing. I was heading over to Trent's case worker and I can drop you off at the Liberty Center on my way."

"Who's Trent?" Cassie asked with a smile. She had a feeling she knew the answer.

"Tagger, of course. I told him no gang names in my house."

"How'd he take that?"

"Not so happy at first. Also not so happy about eating real food, setting the table, or not wearing that god-awful hat of his inside the house. But he's back in school and came home yesterday laughing and excited about a big art project his teacher is planning. Spent all night sketching ideas."

"Good." She made a mental note to ask Drake to stop by to see Tagger, maybe give him some encouragement. "And Baby Jane?"

"Gained almost half a pound already. Once her temperature

stabilized she turned out to be a champion eater. I'm working with CYS on bringing her here. That way Athena can visit both her and Trent."

This was what Cassie admired most about Natalie. The woman never gave up on anyone, not even a girl the police had labeled their number one suspect in a homicide.

They pulled up to the Center and she was relieved Tony's van wasn't there. She wasn't sure how she felt about knowing Richard had paid Tony to watch over her—or how that colored the ex-cop's affection for her. Richard sure as hell didn't pay Tony to kiss her the other night.

Natalie drove off with a jaunty beep-beep as Cassie ran inside, glad to be back in familiar territory. Tammy was out front putting up shelves in the reception area, her radio playing her favorite, Alicia Keys.

"Want some help?" Cassie asked, reaching for her tool belt from the peg where Tammy had hung it. The woman was always cleaning, sorting, or straightening something.

"Cassie, you're back!" Tammy rushed over with a big hug. "Are you okay? I heard about your house. I'm so sorry."

"I'm fine. Just a few aches and bruises."

"Hmmm . . . wish I could say the same about your hair."

"Tagger helped me cut it."

"Yeah, well, we can do better than that. Let me finish these and we'll go over to Miss Leila's down on Centre. She does real nice work. My treat."

Cassie hated sitting in a hair stylist's chair. It was one of the reasons why she wore her hair long. She never knew what to say, and the small talk made her nervous. But she couldn't ignore the look on Tammy's face. "Okay. Sounds like fun."

"Good. I won't be long here."

"I'm going to run upstairs and finish painting that last bit of trim in the day care. Just grab me when you're ready."

It was amazing how therapeutic something as simple as painting trim could be, she thought as she carefully swished the brush back and forth. Rosa was right. As usual.

She'd just finished the tricky bit in the far corner—without even splashing any on the floor—when Tony Spanos rushed in.

"Thank God you're here. It's that girl. She's been hurt. I was afraid to move her."

Cassie climbed down from her ladder. "Athena? What happened?"

"She was over in the Stackhouse. Some debris fell on her. It's bad, Cassie. You need to hurry." He ran down the stairs and she followed.

"Did you call EMS?"

"Yeah, but I'm not sure she's going to last that long. I didn't know what else to do, so I took the chance you'd be here—"

They reached his van and she jumped into the passenger seat. "I don't have any supplies."

"Still, better than nothing," he said as he gunned the engine and roared out of the parking lot. "You're her only chance, Cassie."

Chapter 34

DRAKE WASN'T HAPPY TO see Richard King waiting with
Tammy when he arrived at the Center. Damn paperwork took longer
than he'd thought. "Where's Hart?" he asked Tammy, ignoring
King.

"Upstairs in the daycare, painting."

Good. Even Hart couldn't get hurt painting.

"What do you want?" he asked King, not bothering to pretend
at civility.

"We need to talk." King glanced at Tammy, who arched an
eyebrow and crossed her arms over her chest, not budging an inch.

"This way." Drake led King back into the clinic area, not
worrying if the wheelchair bound man would have a problem or not.
Since the ramp led to the rear entrance near the elevator, he assumed
King came in through this way.

"While my brother was in court today, I went through his
office," King started. "Alan paid to bring Elizabeth Reynolds here."

"Did he kill her?"

King looked down as he shrugged. "From his notes it looks like
he paid Tony Spanos to harass you as well."

"Spanos was working with Reynolds." Just what he'd suspected all along. "Do you have proof?" Maybe they could tie Spanos or Alan King to Reynolds' murder as well.

King handed him a thumb drive. "It's all there. But it was obtained illegally, so you can't use it."

"I know that. I just want to check it out for myself. Make sure you're not involved."

"I told you. I only want to protect Cassandra."

"Right." Drake turned, surprised to hear the elevator. Coming up from the basement. Inside was a thin black teenager with a scar across her forehead. Athena Jackson. He wrenched the wrought iron door open and grabbed her by the arm before she could bolt.

"What are you doing here?"

"I was in the basement and heard the man's voice. The one from the other night."

He whirled on King. "You. I knew—"

Athena tugged at Drake's arm. "No, not him. The man who just left with Doc Cass. You have to warn her."

"Left?" Drake jogged to the front of the clinic. "Tammy, didn't you say Hart was upstairs?"

"Yeah, I thought so. She and Tony were—"

"Spanos. Hell." He raced back to Athena. "Where were they going?"

"He said something about the Stackhouse. That I was in trouble. But I was right here."

Drake grabbed his cell, already dialing the station house as he flew past King. He'd only taken a step out of the door when a shot rang out, hitting the brick wall beside him. He ducked back inside, searching for the shooter.

A bunch of kids stood at the alley across the street. Rippers. They pushed a car into the street, blocking the alley. Flames blazed into the air as they set it on fire and cheered. More shots flew through the air. None of them seemed to be aimed, they were just shooting for the thrill of it.

Same thing happened last time the Stackhouse burned. One gang blocked the streets so EMS and Fire couldn't get there, while the other fought their way out. Leaving innocent women and children behind to die.

Black smoke billowed into the sky beyond the warehouse across the street. Coming from the direction of the Stackhouse.

The humid July air was sucked from his body, replaced by an arctic blast of fear. He ignored the potshots and ran out onto the landing. More gunfire came, this time aimed at him. He jumped back behind the cover of the door, gauging the angle of the gunfire, calculating a path to the van.

To his surprise, King rolled past him, speeding down the handicapped ramp.

"Throw me the keys," he shouted as he neared Denise's van. Drake tossed them to him. A few moments later, gunshots pinging all around them. King backed the minivan up close enough for Drake to jump in.

"Are you crazy?"

"We've got to get to Cassandra."

"You don't stand a chance against those gangbangers."

"Neither does she. Not unless we help her." King peeled off down the street and around the corner, searching for an alternative route to the Stackhouse. He glanced over at Drake. "You want out? I'll go alone. But Cassandra has a better chance with both of us."

King might be crazy, but Drake couldn't argue with that.

—◠◡◠◡◠◡◠—

TONY DROVE THEM TO the Stackhouse. There were Rippers

gathered on street corners everywhere, but they ignored the van.

"Gangstas are coming. It's going to be war," Tony said. His tone was one of glee. Or maybe it was fear of getting caught in the crossfire. "We need to hurry."

He screeched to a halt at the front door of the Stackhouse. "She's upstairs."

Cassie followed him in through the foyer and up the partially burnt staircase. They had to climb it with their backs pressed against the supporting wall and jump over several missing steps, but thankfully, it held.

Once they made it to the landing, he stepped aside, allowing her to duck under a fallen beam and enter the room. She aimed her flashlight into every corner. No Athena. Only a rolled up piece of carpet thrown in the corner and a tremendous stink that gagged her even worse than the smell downstairs.

"Where is she?"

Tony came up behind her and reached for her arm to direct her flashlight beam. Suddenly he snapped a handcuff onto her wrist.

She pivoted away, but he cranked her wrist behind her, bending it so she had to move in whatever direction he wanted. The pain was excruciating, firing up her nerves into her shoulder joint.

"Tony—"

"Shut up and move." He forced her into the room and down on her knees where he handcuffed her wrist to a radiator.

"I don't understand," Cassie said. Only she did understand, all too well. Drake had been right all along. Fear threatened to engulf her, but she thought of Drake and forced it down.

Drake was meeting her at the Center. Tammy knew she'd left with Tony. Surely someone would come, if she could just buy some time.

"You and Drake. Such idiots. You think the whole world

revolves around you and your little love fest, don't you? You never
stop to think there are other people out there. People whose lives
you ruined."

"This is about Pamela and Drake?"

"No. It's about me. I was with Pamela the night before she
died—before Drake. She tells me all about the HIV, doesn't give
a shit that we just fucked and that maybe I'm fucked. No, all she
cares about is how is she gonna tell Drake and what will he think
of her and now she's never gonna get him back. A load of crap. But
I listen. And I tell her she's right. There's only one way she can be
sure she'll always have Drake, that he'll never ever let her go.

"I even showed her how to use a gun and where to aim to make
sure she didn't screw it up. Dumb bitch."

"You convinced Pamela to kill herself? Why? To get back at
Drake?"

"Drake's a fuck up. Always has been. I don't know why Miller
kept him on as long as she has, unless he's screwing her, too. I
thought with him gone I might have a chance at plainclothes, show
Miller that I had what it took. Who knew Drake would land on his
feet the way he did, son of a bitch." He paused. "And then you came
along. Little miss perfect. You humiliated me. I try to do the right
thing, warn you about Drake, and you humiliated me. In front of
my guys. Then I lost my job because of you. The only thing in this
whole goddamn world I give a shit about and you take it away from
me."

It wasn't her fault he lost his nerve during a hostage situation—
except she'd been the hostage. "But—"

"Shut the fuck up! I'm talking here. Did you really think it was
a coincidence you were having such a bad week, Cassie? It was so
easy. Once Reynolds was on board, I hooked her up with Alan King.
Slipped him the info on the Brickner case, let him think he was

using me to spy on you. He figured there was more going on but he didn't care as long as he could destroy you, restore the family honor. Of course, I never figured Drake would run off. Plan was he'd be here to watch me kill you, nice and slow. Reynolds would take the fall and I could get the one thing I love more than anything—my job back. As usual, you screwed things up. Now we have to do it the hard way."

"You killed Elizabeth Reynolds?"

He laughed. "Bitch was crazier than her sister. Guess brain cancer will do that to you. She loved seeing Drake squirm. Came this close to getting him into bed with her. She didn't even give a shit about dying as long as Drake paid for what he did to her sister. It should've worked. Would've worked, if it wasn't for you."

Cassie doubted Elizabeth Reynolds went voluntarily to her death. Like all of Tony's accusations, it was what his warped brain needed to believe. He was the victim here, it wasn't his fault—how many times had she heard that from patients in the ER?

"This time I get to play hero. They'll give me a fucking medal after tonight. Too bad neither you or Drake will be alive to see it. He'll live long enough to see you buried, and then he's mine."

"It's me you want, Tony. I'm the reason you lost your job. Please, leave Drake out of it. Let him live. I'm begging you."

"You know the hardest part of this whole damn thing?" he asked with a sneer. "Kissing you on the roof the other night. Playing at being your friend, infatuated. I wanted to puke after."

"Tony, please. There's no need—"

He slapped her hard. Just once, but once was enough for her to see he would never listen to reason. She thought back to every other encounter they'd had. Tony had always showed himself to be a bully, caring only about himself, but she'd ignored it, and thought he'd changed. How could she have been such a fool?

"No going back now, Cassie."

He turned to kick a rolled up carpet away from the wall. That's where the stink was coming from. Urine, vomit, blood, and . . . lighter fluid? Tony kicked it again and a muffled scream came from inside. He unrolled the top layer.

"Meet your favorite fire starter."

Ronald Brickner lay facing Cassie, face bruised and swollen, his body encased in the layers of carpeting. "Please—"

His pleas were cut short by another vicious kick. Tony crouched low, taking a squeeze bottle of lighter fluid from the floor and spraying it over Brickner's face and the carpet.

"You've been a very naughty boy, Ronald. No one told you to set Cassie's house on fire. You almost ruined everything."

He picked up a plumber's blowtorch and lit it. "Time's up Cassie. No more second chances. For either of you." His grin was ghastly in the light of the flickering blue flame.

"Tony, turn off the blowtorch," Cassie yelled, trying to break through to whatever reason was left in the ex-cop. "The fumes. They'll ignite."

"Shut up, Cassie. It's finally my turn to have fun." He lowered the plumber's torch, aiming at Brickner's eyes.

Brickner screamed. His voice was hoarse, choked with blood and mucus. Before Tony's flame touched his skin, the air beyond Tony's hand caught fire. Brilliant blue and gold flames danced onto Tony's arm, racing up his sleeve.

Tony dropped the torch and fell to the ground, cursing. The torch hit the floor and the flames spread, one wave towards the carpet where Brickner struggled, simultaneously trying to roll away and free himself. The other towards Cassie.

Cassie struggled with her bonds. The handcuff held her tight to the radiator. She tried to rock it, pull it free, but it barely budged.

A few streaks of fire came close but she was able to kick them out. Thank God none of the lighter fluid splashed over here.

Tony ran from the room, cursing, holding his arm to his chest.

The room filled with smoke, choking her. She bent over double, keeping her face as close to the floor as possible. Brickner's screams filled her head but she couldn't see him through the smoke.

Flames crawled up the walls, eagerly feeding on them, then blossomed over the ceiling. Everywhere Cassie looked was black smoke and flames.

Chapter 35

TO DRAKE'S SURPRISE, KING maneuvered the minivan fairly well using the cruise control as accelerator and his left leg, the stronger one, for the pedals when needed. They sped down Ravenna and cut over to Ruby Avenue where the Stackhouse was located.

The smoke Drake spotted wasn't coming from the Stackhouse. Instead, an abandoned row house was ablaze. Women and children ran down the streets while Rippers gathered in groups. Drake spotted one kid, maybe all of twelve, standing guard on a corner, holding a Mac-10, while his compatriots rolled a car onto its side and set it on fire, blocking another side street.

"Why are they torching their own territory?"

"You asking me?" King answered in a loud voice fueled by adrenalin. "I'm more concerned about how we're going to get past that."

He pointed through the windshield to the pickup truck pulling out in front of them, its bed filled with burning tires. It rolled to a stop across both lanes of the street, half a block from the Stackhouse.

"Got your seatbelt on?"

King buckled up, grit his teeth, hunched forward, and shifted his good foot to the accelerator. "Hang on!"

The last thing Drake thought before they hit the truck was Denise was going to kill him if he made it out of this alive.

King aimed for the rear bumper of the truck. They rammed it at high enough speed that the truck flipped as it spun, spilling its fiery cargo.

The minivan sped through the flames but the airbags deployed on impact, obscuring their vision. King lost his grip on the steering wheel as they skid out of control. Sparks flew as they slid along the side of a car parked on the side of the street.

Finally, they jumped the curb and stopped. Drake batted away the deflated air bags, squinting through the smoky haze they left in their wake. King was stunned, bleeding from his forehead, but otherwise looked okay.

What Drake didn't like the looks of was the crowd they'd attracted. Eight Rippers formed a circle around the front of the van. All armed. All smiling.

"Can you shoot?" Drake asked King.

King blinked and stared at him like he was having trouble hearing. Drake didn't waste time trying to explain. Instead, he drew his backup Glock-27 and handed it to King. "If they get close, just point at the chest and pull the trigger."

"Don't you have to fire a warning shot? Or aim for their legs or something?"

"Only if you want to get killed. You aim that at them, it's warning enough. They don't back off, you shoot. Can you do that?"

King's Adam's apple bobbed up and down. "Yes. Go get Cassandra."

Drake did the math. The Baby Glock had nine bullets; there were eight Rippers. Hopefully if it came to shooting, they'd

scatter fast. But if they returned with reinforcements . . . He took
the smaller Glock from King and gave him his duty weapon, a
Glock-22, and a spare clip instead. That more than tripled King's
ammo, leaving Drake with one full magazine of fifteen and the nine
bullets in the Glock-27.

Even as he made the switch, more Rippers arrived. Bullets
weren't going to be the answer here, speed was.

"I'll be as fast as I can. Backup is on the way."

"Don't worry about me. Save Cassandra."

CASSIE COUGHED AND CHOKED, knowing that with each
breath she sucked in poisons like cyanide and carbon monoxide.
She slid her wrist down to the base of the cast iron radiator and put
her shoulder as low to the floor as possible before trying to lift it up.
The handcuffs were attached to the water inflow pipe, and if it had
fared as well as the other plumbing she'd seen in the Stackhouse,
there was a good chance it had been cut and scavenged. If she was
lucky . . .

The radiator tilted and she spotted the bottom edge of the
pipe peek through the rotting floorboard. Just an inch more . . . the
radiator rocked back into place before she had enough room to slide
the handcuff free. She took as deep a breath as she could, adjusted
her position to get the best leverage possible, and tried again.

This time the handcuff was halfway free when she couldn't hold
the weight any longer. But the third time was the charm. She yanked
free just before the radiator landed.

Cassie looked around, but was totally disoriented. Her first
thought was to save Brickner, but she realized that was hopeless—
not only could she never find him in the smoke, there was no way
he could have survived that blaze. Instead, she concentrated on

finding the door.

The fire itself guided her as flames spread over the ceiling, down a short way, then disappeared heading out of the room. She crawled in that direction.

Flaming pieces of the ceiling dropped down but were small enough to knock aside before they did any damage. She made it through the doorway to the landing. There was less smoke here but the ceiling roiled with flames, its surface bubbling black. It would only be a matter of moments before it came crashing down.

"Cassie, help me!" Tony had fallen through the damaged flooring on the landing and was clawing at floorboards, fighting to keep from falling.

She hesitated. Part of her wanted to pretend she never heard him. But she had. He'd tried to kill her, had killed two people; he didn't deserve to live.

But she wasn't a killer. Except she was. Memory flooded through her. When she first met Drake, when they were fighting for their lives, trapped, and she had no choice but to kill.

This time she had a choice.

She crawled towards a length of metal latticework that had torn loose from the railing. She couldn't risk falling through the floor by getting too close to Tony, so she extended the metal railing towards him. "Grab hold."

A coughing fit overcame her and the world blurred as tears obscured her vision. The flames began eating their way down the walls. If she didn't move fast, the stairway would be blocked.

Tony took the end of the railing. It took all her strength to anchor it in place as he struggled to heave his body up and out of the hole in the floor. "Pull, damnit!"

She tried, but couldn't. Red blotches floated through her vision and her head pounded. The world kept going in and out of focus and she couldn't catch her breath.

Tony managed to pull himself part of the way out. Just as he leveraged one knee up out of the hole, the ceiling collapsed between them, a shower of sparks and wood crashing onto the landing.

The floor beneath Cassie buckled and groaned. Tony screamed as it gave way around him and he fell, pulling the metal railing from her grasp.

Cassie backed away from the flames and heat, trying to find the stairway. The air quickly grew hot. Too hot to breathe. She covered her mouth and nose in the crook of her elbow. Don't stop. If you stop, you die.

She reached the steps and settled her knees on the first one when the landing collapsed. Throwing her weight to the other side, the side protected by the wall, she managed to keep from falling. But her vision was darkening and every breath was a struggle.

Crawling backwards, she made it down two more steps before she slumped forward, gasping for air and finding none.

Her body slid towards the void on her right, mere inches away. She felt herself going, but was powerless to stop. Her mind filled with Drake's face. The way he'd looked last night when proposing, they way he'd looked this morning when we woke together.

Live a fool, die a fool. That's what Rosa would say. Should've told him she loved him, was her last thought floated through her oxygen-starved brain.

Then she was falling . . .

Chapter 36

AS SOON AS DRAKE jumped out of the minivan, the Rippers began firing. Good thing none of them ever bothered with target practice.

Drake hunched low to the ground, zigzagging across the sidewalk that separated him from the nearest cover, while the Ripper's modified automatic weapons pulled high, showering the air above him with bullets, but left him unscathed.

He reached cover, a narrow brick doorway in the building beside the Stackhouse, and returned fire, dropping three of them with six shots, and scattering the rest. Hopefully he bought King some time, he thought, as he rushed across the alley and up the steps into the Stackhouse.

More gunfire came from behind him. He flattened against the wall and looked out. From the other end of the street came the growl of engines and shouts of angry men. The Gangstas had arrived to the party.

In the other direction, Denise's van was surrounded by Rippers intent on toppling it. They swarmed against the side, trying to rock it off its wheels, when one, then two, of them dropped. King's work.

Nice to know the asshole had his back.

A thunderous crash stole Drake's attention. The landing above caved in, showering flames over the foyer.

A man screamed and fell past him, crashing through the first floor and into the basement. Drake ran over, weapon at the ready. It was Spanos. Fiery debris covered his legs, but his face was clear and his shrieks of pain ear splitting.

Then Drake saw the cause: he was impaled on a broken wall stud. The jagged wood emerged from Spanos' abdomen.

Drake jumped back as more debris fell from above. Black, oily smoke rolled out in waves from the second floor. When he looked back down, Spanos had stopped screaming.

Hell with Spanos, where was Hart? He holstered his weapon and used both hands to climb through the smoke filling the stairway. One hand held the wall, the other searched the space before him.

He tripped over her just as her body slid into the empty space. He knew he shouted something but as soon as he said the words, they vanished from his mind. All he could think about was getting Hart out of here.

They made it to the stoop before gunfire pushed them back inside the foyer. The fire found the stairs, but a lot of the flames were taking a short cut down the walls, devouring the wallboard and leaping onto the carpet and furniture strewn around the foyer.

Drake hauled Hart over one shoulder, drew his weapon, ducked, and ran. Before he got two steps a body crashed into him, pushing him against the Stackhouse's wall. Bullets whizzed past the empty space where he and Hart had been standing.

He looked up, aiming his gun, but then lowering it. Their savior was Athena.

The girl met his gaze, said nothing, but put her arm around his back, stabilizing Hart's weight and steering him back onto the street.

"Thanks," Drake gasped.

A car sped by going the opposite direction, a Ripper standing up through the sunroof, firing his gun at the roof of a building down the street. The fight seemed to have moved past them, at least for the time being.

The minivan was riddled with bullet holes but the Rippers had left it upright. They managed to yank the side door off its track, so it hung half open, one edge scraping the pavement. He threw Hart in back and ran around to the driver's side.

Shell casings littered the ground. He found King face down in the gutter where the Rippers had dragged him. His skull was caved in, brain matter showing. One of his arms was twisted backwards, obviously dislocated. Drake rolled him over to check for signs of life. The other hand still held the Glock, its magazine emptied.

No pulse. He'd gone down fighting. Giving Drake the time he needed to save Hart.

Athena helped Drake drag King's body to the van—it really didn't take more than an extra second or two, and he couldn't just leave the man there. No matter how much of a jerk he'd been in life, Hart had once loved him, and that meant something.

"Get in," he shouted over the roar of sirens and gunshots. Athena shook her head.

"I've got to see that Lucien gets what's coming to him. Once and for all." She took off running before he could stop her.

Drake jumped into the driver's seat and started the engine. It protested and whined, but perked up once he shoved it in reverse and hit the accelerator.

Time to get the hell out of Dodge.

⎯ᴧᴧᴧᴧᴧᴧ⎯

THANKFULLY, ED CASTRO WAS on duty at Three Rivers. The

ER was swamped with casualties from the fires and gang war, but when Drake carried Hart in, everyone dropped what they were doing to rush her into a treatment room.

Then they shoved Drake out into the hallway. To wait. Like any other victim's family.

Damn, he hated waiting.

Finally, Ed emerged from the treatment room. Drake got to his feet, surprised by a sudden rush of light-headedness.

"I know Cassie misses us, but she really doesn't have to keep bringing us all this business," Ed said. But his smile didn't reach his eyes.

"So, she's going to be okay?"

"Too early to say. We treated her for cyanide toxicity. She didn't suffer any severe burns, but there are two things to worry about."

"What?"

"Her lungs. She has swelling around her airway and we had to intubate her. But I suspect, given it's not progressing and the way her gases look, that with a little time, that will improve and she'll start breathing on her own."

"She's not breathing?"

"We've taken over the work of breathing and put her on a special ventilator to protect her lungs from any edema. Usually in two to three days, if the swelling improves, the lungs will heal."

Okay. Two to three days. Knowing Hart, she'd go for a record and be off the damn machine in one day. "What's the other thing to worry about?"

"Her brain. We're prepping the hyperbaric chamber to treat her for carbon monoxide poisoning but her levels are pretty high. Nowhere near lethal," he hastened to add when Drake rocked forward, "but high enough her brain might have been oxygen deprived for too long."

"Like Richard King's was after his overdose."

Hart ending up like her ex—could she bear to be disabled, at the mercy of others attending to her needs? Hell, she wouldn't even let him hold the damn car door open for her. And what if it wasn't just physical? What if she lost cognitive function or parts of her memory?

Drake felt for the wall behind him, not sure he could keep standing on his own. Ed placed a hand on his elbow and guided him to a chair, then sat down beside him.

"Don't start rushing to think the worst," Ed said. "We're getting to her early. And you know Cassie. If anyone can beat the odds, it's her."

Drake nodded, unable to form a coherent sentence. He jerked his gaze up as the nurses wheeled Hart from the treatment room. "Where are they taking her?"

"Hyperbaric. She's going to need several treatments over the next few days."

"You mean that glass torpedo thing in the basement?" Hart had showed him the hyperbaric chamber once while giving him a tour of the hospital. "No way. You can't lock her in there."

"She's sedated, she won't know what's going on."

"Are you sure? Can you 100% guarantee that?" Drake stared down the older man. "Ed, she has claustrophobia. She'll go nuts in there."

"Claustrophobia? She can't—she goes up in that damn helicopter all the time . . ." Ed trailed off as Drake nodded. "You mean, she, shit, Drake, why didn't she say anything?"

"She hated the thought of letting you down. So she took it. Every single time she took off in that helicopter she thought she was going to die."

"Jesus. I never knew."

"Please. Ed. Let me stay with her. Hold her hand, talk to her. It doesn't matter if she can't hear me, but if there's the slightest chance that she can—" Drake hated to beg, but it did the trick.

"It's totally against the rules, but to hell with them. Least I can do. For both of you."

CASSIE WAS SWIMMING BUT there was no water. Instead she was floating in air, as graceful as a ballerina. Drake was there, too. She couldn't see him, but she heard his voice, felt his hand in hers. Somewhere in the back of her mind, she knew she should be scared, wanted to fight, started to panic, but then he'd start talking again and peace would descend.

He was there again when she woke, struggling against the tube down her throat and the machine forcing her lungs to expand. He bent close, his breath soft against her face, his lips on her cheeks, and she slept some more. He whispered that everything was all right and she believed him.

Chapter 37

IT WAS SIX DAYS before they let Cassie leave the hospital. She'd even missed Richard's funeral—not that Alan and his family would have wanted her there. They wanted her to do another round of pulmonary function and psychometric testing, but other than feeling sore and hoarse, she was fine.

Finally, she threatened to walk out on her own and backed up her threat by making it all the way to the front lobby, patient gown flapping behind her.

Drake brokered a peace of sorts, setting up outpatient appointments for her and getting a bag full of inhalers, inspirometers, and other shit she vowed not to need or use. Then he drove her to the Liberty Center.

"Athena turned herself in this morning," he told her.

She vaguely remembered him telling her that Lucien, the leader of the Rippers, had been killed in the gang war. "Did she kill him?"

"No. Car he was in did a head on against a cement pole and he was ejected. Nothing to do with her. She's in the clear."

"So she can get her baby back?"

"Given time. Natalie is working with Children and Youth." He gave a mock frown. "Also conned me into teaching a painting class to Tagger's class. That's gonna go over real good with the guys at work."

She knew he expected her to laugh, but it took all her strength to sit up straight. They arrived at the Liberty Center and he practically had to carry her up the steps after she refused to take the elevator, and ran out of steam after half a flight.

But he was patient. He didn't chide or scold or even yell. She wasn't sure what the hell was wrong with him, but hoped he got over it fast.

He led her inside and across the living room to the bedroom door.

"Close your eyes," he insisted, holding the door closed.

She sighed. All she wanted to do was to crawl into bed with his arms around her, and sleep about a thousand years. "Drake, I just want to go to bed. Any bed, I don't care—yours, the guest room, hell, I'd settle for the recliner in your studio. Can't we do this later?"

The boyish grin on his face slipped a bit and she regretted her harsh words. "All right," she said. "My eyes are closed."

He guided her inside the room, then his hands left her. "Okay," his voice was tight with anticipation, "now open them."

What had he done? she wondered before complying. She envisioned a large basket of flowers, a box of McIntyre's chocolate, maybe a new painting to replace the one she lost in the fire.

She inhaled. No flowers, just the faint scent of lavender mingled with Liquid Gold and fresh sawdust.

Sawdust?

Her eyes fluttered open. To a sight she never dreamed of. Padraic's bed—a bit battered, with a new dark scar running down the middle, but the singed wood only made the intricate carvings stand out more dramatically. Rosa's quilt, clean as new, spread over top the mattress, inviting Cassie to dive under it, to wrap herself in its warm memories. Hennessey lay in the center, her expression regal and possessive, as if she'd always lived here.

Cassie traced her fingers over the headboard, coming away with the oily tinge of furniture polish. "How did you? When did you?"

Drake stood beside her, his face as eager as a boy's on Christmas morning. "Jimmy and I rescued the headboard. Working on it the last few days kept me sane."

In between his shifts watching over her in the hospital. She looked at him again, this time with the eye of a clinician. Dark circles ringed his eyes and beneath the stubble of his beard, his complexion was pale. He was as physically and emotionally exhausted as she was.

Yet still, he had done all this. For her.

"I was hoping," he said, "you'd make this your new home. With me."

She sank onto the bed, her hand automatically stroking the soothing velvets of Rosa's quilt, and then ruffling the cat's fur. To her surprise, he sat beside her, and took her left hand in his.

"I know how you feel about marriage," his said, his voice uncertain, but his hand firm as he slid the sapphire onto her ring finger. Another treasure resurrected from the ashes. "But I'd like you to wear this—not as a commitment or a promise—just because it's important to me that you always have something of mine . . ." He trailed off, obviously at a loss for words.

Cassie looked from the gleaming gemstone to his eyes, both the same color, both glistening. Were those tears in his eyes? A pang speared through her. He'd given her, offered her so much—and what had she returned his love with? Fear, apprehension, specters of her past failures.

He deserved better from her. Or else she might lose him.

That thought made her decision for her. She'd lost everything, but it was inconsequential to the idea of losing Drake.

"Will you marry me?" she asked him, her gaze fixated on their joined hands, unable to look at his face for fear he might reject her.

Was it this hard for men? she wondered, regretting her earlier refusal of his proposals. Her stomach did a flip-flop as he drew in his breath to answer.

"Why?" The single syllable was all he said, but his free hand lifted her chin so that her eyes met his. "Not, because of this—" He gestured to the bed. "I can move into the other room if you want—"

Silly man, that was the last thing she wanted. As she tried to find the words to answer his perfectly valid question, a deep, soul-stirring laugh bubbled up out of her, releasing itself into the air between them, taking her anxieties with it. His eyes widened as she fell against him, laughing so hard tears flowed from her eyes.

He held her in stunned amazement, arms circling her, cautiously, as if she might break.

"Are you all right?" he asked when she finally stopped to draw her breath again.

"I want to marry you," she replied, now staring him straight in the eye. "I need to marry you. I need you."

She'd said it, consequences be damned. It was the simple truth. About time they both admitted it. She wasn't strong or brave or any of those things he thought she was.

She was scared and haunted by nightmare demons and things that went bump in the night and fears that she could have, should have done more for those she had failed in the past, present and future.

Most of all she was terrified she would fail him, hurt him, or disappoint him.

None of that seemed to matter when he was there, by her side, lending her his strength, granting her the power of his vision, joining with her as a partner, and sharing everything.

"I love you, Drake," she whispered into the lengthening silence. "Only you, always you."

For once he was the speechless one. He framed her face with his hands, his lips capturing hers as his tears flowed onto her flesh, mingling with her own.

Cassie plunged into the kiss, offering him everything she had. Rosa's voice echoed in her mind. *Life is love.*

At least she thought it was in her mind. Maybe she actually said it—or Drake did. Because he pulled away for a brief moment, his head tilted as if he, too, heard the ghostly whisper.

They were both laughing, crying, their joyous noises echoing from the high ceilings above as they fell together onto Rosa's quilt, the thick, velvet folds embracing them.

About CJ:

AS A PEDIATRIC ER doctor, New York Times Bestseller CJ Lyons has lived the life she writes about in her cutting edge Thrillers with Heart.

CJ has been called a "master within the genre" (Pittsburgh Magazine) and her work has been praised as "breathtakingly fast- paced" and "riveting" (Publishers Weekly) with "characters with beating hearts and three dimensions" (Newsday).

Learn more about CJ's Thrillers with Heart at www.cjlyons.net

Legacy Books

Manufactured by Amazon.ca
Acheson, AB

14262763R00192